THE SILVER LADY

THE SILVER LADY

James Facos

F
FAC

Chivers Press • Thorndike Press
Bath, Avon, England   Thorndike, Maine USA

EdS RR ER LE EdS ZE RD BM PT

This Large Print edition is published by Chivers Press, England, and by Thorndike Press, USA.

Published in 1995 in the U.K. by arrangement with the author

Published in 1995 in the U.S. by arrangement with James Facos

U.K. Hardcover ISBN 0–7451–2797–5 (Chivers Large Print)
U.K. Softcover ISBN 0–7451–2865–3 (Camden Large Print)
U.S. Softcover ISBN 0–7862–0488–5 (General Series Edition)

Permission has been granted by the publishers to quote material from the following songs:
Paper Doll
By Johnny Black
© Copyright E. B. Marks Music Corporation
I'll Get By (As Long As I Have You)
Words by Roy Turk; music by Fred E. Ahlert
TRO © Copyright 1928 and renewed 1956 by Cromwell Music, Inc., and Fred Ahlert Music Corp., New York, N.Y.
I'll Be Seeing You
By Irving Kahal & Sammy Fain
© Copyright 1938 by Williamson Music, Inc.

The text of this Large Print edition is unabridged.
Other aspects of the book may vary from the original edition.

Set in 16 pt. New Times Roman.

Printed in Great Britain on acid-free paper.

British Library Cataloguing in Publication Data available

Library of Congress Cataloging-in-Publication Data

Facos, James, 1924–
   The silver lady / James Facos.—Large print ed.
      p. cm.
   ISBN 0–7862–0488–5 (lg. print : lsc)
   1. World War, 1939–1945—Fiction.   2. Large type books.
I. Title.
[PS3556.A3S55   1995]
813'.54—dc20   95–14544

*For Chi
with love
always*

PERSONAL NOTE

There was, of course, an actual *Silver Lady*, a Flying Fortress with a very real and wonderfully human crew—a crew of instant courage, vital spirit and blessed luck. And they *do* have a story—an incredible one—but it is not the one told here.

I have used the name of *The Silver Lady* simply in tribute to the real *Lady* and to the spirit of her crew; for she was most certainly a ship to be remembered, and they, a crew beyond forgetting. Also, I had found in the name a symbol that fitted well the design of this novel; for while it is based on the spirit and times of the original *Lady*, this work *is* nevertheless a novel. Consequently, the background is real, rooted in the memories of the actual historical events; but the people are, naturally, fictional and are not, under any circumstances, to be confused with the crew of the actual ship.

I wish, however, personally to acknowledge my indebtedness to the entire crew of the real *Silver Lady* both for the inspiration of this work and, incidentally, for my life: to Gibson, and Koenig, and Gilmore; to Mielke, Bragg, Grossman, Harris and Chapman; and most of all to Arthur L. Moreland, skipper of the true *Silver Lady*.

To each and all, my thanks, gratitude and admiration.

J.F.

CONTENTS

ix

PART ONE

CONDITION RED
March 1, 1944

CHAPTER ONE

Lieutenant William Starrett—a compactly built man, with wavy sunburnt hair, grey eyes and a wry-smiling mouth—leaned back on his pillow, his hands behind his head, thinking of Chance.

Over his bunk the narrow window of the Nissen hut was opened. The English sky was a square of sunlit blue, clear with a crisp first-of-March wind blowing across the morning. From the line the cough of a sick engine cracked explosively, caught and revved thundering up, then cut again and died with a hacking sputter. Overhead a Spitfire droned in low, flashed beyond the window and was gone again.

Starrett stared wondering at the curved, corrugated roof arcing the room. Chance in combat (especially in aerial combat, he thought) was a fundamental fact. It was a fundamental fact in ordinary life, too, he knew; but war italicized it. Fate, Luck—call it what you would, it was still the unpredictable, the circumstance beyond control. It either favored or shafted you, and there was nothing you could do about it. And that was that.

But Chance wasn't the All of it. A good skipper (and Starrett thought of himself honestly and coldly as a good skipper) did all he could to shape a slick crew—one that meshed, from navigator to tail gunner, into a single, smooth-functioning unit of action. With such a crew, whatever Chance might do, he could at least reduce the possibility of accident, or carelessness, or panic, within a manageable sphere, and as far as that, insure their coming through. And that, clearly and succinctly, was his duty.

Starrett had, he felt, a clean, tight sense of duty, and a fierce pride, rooted in the Old Army tradition, and in the sure knowledge of who and what he was. He had served in the Old Army before Pearl Harbor and had, rather late, decided to transfer to the Air Corps. He was twenty-eight—older than usual for a bomber pilot—when he received his assignment to Ardmore, Oklahoma, to pick up his crew and train them for Flying Fortress duty.

That had been five months ago. Five months of intensive flight and ground work with the crew: five months of living with them, working with them, studying them under shifting conditions, listening to them, feeling them out, wondering, deciding. And only one had he had to reject of the original nine: his first co-pilot, Wozek.

He remembered that incident for more reasons than one, graphically. It had happened last October, at Ardmore, at the end of a long, exhausting flight—a massive wingding simulating a full air operation coordinating squadrons from far-flung fields. They were finally coming in for their landing, wheels down and locked, approaching the runway. He had called, 'Lower flaps,' but Wozek's coordination was off, his mind fogged with other thoughts: whatever the reason, Wozek pulled the wrong lever. He raised the wheels instead of lowering flaps as the ship sped in toward the runway.

Even at best, Ardmore had been poorly situated for Fortress maneuvering. The hills were too high, too many and too near.

He remembered shooting a quick glance at Wozek; then, in an instant reaction, tightening on the controls. The ship hurtled swift in its descent. The whole sped-weight of the plane, the heavy accelerating pressure, strained shivering through his tensing grip as if balancing on his slightest touch. Bracing in every sinew, slowly he drew back on the controls, forced the ship into vibrating strain and guided her level for the hills directly ahead; then, drawing tighter back, with calculated, gut-busting tension, pulled her up, grazing trees, easing just over the height, up into the open, clear sky.

The next day Wozek was off the crew.

Starrett remembered that incident for more than Wozek. He remembered it because of the crew. Every man, from Kramer the navigator to Swacey the tail gunner, had been aware

5

acutely of the death threat. From nose, waist and tail positions they had seen the ambulances, fire trucks and crash teams careening in emergency pursuit down the runway under them. They had seen the hills racing in to shatter them. They had felt the buffeting tensions of his fighting the ship into clear air. And not one man had panicked, or jammed intercom, or in any way deflected his concentration. From all he had later learned, they had merely trusted to his wit and ability, and braced themselves for the recovery—or crash—to come. And from that moment he knew he had the crew he wanted.

True, there was still the question of Wyatt, the ball-turret man, and, for a week now, of the new right-waist gunner, Hagen—

'If they were on my crew,' Aronson had drawled that morning here in the hut, 'I'd bounce them both—pronto.' He aimed a dart at the board on the far wall.

Aronson was skipper of *The Queen O' Reno*, a tall man and bony, with a sharp nose and jutting chin and blue, quick-laughing eyes. His leather jacket was a blaze of color, with *The Queen O' Reno* in scarlet painted across the top, a cartoon of the queen of diamonds in the center, and an even line of seven yellow bombs stenciled below, one for every mission.

'I mean that,' Aronson said seriously. 'Before it's too late.'

'Wyatt's come this far,' Starrett said. He

6

picked up Aronson's harmonica from the table and turned it over in his hands. It was Aronson's good-luck piece: he called it Clementine—after his wife.

'But,' said Aronson, 'from here on in it's really going to be rough. They're talking of hitting Berlin already—by daylight.'

Starrett nodded and set the harmonica down again.

Aronson refingered the dart, squinting at the board. 'What about Hagen?'

Starrett frowned. 'I don't know,' he said. 'It's just a feeling I've got—'

Aronson threw the dart. It hit near center. 'Bounce them,' he said.

'Just like that?'

Aronson glanced to Starrett. 'Think of it as a job,' he said. 'And keep it that way.' He turned back to the darts again. 'You haven't got much time, you know. We got the ass shot out of us yesterday.' He held the next dart out at arm's length, and smiled. 'Your crew's the only logical replacement.'

'Thanks,' said Starrett. 'But we've still two or three weeks' training—'

'Like hell,' said Aronson. 'We've had the shit kicked out of us, man.' He tossed the dart. It struck left of center. 'You'll go up green,' he said flatly.

'Well, if that's the way it goes—'

'You got a name yet?' Aronson asked.

'No.'

7

'It's time you thought of one,' Aronson said. 'It's good for the crew. Good luck, too.'

'We'll think of one,' Starrett said.

Aronson nodded. 'You going to bounce Hagen?'

Starrett smiled. 'You ever bounce anyone?'

Aronson shook his head. 'Nope.' He took aim again. 'But it takes just one—just one—to wreck a crew. And you, man—you've got two.'

'It could be worse.' Starrett grinned. 'It could've been a crew like yours.'

Aronson shrugged. 'We do all right,' he said, 'considering we only lost two so far.'

He flung his final dart. It clanked against the metal wall and dropped to the concrete floor.

Starrett looked up, surprised.

Aronson frowned, his lips puzzled. He rubbed his hands down the sides of his trousers and shrugged. 'Happens to the best of them,' he said wryly and went to the dart board. He pulled out the two near-center darts slowly; then, studying the fallen dart, 'To the best of them.'

*　　*　　*

Starrett glanced to his watch. It was twenty to eleven. At eleven he was to see Cronin, his crew chief, at the gunners' shack, to check on things, to see how they were doing there. Like Wyatt.

Starrett had often wondered about Wyatt, about the wisdom of keeping him on the crew,

8

for his own good. Physically, Wyatt was just five-two, but trimly built, dark haired and quiet-eyed. He was a very green nineteen, an only son, but, from all evidence, with only the thinnest of family ties. He rarely wrote and rarely received letters. He had no girl.

From the practical point of view, Wyatt was a competent gunner who knew and did his duties efficiently; but from the emotional standpoint, he seemed a risk. He was shy, withdrawn, sensitive—perhaps he would be too sensitive, too keenly responsive, inwardly, to the shocks of combat to come. He spoke little and that haltingly, as if unused to talking. He read constantly, and had the look about him of one having thought things out a level or two below the apparent.

Nor did he mix with the crew, but always seemed, while a functional part of them, yet isolated from them—the way he was isolated from them by his very position in the ball turret, which, while a functional part of the ship, hung suspended below and outside it—a lone, interior world of itself.

Yet there was about him, too, a terrier spirit and a pride (so like Starrett's own) in the crew: a belief in them, and a trust, that Wyatt seemed determined to hold, take what it would. And it was this spirit, quiet yet urgently known, that had so far centered Starrett's decision to keep him on the crew, to take the chance.

But now, here in England, the nearer they

came to actual combat, the darker his doubts became, for it seemed more and more evident to Starrett that in a silent, interior way the war Wyatt was fighting within himself was mounting. And Starrett wondered how many wars a man—especially a boy-man like Wyatt—could fight without breaking.

*   *   *

But Hagen was a different matter.

Starrett had met the type before: cocky, calculating, predatory, out for all he could get; yet, according to the crew reports, sure and confident ('better than Dober') in his duties as the right-waist gunner and armorer.

Dober had been the original right-waist man; but only a week before, cycling through the base blackout, he had crashed with a lorry. The truck had run over his left leg. The next day Hagen had been assigned from the Gunners' Pool as replacement.

Chance again, thought Starrett. Well, if there *was* anything behind Chance (and he had never been quite sure), it made him wonder now; for even from his first meeting with Hagen, he had sensed, like a faulty electric current, a quick shock of distrust between them—on his part, as if in Hagen there was an element dangerous to the crew...

*   *   *

Starrett looked to his watch again. It was ten to eleven. Time to see Cronin. Deftly he swung from his bunk, snapped his cap from the nearby chair and slipped it on; then, from the foot of the bunk, picked up his leather flying jacket and, pulling it on—his gestures laconic, simplified to purest action—he started out.

The back of his jacket was bare.

*   *   *

Ten minutes later at the gunners' shack, he was leaning back in a chair, watching Tech Sergeant Cronin sweeping up eddies of dust. Cronin was his flight engineer and crew chief, a lean, agile Iowan with cornsilk hair and a thin, high-boned face. He had just had a run-in with Lieutenant Waverly, the area CO, a brittly defensive ground officer tensed in a world of airmen. Starrett had seen him at the Officers' Club, a precise, spit-and-polish man with an official sense of himself.

With a grunt, Cronin picked up a crushed cigarette butt and flipped it into the coal scuttle by the stove, then flicked his broom over the spot and scattered the ashes.

'Inspection, my ass,' he muttered. 'Came in here with Finch and started chewing me out. Said he was going to gig the whole fuckin' hut 'less we shaped up. Said just because we're combat's no reason to slack off and live like pigs—I'd sure as hell'd like to see that bastard

11

in combat.'

'When's inspection?'

'Any damn time he wants to, he said.' Cronin looked about the hut they shared with the crew of the *Miss Fire*. They had called it the Sad Shack, and it looked it.

The sharp, peppery tang of wood smoke and coal dust spiced the dim air. The aisle between the bunk rows had been swept clean. A potbellied stove glowed ruddy in the center. Along the walls down both sides, uniforms hung crowded, shadowy in the grey light. In the corner, a pair of yellowing long-johns and heavy socks were drying out. The splintery doors at either end were covered with pin-up girls, mostly from *Yank*. The torn blackout curtains had been drawn back, and through the opaque windows on either side the doors, a murky sunlight slanted in.

Cronin reached into his jacket for a cigarette and lit up. 'Anything new?'

He seemed uneasy, uncomfortable, as if, for some reason, there was a barrier between them, and Starrett wondered why. 'We may go up green,' he said. 'Any time now.'

Cronin sat at the rickety table by the stove and fingered a deck of greasy, worn cards. 'The *Miss Fire*'s up,' he said. 'Their fifteenth run.'

'Together?'

Cronin shuffled the cards. 'They lost four.'

Starrett got to his feet restlessly, wondering what was eating Cronin. 'How's our bunch doing?'

Cronin shrugged. 'Okay, I guess.' Then, 'Wyatt doesn't sleep much.' He looked up evenly.

Starrett nodded.

'I can't figure him for shit,' Cronin said and started to play solitaire. 'Can you?'

Starrett shook his head. 'Not all the way.' He started to amble down the bunk row, waiting for Cronin to open up. 'Who's closest to him now—since Dober?'

'Bayer. Ball-turret man on the *Miss Fire*.' He pointed to a lower bunk by the stove. 'That's his there. Under Wyatt's.'

'On the crew, I mean,' said Starrett.

Cronin thought awhile; then, 'No one, I guess. Why?'

'Just wondered.' He was by Nelson's bunk now. Nelson was his left-waist gunner. 'How's Nelson's wife doing?' The last time Starrett had seen her, she was just beginning to show.

'Due next month,' said Cronin. 'He's getting edgy about it.'

'Who wouldn't?' said Starrett. He stopped at the corner bunk by the door and read the name tag. 'Might've known it,' he said. Pictures and snapshots of a dozen women—two of them completely nude—had been posted by the window wall. All had been signed intimately to Hagen.

Starrett studied them appreciatively. 'He sure gets around, doesn't he?' He glanced over

13

the bunk (the blankets pulled quarter-bounce tight) to the uniforms, creased sharp and clean, hanging by the back wall. On the shelf overhead were Hagen's toilet kit, hair oil and half a bottle of after-shave cologne.

'He makes out,' Cronin said.

'What did he say about his new assignment?'

There was a pause, too long a pause.

Starrett turned. Last night, after a talk with Wyatt, he had given Cronin Hagen's new flight duty: checking the turret when Wyatt was in the ball—keeping the ring cleared, noting the oxygen supply level—things Wyatt would have no control of while in position.

'I didn't tell him,' Cronin said uncomfortably; then, bluntly, 'I didn't tell him because I didn't see him. He didn't come in last night.' He flung down the cards and rose angrily.

Starrett frowned, eyeing Cronin. Then, 'Was he on base?'

'I don't know—dammit, he should've known better!'

For a full moment Starrett waited. He understood now Cronin's odd uneasiness with him, the barrier between them.

Cronin looked at him.

Starrett shoved his hands into his back pockets and shook his head, his lips tight and tensing.

'Maybe he's got an explanation,' said Cronin.

Starrett glanced up. 'It had better be a good one.' He looked to his watch; then sharply, 'When he comes in—and he'd better—tell him to report to me at fourteen hundred. Or else!'

Cronin nodded. 'Yes, sir.' He spun his cigarette butt into the dust pit under the stove. He seemed relieved.

But Starrett's eyes were brittle, his whole body tensed as, turning, he strode out.

CHAPTER TWO

It was twelve thirty when Hagen finally breezed in. He tossed a loaf of fresh, warm-smelling bread to the table.

Cronin was reading *Yank*, tilted back in a chair against his bunk. He glanced up and saw Hagen coming down the aisle. 'Where the hell you been?' he said.

'Where're the guys?' said Hagen.

'Chow. Where you been?'

Hagen looked at him. 'Why?'

Angrily Cronin flung the *Yank* aside. 'Because Starrett wants to see you,' he snapped. 'Two sharp.'

'What about?'

'Last night, god-dammit!'

Hagen frowned. 'How'd he find out?'

'I told him,' said Cronin.

Hagen looked at him darkly. 'Thanks,

15

buddy.' He went to his bunk, sore. His stride was tensed, rhythmic with athletic ease, his body tapered in tough, sure lines.

He took off his cap and jacket and threw them on his bunk; then hoisted himself up and stretched out, straining his whole body taut in a single gesture and, suddenly, with a grunt, went limp.

He turned his head, eyeing Cronin down the shack. Cronin reached for the *Yank* again.

Hagen's face was bronzed and finely chiseled, proud with a straight aquiline nose, a cynical mouth and a strong chin. His hair was a mass of black curls; his eyes a lucid, glinting blue.

'Is it the bounce?' he said.

'How the fuck should I know?' muttered Cronin. 'That's between you and him.' He rattled the paper as he turned a page.

Hagen looked at him closely. 'How come you didn't cover for me?'

'With Starrett?' Cronin shook his head. 'Not me, brother.'

Hagen rolled on his back and, frowning, drew a cigarette and a match from his shirt pocket and lit up.

He needed a crew. That was for damn sure. A good, tight crew like Starrett's. Not like the crew he had been on—a real fuck-up crew, from pilot to tail. The pilot and co-pilot had crashed three weeks back in a checkout flight. ('It figured,' Hagen had said.) He had been at

16

The Wash at the time, taking final gunnery training. When he came back, he had been sent to the Pool with the rest of the crew gunners.

Hagen's frown deepened. A guy didn't have a chance without a crew. Like Ralegh at the Pool. Ralegh had been there since last November and still had fourteen missions to go. And every time he had gone up, it had been with a different crew. 'Guys I didn't know,' he said. 'Strangers. Like fighting the whole fuckin' war alone.' And he looked it.

But Ralegh at least had come back, thought Hagen. Not like the others, the too goddam many others, who hadn't come back—all, like Ralegh, temporary fill-ins. The cut of luck narrowed then. With every strange, new crew you went up with, it cut down just so much more. So no matter how you looked at it, the breaks were against you in the Pool. And the only real way out was permanent assignment to a crew.

A *good* crew, Hagen insisted. Well, he *had* been assigned—he was one of the lucky ones—and even though he hated Starrett's guts (and the guts of every other bastard with bars on his shoulders), he knew Starrett had something in his crew. And now, god-dammit, he had fucked it up but good—again.

Hagen took a long drag on his cigarette; then, wondering, he turned toward Cronin again. 'Hey, Cronin—tell me. Did he ask you, or did you just tell him?'

Cronin got up, stretching, and tossed the *Yank* on his bunk. 'He asked.' He met Hagen's look and started down the hut to him. 'I told him you probably had a reason—'

Hagen snorted, almost laughed; and swinging himself up, sat on the bunk edge, crushing out his cigarette on the iron rim post. 'Oh, sure,' he said. 'Some reason.' He gestured to the bread on the table. 'Phyllis.'

'Phyllis!' Cronin looked at the bread, then back to Hagen.

Hagen shrugged. 'Any port in the storm.'

Actually, though, Phyllis was more than a port in the storm. She was homely, a stocky blonde, squint-eyed (but jolly) with chipped teeth. But being the daughter of the village baker, she meant also fresh bread, and jam sometimes, and even occasionally eggs— nights when a guy felt hungry and the chow lines were closed and the canteen was too far away. She was a means to an end. She was also Moody's girl.

Moody was right-waist man on the *Miss Fire*. Ever since Hagen had come to the Shack and had found out Moody's source of food supply, he had been buddy-buddy with him. Two nights ago Moody had brought him (through the field east of the hut, down the cow path, through the thicketed woods and into the town road) to the cottage at the fork leading into the village.

'Moody ain't going to like it,' Cronin said

18

quietly.

'Tough shit.' Hagen dropped to his feet.

'Thought you two were buddy-buddy.'

Hagen rubbed his chin, feeling the day-grown stubble, and decided he had better shave. He took off his tie, loosened his collar and reached for his toilet kit.

'Moody's been through a lot,' said Cronin, watching him. 'Schweinfurt. Regensburg. He takes things hard.'

Hagen snapped his towel from behind the bunk. 'That's his tough luck,' he said and, flapping the towel over his shoulder, went out.

*   *   *

At quarter to two Hagen zipped up his jacket and started down the path outside the Shack.

The Shack was the last of four Nissen huts on Gunners' Row, Section C, two areas from the Officers' Quarters. A cinder path, bordering a quadrangle of muddied grass, led past the other three huts, turned right under the oak by the latrine and ended abruptly where the warped tar road began. The road went north by Quartermaster's, skirted the rest of the gunners' area and, by the Squadron Orderly Room, branched out in two directions.

Hagen turned left by the row of oaks, to the BOQ section.

Starrett's quarters, like most of the buildings

19

on the base, was a Nissen hut, like a giant steel barrel cut in two and set lengthwise and flat along the ground. The walls were corrugated, painted a drab olive green, and ventilated by windows built into the sides. The front and back sides, like the enlisted men's huts, were wood, with two small windows cut in beside the doors. A grimy stovepipe, with a thin drift of smoke trailing out, jutted from the roof. A bicycle leaned against the wall. Hagen glanced at it quickly, then opened the door and went inside.

The hut was empty. Hagen looked at his watch—five-to-two—unzipped his jacket and strode down the row of cots to the one tagged LT. WILLIAM G. STARRETT.

A small writing table, facing an opened slide-back window, stood beside the cot. Outside, an old moss-grown oak stirred against the clear sky. There was a light wind blowing in, edged now with a faint warmth. The feeling of an early spring tinged the air.

Hagen pulled back the folding chair and sat down, frowning. On the table before him lay a manila folder labeled THE CREW. The printing was fine and even.

Hagen flipped it open and studied the first page, a typed list of the crew, their names and positions. Hagen's frown deepened. The list started with the co-pilot, but the first name— ruled through—was strange to him: *Lt. Bruno Wozek.* Hagen wondered what had happened

20

to Wozek. The bounce? Accident? he recognized the newer name:

Lt. Dan Kirby	Co-pilot
Lt. Lyle Gillis	Bombardier
Lt. Jim Kramer	Navigator
S/Sgt. Lee Cronin	Engineer, Crew Chief
S/Sgt. Sid Golden	Radioman
Sgt. Lindy Nelson	Armorer, Left-waist
Sgt. Tom Wyatt	Armorer, Ball-Turret
Sgt. Tom Swacey	Engineer, Tail

Another name had been neatly ruled out: *Sgt. Stan Dober, Armorer, Right-waist.* And in its place, inked in over it, was his own name: *Sgt. Mitch Hagen, Armorer, Right-waist*—with a small penciled question mark beside it.

Hagen studied it, his lips drawn tight.

The list had been made up some time back. The page was dog-eared, and the enlisted ranks had been upped since then. Cronin and Golden were Tech Sergeants now, and all the others Staff.

His eye went back to the question mark beside his name.

The door down the hut opened and was shut abruptly. Hagen glanced up, startled.

'Sorry I'm late, Hagen.' Lieutenant Starrett came down the hut, taking off his cap. He looked at Hagen, quickly noting the open folder.

Hagen flipped the folder shut and stood to a

stiff, guarded attention.

'At ease,' said Starrett.

Hagen relaxed.

Starrett had his jacket off now, dropped it across the bunk and whipped off his white silk scarf. He motioned Hagen to the cot, slid the folder under a writing pad and sat down, facing Hagen.

'You'd been a cadet once—'

'That's right.'

'And washed out—'

'That's right.'

Starrett nodded, his look cold. 'Why?'

'I missed a bus one night. They reported me AWOL.'

'Like last night?' said Starrett. His eyes were grim, steady.

Slowly Hagen reddened. Then, brittly, 'Yes, sir.'

Starrett nodded again, 'Then why—'

'Is this the bounce?' snapped Hagen.

Starrett frowned, searching Hagen's face. 'If I had my way,' he said evenly, 'I'd have had you off the crew last week. But the others think you'll work out.' He studied Hagen as if, even now, weighing a final decision. Then: 'What do you think of Wyatt?' he asked curiously.

'Wyatt?' Hagen's eyes narrowed. 'Wyatt, sir?'

'Yes, Hagen. Wyatt.'

Hagen was uneasy—the way he was when playing chess with someone new, wondering

22

about the effect of the next move, how his opponent might meet it. 'He'll crack in a week,' he said flatly, and waited.

Starrett leaned back, his eyes still intent, still inscrutable. 'You think so?'

Hagen nodded. 'He's too quiet.'

'He's always been quiet,' said Starrett. 'Even back in the States.'

Hagen shook his head. 'Nobody's that quiet,' he said. 'He's all wound up inside— tight.'

Starrett pursed his lips, wondering; then, 'You don't like Wyatt, do you?'

'No, I don't,' said Hagen.

'Do you trust him?' asked Starrett.

'No, sir! Not on your life.'

Starrett's lips smiled, but his eyes were steady. 'He's willing to bet *his* life on you,' he said.

Hagen paused, then quietly, 'He's got the better odds,' he said.

Starrett's smile went. Brusquely, 'Your new assignment,' he said, 'is checking Wyatt in the turret. In flight, when he's in the turret, you'll keep a constant check on him—especially on his oxygen supply and on the turret rings. Make sure they're clear at all times. He's the only one of us locked outside the ship. If anything should go wrong—' he eyed Hagen sharply—'be there to get him out.' Starrett looked to his watch. 'Wyatt's up on the line now. Report to the armorers' shed. Work with

23

him. Get to know him better.' He paused. 'And tell him we're operational.'

Hagen started. 'Operational?'

'I just got the word,' Starrett said. 'We'll be going up any day now. Tomorrow maybe. They're assigning us a ship now.'

Hagen frowned. 'But your gunners—they haven't even been to The Wash yet. They're not even checked out—'

'They're as checked out as they'll ever be,' Starrett said and, with a gesture of dismissal, got to his feet.

Slowly Hagen rose and zipped up his jacket. 'Anything else?'

'Yeah,' said Starrett, and eyed Hagen squarely. 'Crew or no crew, one more trick like last night—just one—and it'll be your ass.'

Hagen turned and, putting on his flight cap, strode angrily down the hut. At the door he glanced back.

Starrett was still looking at him, steadily.

*　　*　　*

The armorers' shed on the line was vague with shadow, cold with the smell of oil and metal and fusty rags. The door was opened to the slow wind blowing across the sunny field. The single bare bulb, glaring above the workbench, burned with a dim, greasy glow.

The counter before Wyatt was strewn with cotton patches, brass brushes, cleaning rods,

24

gauges, and parts of a caliber .50 machine gun soaking in pans of oil.

Hagen watched as Wyatt, perched on a high stool, checked and fitted the parts deftly together, his hands glistening, his face intent on the practice checkout.

Wyatt was scarcely five-two in height—the shortest and youngest of the crew—with dark, unruly hair, a ruddy complexion and wide, quiet eyes. He was wearing a heavy green sweater, dirtied fatigues and no cap. The week before—in a series of thefts in the gunners' area—somebody had stolen his leather flight jacket. His grey windbreaker hung from the door.

Hagen had never thought of Wyatt before, except to dismiss him as unusable. He noticed that even among the crew members Wyatt had stood apart, never quite drawn into their rough-and-tumble, give-and-take interplays—not that they had excluded him, but that he seemed never to know how to become a part of them. He seemed even more a stranger among them than Hagen was. And always there was that sense of control about him—a tight, constant, guarded control, Hagen felt, all wound up.

Yet, Hagen had noticed, from the rough-and-tumblest of the crew, Swacey the tail gunner—and from Starrett himself, and Kramer the navigator, and Gillis the bombardier—there was a warm, real liking for

Wyatt, almost an appreciation, as if they had sensed something about Wyatt that was—for the time anyway, Hagen felt—beyond him.

Already he had found out that he had been Wyatt's choice, not Starrett's, for outside turret man.

'How come?' He leaned back against the bench, watching Wyatt closely. 'How come me?'

Wyatt shrugged. 'It was the best answer I could think of at the time.'

'Why not Nelson?'

'He wasn't in question,' said Wyatt.

'And I was?'

Wyatt wiped his hands carefully. 'He wanted to know if I trusted you.' He started to screw the gun barrel into the barrel-extension unit. 'Under the circumstances, it was the only answer I could have given.'

Hagen handed him the bolt group. 'Anything special I should know?' he asked. 'About you in the turret?'

Wyatt slid the bolt into place. 'One thing,' he said. 'I wear a chest chute—but I leave the pack in the corner—just by the turret.'

'*Outside?*'

Wyatt looked up. 'Ever try wearing a chest pack in the turret?' He shook his head. 'I've got it timed, though. I need only fifteen seconds.'

'Fifteen!' Hagen frowned at him. 'What happens if you've only got *two*?'

Wyatt shrugged again. 'If it's that bad,

26

chances are I'd have had it anyway.' He checked the final assembly of the gun carefully. 'If the ship dives, the pressure'd force me—' He started to oil down the gun. 'We dove once—in a wingding, back in Ardmore—about a hundred, two hundred feet. A guy nearly rammed us in formation. The pressure jammed me in the turret. Like I weighed a ton to every inch. I couldn't manipulate. So—' he reached for the canvas gun cover behind the oil pan—'I realized I'd have to figure that in.'

'Figure that in what?'

Wyatt slid the gun into its jacket and shoved it into its rack under the counter.

'I tried a seat chute,' he said, 'once. But I didn't like it. Too bulky. Besides, there'd still be the pressure of the dive. I'd still have to unlock the turret, unplug oxygen and intercom, and flip into a back tumble to clear out. Meanwhile,' he said lightly, 'the plane is still diving—and this supposes the turret's still *with* the ship.'

He shook his head again and started to mop up the counter with a rag. 'My only hope is that Starrett can keep her steady for fifteen seconds *after*—'

He tossed the oily rag into the corner pile. 'The point is,' he said, 'make sure the pack's always in the corner. Sometimes a guy might kick it, or move it aside, by mistake.'

He started to collect the cleaning rods and brushes.

Hagen watched, frowning.

'On top of that—' Wyatt grinned—'I'll need all the space I can get down there. Bayer says I'll be from six to nine hours at a stretch in it.'

'But what if—' Hagen moved out of his way—'Starrett can't give you those fifteen seconds?'

Wyatt paused—for only an instant. Then quietly, 'He'll give it a good try,' he said.

Hagen frowned again, thinking, remembering Starrett's orders: *If anything goes wrong, be there to get him out.* But, Christ, *fifteen* seconds! In a hit plane? He looked at Wyatt busily wiping down the cleaning rods, then turned and, leaning against the door, looked over the field, thinking.

From the doorway of the armorers' shed he could see most of the base spreading out over the dips and rises of gently hilly terrain. Nissen huts and sheds, tents and shacks, and a few grounded Fortresses dotted the far-flung field. To the south the hangars and towers of the flight line, built on the nearest of the rises, gleamed in the sun. From Operations the perimeter track stretched in a dark, undulating road through the new grass and wound its far way by the dispersal areas, skirting the crosswork of runways and landing strips, as far north as the forest line and as far east and west as the pasture and farmland bordering the base.

The cow-lazy meadows and furrowed fields

28

rolled out from every side, reaching away, like a quilted design, to sunny, greening counties. In the distance, above the trees, towered the spire of a Gothic church.

'He's a great guy, Starrett, I suppose,' said Hagen, almost casually.

Wyatt nodded, wiping his hands dry again. 'I'd fly clear through Hell with him,' he said. 'And from what Bayer tells me, that's just where we're going.'

He crossed to the door for his windbreaker.

'We're operational,' Hagen said.

Wyatt looked up, a sudden shadow in his glance. Then, as suddenly as it had come, it went. 'I suspected it,' he said, 'from what Bayer told me. We got a ship yet?'

Hagen shook his head. 'They're assigning us one now.'

'Hope it's a new job,' said Wyatt, slipping into his windbreaker. 'One of those silver ones.'

'But all in all,' said Hagen, 'I suppose he's a great guy—Starrett.'

'The greatest,' said Wyatt. He started to zip up.

'In spite of his weak points,' Hagen said, eyeing the field.

Wyatt turned, his look sharpening. 'Like the way he feels about the crew?' he asked. His eyes were steady.

Hagen shrugged. 'That's his strongest point,' he said carefully, and glanced aside to

29

Wyatt.

'Is it?' asked Wyatt evenly.

Hagen shrugged again. 'I don't know,' he said. 'Seems like he's out to prove something.'

Wyatt pulled a knit cap from the pocket and slid it on. 'He doesn't have to prove a thing,' he said. 'It's others—that have to prove things.'

Hagen turned, tensed. 'Meaning?'

'Others,' said Wyatt. 'Not the skipper.'

'You, for instance?'

Wyatt's eyes were quiet again. 'Maybe.' He looked at Hagen wonderingly.

'Shit!' said Hagen uncomfortably and glanced away. Suddenly—'Jesus Christ! Look!' He nodded eastward toward the church tower.

Brokenly a Fortress was veering in toward the base, its wings straining, one of its engines dead. The tail letter was partly shot away. It struggled for altitude.

'He'll never make it,' said Hagen.

Wyatt's face was tight and drawn.

The Fortress rose unsteadily, held wavering a moment; then, its engines sporadic with fractured thunder, it trembled and dropped again, lower.

They stood, fixed, side by side, silent, and watched.

Shakily the Fort drew in, nearing the edge of the field. It sheared the highest boughs of a tree and droned in, louder.

A red flare shot out from the waist, arced up

30

like a rosy comet and fell sharply, trailing a wavy pink cloud.

'Wounded aboard,' said Wyatt.

Suddenly another prop fluttered and cut. The ship flung up like a windy leaf, tossed swiftly, crazily atilt, and plunged for earth, spin-crashing wing-end-up in a deafening roar.

Shock waves snapped out, ripping across the field. A black, billowing cloud erupted from the main wreckage.

'Christ,' muttered Hagen. 'What a send-off.'

He turned and saw Wyatt watching the scarlet flames spiraling through the smoke, his eyes dark and quiet, his face taut with control.

CHAPTER THREE

The smoke swirled, towering thick and black, smudging in the wind as Wyatt watched, aware of Hagen's searching look—aware, too, of the tight coolness, like a sudden, subtle guise, masking the dry, dark hollowness within.

He had seen death before, like this, swift and violent, in the crashes at Ardmore: the fire-blasted slopes, the wreckage-strewn scars cut black into the landscape.

And he had seen death come slow in the malingering, steady absorption of life in an antiseptic room ... his Uncle Seth, of the warm, bright-grey eyes and the loving-gentle smile ... first teacher and earliest companion ... cancer-ridden, edging into death gradually through a long, lovely summer... *But death is not the end, my boy. Oh, no. Death is not the end... Tears, Tommy?... You're a man of twelve now... Courage... There is no death. Believe me. And no fear... Only ... the going across to Him ... in His time ... in His way... Even the pain ... is bearable ... as yours must be, if you believe... Believe, my boy, and the courage ... is yours ... to endure all things ... even this...*

And the light fading from the windows across the white bed, and the worn hand, holding his, going gently still...

And now the other death—the silent death within, of belief, and of that courage—

'Going back?' asked Hagen.

Wyatt nodded.

They started across the grass to the perimeter track, curving back to the main base.

Already across the far field the crash crew had brought the flames under control, and the ambulances were veering about and speeding back down the line.

'She must have aborted,' said Hagen, 'coming in alone like that.'

Wyatt burrowed his fists into his windbreaker pockets. He felt cold.

Suddenly a horn honked behind them. 'Wanna lift?'

They turned. A sergeant in a line jeep pulled

32

over to them.

'Sure thing,' said Hagen and leaped in.

'You go ahead,' said Wyatt. 'I need to walk.' He waved them on. The sergeant nodded and, shifting gear, swung the jeep ahead of Wyatt and sped on down the perimeter track, with Hagen looking back at him.

If only we could all be Hagens, thought Wyatt. The kind that don't question, that just act and make the most of the consequences, to whom there is neither meaning nor purpose, only the physical Now of things, and only the sensual self.

A deep, uneasy sigh forced through him. He shook his head and started the long way down to the Shack.

Life was too transient to Wyatt, and death too present, for him not to believe there was something beyond; and life, brief, intense as it was in a world precise with miracle, surrounded by infinite wonder, was in itself too much a miracle for him to believe it chance or accident. Somewhere, somehow, he felt, there was a purpose in his being here now; but whatever that purpose was, it still eluded him, fading always beyond the horizon of his searching thought—the insight that would bring again the conviction he needed if he was to hold together for the missions to come.

He remembered how once his Uncle Seth had told him that a man grew in two ways, by insight and decision. Well, he had had the insight to know what he was and what he had to do, in spite of all opposition. He had known he could not, in all self-honesty, be the conscientious objector his folks had urged him to be, like his cousins, and let another man fight—and possibly die—in *his* place for the rights he would enjoy.

So he had made his decision and had had the courage to stand his ground in the consequences of that decision, his family's alienation. He had had the conviction then, and for the long months after, that what he was doing was the right and only way for him. He had believed in himself.

But now, the nearer he got to combat, to the daily reality of death, the more intense life had become. It was simply and starkly the fear of death, the ending, the finality of life, that had given him the surging, almost overwhelming desire to live that tore like an ascending scream through every hour and fiber of his being.

What if he (and Uncle Seth) had been wrong, and death *was* the end of life; and life was only this instant of time here on earth? And what if he should die now, this young, when he might have chosen differently? *Was* he right to do as he had done, to be here now on the eve of combat? What if this *was* the All of it, and he was flinging that All away for a principle, an ideal, that had been in reality *not* an insight but a delusion, a trick of the mind only, a rationalization?

Wyatt's mouth tightened. He dug his fists deeper into his windbreaker pockets and quickened his steps.

Life was too precious to throw away on a mistake of judgment, a trick of mind. Lately he had found himself acutely, desperately aware of living: of food and sleep, smells and taste and sounds, the world about him, grass and sun and wind. He had found himself touching bark, rusted iron, wool; staring at grass and the gritty earth between, flowers and the cows in the fields, and the faces about him; breathing in the smoke of the Shack, the clean morning wind, the tangs and tars of the hangars and line—all in a strange, new way, as if for the first time.

The will to live was rising, growing now daily more intensely real as the belief he had had in himself faded, and the once-certain courage had steadily ebbed away, like wind into stillness, until now there was nothing left— neither belief nor courage—to face the threat that was to come: nothing but the dry, dark hollowness within.

Wyatt shivered, feeling the wind chill across the field.

*   *   *

It was ten past eight by the clock over the bar of the Rocker Club—the squadron's club for gunners and groundmen, staff sergeants and up. It was built of three Nissen huts in an H formation, with a bar in one wing and a lounge in the other, three areas away from Squadron Mess.

Quietly Wyatt eased back in his chair and looked about. The dry haze of smoke, swirling thick and yellow in the air, stung his eyes.

The club seethed with motion now, crowded with men jostling to the bar and back again, glasses foaming and slopping over. On every side the men slouched about the tables, joking, arguing, their arms waving and swooping in and out, hangar-flying the day's raid.

Glasses clinked and clicked over the gushing taps. Chairs scraped back and forth. The steady droning hum of talk flowed on through the bursts of laughter and shouted calls, sharp and shrill across the din.

The wet, bitter smell of brew mingled with the leathery smell of jackets and sweat and sour, dank fleece. Under the shaded lights, clouds of stale smoke hovered in curling drifts against the low, arced ceiling.

Wyatt leaned forward, resting his arms on the table, noting that Bayer's gnarled, hairy hand trembled as it struck for a light. The flame wavered gently as Bayer cupped his hands and, squinting through the smoke, puffed until his cigar end glowed. Then flicking out the match, he tossed it into the butt can on the table.

Bayer was ball-turret man on the *Miss Fire*, a tough, weathered old-timer. His face was

36

stubbled and gaunt, etched, Wyatt thought, with unaltering sadness. His lips were drawn thin, without full color. His small, sharp eyes were oddly bright with the quick blue-grey look of sudden aging.

'They should have made for the emergency strip,' he said, almost to himself. 'It's just this side the Channel. They could have made it easy.' He looked across the brew-stained table to Wyatt. 'But—' he shrugged—'that's the way the song goes.' He turned abruptly, scanning toward the bar; then, sharply, a shout, 'Hey, Lyzak—get the lead out!'

A cry went up. 'Hey, Lyzak—your date's getting anxious.'

Laughter rang out.

Bayer grinned at Wyatt.

Bayer and Lyzak were a pair. Lyzak was left-waist man on the *Bombay*. Their crews had flown together since Stateside training; they had flown trans-Atlantic in the same flight; and had, ever since becoming operational, been flying combat together, raid for raid. Both had now fifteen bombs to their jackets.

They even shared the same girl, Dory, barmaid at the village pub, The Swan.

'About time,' Bayer grunted, seeing Lyzak maneuvering from the crowd, two brews and a Coke in hand. He kicked out a chair for him.

'Next time,' said Lyzak, 'you go,' and slid the glasses across the table. They slopped gently.

37

Lyzak was ruddy-faced and freckled, his nose stubby, his mouth lopsided, with a jagged scar twisting his left cheek—from a crash at gunnery school. He was redheaded and blue-eyed, his hands thick and heavy. He nodded toward the bar. 'They're talking about the *Shy Ann*,' he said. 'Their thirteenth run. Lucky thirteen.'

Bayer turned his glass in its wet circle. 'Wyatt saw her come in.'

Lyzak cocked his head at Wyatt. 'Bad, huh?'

Wyatt nodded. 'Yeah.'

'The homing instinct,' said Bayer grimly. 'We all get it.' He looked at Lyzak. 'Bet that's why they didn't try the emergency strip.' He grinned sadly to Wyatt. 'You'll get it, too,' he said. 'You'll see. No matter how bad it'll be, you'll make for home base. Even if it kills you.'

'But why?' asked Wyatt.

'Damned if I know,' said Bayer. 'It just happens after a while. That's all.' He shrugged. 'Watch.'

He sipped his brew, quiet; then, to Lyzak, 'Any word yet?'

Lyzak shook his head. 'No. It's still white.'

Wyatt glanced to the bar, to the panel of three lights just under the clock: the Mission Signal Board. The red bulb meant Mission, alert for tomorrow; the green, Stand-down, no mission (a day to breathe); and the white, Stand-by (and sweat it out). A phone call from Headquarters would tell the barman the signal

38

to switch on. The white bulb was still glowing, Stand-by.

'Hope it's green,' Bayer said tightly.

'Want a bet?' said Lyzak. 'We got another Big Week coming.'

'Says who?' snapped Bayer.

'It figures,' said Lyzak flatly and drank his brew.

Bayer frowned, turning his glass, uneasy. 'Does it?'

Quietly Wyatt watched him, wondering.

Even now the wind of the war was rising. Rumors of an Allied invasion were being scattered about. Invasion was the dark army crouching beyond the horizon. But between the rumors and the event rose the Luftwaffe. Before any invasion could be made, the Luftwaffe, now at its towering height, had to be broken.

Already, during the Big Week—ended only a few days back—the challenge had been hurled. Group after group had winged defiantly in, for seven straight clear days, to blast away at the High Priority targets deep within the Reich. And ever since last August in the skies over Schweinfurt and Regensburg the challenge had been met and parried, with losses heavy and the balance still to be turned.

But the tide of the wind was rising. Any week now, any day perhaps, the storm would break.

'Berlin's the day,' said Lyzak, nodding. 'Watch.'

'I'll do that,' Bayer bit out.

Lyzak glanced up at him quickly.

Wyatt watched.

Then slowly Lyzak raised his brew and took a long swallow.

Dismally Bayer chewed on his cigar. 'We got flak leave coming,' he said. 'Hope they time it right.'

'Like when they hit Berlin?' asked Lyzak. He reached in his pocket for a cigarette and lit up.

'I could use the rest,' said Bayer. 'A week away from here—I'd be a new man.'

Lyzak shook his head. 'I don't know,' he said doubtfully. 'I don't trust flak leave. Nobody's the same after.' He looked to Bayer. 'Gives a guy too much time to think.'

'Some guys,' said Bayer. 'Not me. I just need to rest.'

'At the flak home?' asked Lyzak. 'Or with Dory?'

Bayer grinned. 'I don't know. With Dory maybe.'

Lyzak shrugged. 'Okay by me,' he said. 'Only, the next time you buy her a dress, don't make it blue.' He flicked an ash into the butt can casually. 'It's my wife's favorite color.'

Wyatt and Bayer laughed, and drank.

Suddenly a hard, jolting shove from behind jarred Wyatt's head. His teeth clicked sharp against his glass. The Coke splashed his face and spattered his windbreaker. He slammed down the glass and wheeled angrily.

Behind him a tall, lanky tech sergeant wavered drunkenly, clutching Wyatt's chair for support, his brew pulsing over, dripping through his fingers. His bleary, reddened eyes squinted sullenly, frowning down on Wyatt. His face was clotted with dried blood, cut about the chin and cheeks, and swollen bluish about the nose.

His mouth twisted uncertainly. 'Sorry,' he mumbled, his voice thick and blurred, and tried flicking the brew stains from Wyatt's collar.

Wyatt looked at him, then quietly, 'It's okay, Mac. Let it go.'

The sergeant nodded feebly and peered from Wyatt to Lyzak and across to Bayer. His frown screwed into a look of tight defiance. 'McGill's the best fuckin' pilot you ever saw,' he slurred, his hands tensing hard. 'Got the best fuckin' crew, too—ain't he?' he asked, nodding to Wyatt. 'But *them*—they're shit-eaters,' he said, raising his head again. 'They don't know him like I do.' He looked down at Wyatt again. 'They don't know nothing,' he said and staggered, groping for balance.

Wyatt jumped up to help him. A stinging kick in the shin caught him below the table. He looked to Bayer. Bayer's eyes were on the sergeant, but his hand motioned Wyatt down.

Wyatt sat back.

The sergeant caught himself and stood erect again, his mouth in contempt. 'You're all shit-eaters, too,' he sneered and, turning, veered to a corner table, fell heavily into his seat and slumped forward, staring glazedly into his brew.

'Evans,' said Bayer, with a nod. 'Crew chief on the *Jezebelle*.'

'They aborted again,' Lyzak said. 'Their fifth straight time, at the coast.'

'The skipper turned chicken every time,' Bayer said. 'They racked him out today. Him and the co-pilot. Broke up the crew.'

'And him?' asked Wyatt.

'The Pool,' said Lyzak.

Wyatt glanced at Evans.

'At chow,' Bayer said quietly, 'some guy called the skipper yellow, something like that. Evans tore loose. Nearly killed him.'

Wyatt's eyes darkened. 'He thought a lot of the crew, maybe.'

'Too much,' said Bayer. 'That was his mistake.'

Lyzak slapped the table. 'More brew?' he asked.

'Hey, Wyatt!'

Wyatt looked up and saw Cronin edging through the crowd. Behind him was Swacey, their tail gunner: a stocky Alabamian with light, tousled hair, a lazy smile and shrewd grey eyes.

'We've got a ship!' yelled Cronin. 'We just come from her.' He swung a leg over the empty chair and slid into it.

42

'Where is she?' asked Wyatt.

'Revetment three,' said Cronin. 'Back of the paint shed.'

'One of the new ones,' said Swacey. 'All silver.'

He glanced around for a seat. All were taken. With a shrug, he started to ease Cronin out.

'Here, Swacey.' Wyatt rose. 'Take mine.'

'Where you going?' Cronin asked.

'To the ship,' said Wyatt, and grinned.

'Take the main road up,' Bayer said. 'The shortcut's tricky at night. And take my bike. It's at the Shack.'

'Thanks,' said Wyatt and turned.

The phone at the bar rang twice.

A dark, waiting quiet tensed through the club. Wyatt stopped. Heads turned, listening, toward the barman at the phone—then to the panel of lights, expectantly.

'Got it,' the barman said and, setting the phone down again, bellowed, 'Tech Sergeant Miller—report to the line!'

A burly sergeant rose from a table at the back and, grabbing up his heavy jacket, started out.

Spurts of nervous laughter flickered across the hut.

Suddenly a glass crashed to the floor.

Wyatt spun, startled.

Drunkenly in the corner Evans knocked a butt can clanging against the wall and glared,

43

mean-eyed, around. 'He's yellow!' he burst out, snorting with disgust. 'McGill's the yellowest fuckin' bastard in the whole fuckin' air force!'

The words crumbled in his throat. Wearily he pitched forward, sprawling across the table, his wrecked face twisting in a pool of brew.

Wyatt's eyes met Bayer's. Sadly Bayer shook his head.

Slowly Wyatt started through the crowd again, his face set with rigid calm.

At the door he looked back to the Mission Signal Board. The white Stand-by light glowed steadily through the haze.

*　　　*　　　*

The road in the half-moonlight was dim through shadowed darkness, a world of blackout. Stars flickered, brittle and quick, like chips of light. The cold bit into Wyatt's bones as, carefully, he cycled into the area behind the dope shed and, braking to a halt, got off and leaned the bike to the ground.

He turned and saw looming in the revetment before him the Fortress, towering strange and still.

Uneasily he crossed to her, his fists deep in his windbreaker, his face raw with the wind sharp across the field. He shivered, huddling; then slowly, quietly, he started to circle the ship, his eyes tracing its sleek, swift lines—the wide, tapered wings; the poised, balanced tilt of the body; the high, sloping rise of its dorsal fin; and under her, the globed turret: a ship silver and proud and cold, without identity or meaning.

And yet he knew that, whatever happened now, it would be they, the crew, and how they met the days ahead—themselves never to be the same again—that would give her her meaning. And *if* they were to come through, missions completed, and new and separate ways to go, there would be something gone from each of them—something of them that had become a part of her, because she would be the heart of them.

He touched her gently as if the cold, factual touch brought her into real existence.

She was indeed real.

*   *   *

He was standing there, wondering and still, when the slit-lighted jeep swerved its narrowed beams across the darkness and, with a grinding of gears, veered widely into the moonlit revetment. The lights cut and, from the night, Starrett's voice called out as he swung from the jeep, a flashlight in hand. It clicked on, scanning the ship, and picked up Wyatt, and cut again.

'Wyatt?'

'Yes, sir.'

Slowly Starrett came up to him. 'A beauty, isn't she?'

'Yes, sir. A real beauty.' He waited. He heard another nearing step, a quick, hard stomp on the concrete, from behind Starrett.

Another light flashed on again, blinding Wyatt, then cut.

'Wyatt, this is Greene,' said Starrett as the dark form shaped against the dimness. 'He's ground chief. Greene, Wyatt.'

'Ball-turret, I bet,' said Greene. His hand was sudden and rough; he eased it to a firm, quick shake. 'Glad to know you, Wyatt.'

'Thanks,' said Wyatt. 'Same here.'

Greene turned to Starrett. 'I'll just check the armament, sir.' He opened the waist hatch and hoisted himself, crouching, inside. A light probed the inner dark intermittently.

Starrett leaned against the ship.

Wyatt could feel the clear, cold eyes on him.

Then, Starrett's voice calm and conversational: 'We might go up tomorrow, you know.'

'I know.'

'It'll probably be a milk run.'

'Or Berlin,' said Wyatt.

'Or Berlin.'

There was an uneasy pause.

'You been here long?' Starrett asked.

'No, sir. Not very.'

'Superstitious?'

Wyatt frowned. 'No. Why?'

46

There was a laugh in Starrett's voice. 'Aronson gave me a St. Christopher medal. So did Kramer. Thought you'd like one.'

'No, sir. We—don't believe in that. I mean—my folks don't—' He broke off, uncertain.

Starrett waited.

For a moment Wyatt again felt the need to cover—to lie as he had lied on all his personal records—for convenience: *Religion: Congregational.* But now, in the intimacy of the darkness and of the moment, he knew Starrett was searching for something—something perhaps like the truth.

'They're Quakers,' he said softly.

He noted Starrett's reaction, a quick, startled alertness. 'Quakers?'

'Yes, sir.'

Starrett's voice was quiet, careful. 'I thought Quakers didn't believe in—fighting.'

'They don't, sir. Not this way.'

'Don't they object—I mean, to your—?'

'Yes, sir. Entirely.'

'Then why—?'

The heavy clomping of Greene clanged hollowly through the ship. Violently he swung out. 'Lieutenant Starrett!' It was an angry, seething voice. 'They didn't armor the flight deck!'

'I told them not to,' said Starrett. 'She's heavy enough.'

'But that'll leave you wide open—'

47

'She's heavy enough,' said Starrett. 'Any more armor plating and we'll need a crane to get her up.'

'But, shit, sir—'

'She'll handle the way she is,' Starrett said quietly.

'I *know* that!' snapped Greene. 'It's just—well, shit, sir—the flight deck—'

'Everything else okay?' asked Starrett.

'Sure,' said Greene. His voice dropped. 'You're sure? About the flight deck?'

'Sure,' said Starrett. 'She'll handle fine.'

Greene rubbed his hand along her side. 'She's a sweet job,' he said. 'And a real lady, sir. Like, she's gotta be loved. And then—' he slapped her side, hard—'she'll give you all she's got.' He looked up to Starrett. 'You got her made,' he said. Then, abruptly, 'What're you going to call her, sir?'

'We haven't figured it out yet,' said Starrett.

'Well, make it a good one,' said Greene, and started away. 'Let me know tomorrow so maybe we can paint it on.' Then, pointedly, 'Can't have her going up *all* naked.'

Starrett waved him goodnight.

Greene crossed beyond the revetment, and for the first time Wyatt noticed, just to the left, the dark outline of the ship's engineering tent. He heard a flap thrown back, and Greene disappeared.

Starrett turned, studying the Fortress. 'Any ideas for a name, Wyatt?'

48

Wyatt frowned, shivering with the cold, his eyes on the bomber. 'I was thinking, sir, of what Greene just said.'

'*The Lady*?' asked Starrett.

'Yes, sir. It sounds right—for her.'

The only sound was the wind.

Then quietly Wyatt said, 'Good night, sir.'

'Wyatt?'

'Yes, sir?'

'. . . Good night.'

Wyatt nodded and walked slowly toward the dope shed, to the bike.

Behind him he heard the door of the ship open . . . then close again, gently.

He turned and looked back. There was only the Fortress towering silent, silver and proud as he had first seen her.

But with a difference now.

CHAPTER FOUR

The bulb by Hagen's bunk glared over the chessboard as, grinning, he moved his red queen into Wyatt's ranks and captured his bishop. 'Check.'

Wyatt leaned closer over the board, his lips pursed.

Hagen stretched back, waiting, and glanced to his watch: ten o'clock.

The Shack was quiet.

Nelson, the left-waist man—a tall Nordic blond with large ears and thinning hair—sat on his bunk, writing. A small leather-cased snapshot of his wife lay beside him.

In the under bunk, Golden, the radioman, crouched intently over a paper-backed novel, his dark, Hebraic face serious; his thick, sensual lips half parted.

At the table by the stove Vilano and Wiggam of the *Miss Fire* were deep in a poker game. Vilano was the *Miss Fire*'s radioman—a short, sinewy Italian with a thin, neatly clipped mustache. Wiggam, his fat tail gunner, glinted at him, his beady, piglet eyes flickering shiftily over the shillings between them.

'Your move,' said Wyatt.

Hagen looked back to the game again. Wyatt had shifted his rook, intercepting the queen's threat. Hagen frowned, his eyes darting from one piece to another, calculating. 'Shrewd,' he muttered.

Wiggam's foot started to tap a rapid, nervous staccato, sharp in the quiet.

'For Christ's sake,' snapped Hagen, 'knock it off!'

Nelson looked up from his letter.

Grinning, Wiggam stopped, his eyes fixed on Vilano. He wiggled in his seat. Then slowly his leg started to twitch again, tapping.

Hagen glared up.

Wyatt turned, smiling. 'Hey, Wiggam—take your shoes off.'

Wiggam nodded and slid them off.

Hagen shook his head, moving his knight in for another attack.

Wyatt countered, bringing his remaining bishop across the board and capturing a pawn.

'Not very bright,' said Hagen, satisfied. Quickly he took the bishop with his queen.

Wyatt moved his rook down the board. 'Checkmate.'

Surprised, Hagen's eyes swept over the moves. Hesitantly he shifted his king.

'No good,' said Wyatt. 'The pawn.' He motioned to a pawn checking the king.

Hagen shrugged, looking up. 'Your game,' he said, and his look searched Wyatt's face. It annoyed him to be outplayed, outfigured—exposed, in a way.

'You underestimated the pawn,' Wyatt said quietly.

'Shit,' said Hagen, his eyes dark, and got up, stretching, leaving Wyatt to put the men away.

'Who won?' asked Nelson.

Hagen jerked his thumb to Wyatt. 'The pawn,' he snapped and, crossing to the table, stood looking down at the poker game, his hands in his rear pockets.

Pennies and shillings were piled in the center; but shillings, florins and pound notes were stacked neatly in front of Vilano.

Wiggam had nothing. His face was red and glistening, his eyes glittering on Vilano cagily.

Hagen reached for the bread on the table

51

and started to slice it with the knife. The bread was brown-crusted, floury white, too fresh to cut sharp. He watched the game.

Vilano looked at Wiggam and spread out two pairs—queens and nines.

Wiggam smiled, studied his cards and, with an uneasy laugh, tossed them down, blind.

Curiously Hagen set the bread and knife down and, picking up the cards, fanned them out. He looked to Wiggam and slapped them down again. 'A bluff,' he snorted.

'Yeah,' said Vilano matter-of-factly, and gathered in the coins.

Wiggam shrugged. 'Lend me a pound.'

Vilano shook his head.

Wiggam glanced to Hagen.

Hagen laughed and, cutting another slice of bread, tossed it to Vilano.

A crumpled ten-shilling note bounced onto the table.

Vilano looked up. Hagen turned. Wyatt stood by, his wallet still in hand.

Wiggam picked up the note and smoothed it out, grinning again at Vilano. 'Deal 'er again.'

Vilano, meeting Wyatt's look, shook his head and leaned back. 'It's all you got,' he said and started to munch the bread.

Wiggam studied the money, then glanced to Wyatt, uncertain.

'Call it a loan,' said Wyatt and slipped his wallet back again.

With a shrug Wiggam tucked the ten

shillings into his breast pocket and turned to Hagen. 'Cut me a slice.' He nodded to the bread.

Hagen slid the knife rattling across the table. 'You got two arms.'

Hagen finished the last of his slice, brushed his hands off, and felt for a cigarette.

Vilano savored the bread, chewing slowly; then laughed at a thought. 'Wonder if Moody's set the date yet.'

Hagen looked up sharply. 'For what?'

'Getting hitched,' said Vilano. 'Didn't you know?'

Hagen drew a cigarette from his shirt pocket. 'He mentioned it.'

'He means it,' Vilano said.

'Where's he now?' asked Wiggam, his mouth crammed.

'Where else?' asked Vilano, grinning. 'Phyllis.'

Wiggam stabbed the bread again. 'Then how come we got the bread so early?'

Vilano frowned, puzzled, and studied the piece in his hand; then slowly his face darkened and he turned, looking up at Hagen wonderingly.

Hagen smiled and blew out a match, silent.

Wiggam watched them both, quick with interest.

Thoughtfully Vilano looked to his bread again; then, without a word, flipped it into the coal scuttle beside him, shoved himself up and

53

strode stiffly out, slamming the door behind him, hard.

Vacantly Wiggam fingered the bread in his fleshy hands, almost smiling.

Hagen shrugged, sharp-eyed through the cigarette smoke, and turned away.

Nelson and Golden were both looking at him strangely, curiously. Then, with a grunt, Golden picked up his book and started reading again. Nelson went back to his letter, frowning.

In the corner Wyatt flicked on Bayer's phonograph. The Mills Brothers began singing 'Paper Doll' softly through the silence.

Tautly, glancing about, Hagen snapped his cigarette into the coal scuttle, crossed to his bunk and, getting his kit and towel, marched darkly out.

*　　*　　*

The night now was biting chill, clear. An icy wind whipped across the field. Hagen shivered, stung breathless with the sudden cold. Nearby, the giant oak creaked eerily in the blindness of the blackout. Quickly Hagen strode his way down the gravel path, past the other three huts, toward the latrine at the end.

Suddenly voices broke across the dark: the high, shrilling laughter of Reed, the *Miss Fire*'s engineer; the shouting of Cronin and Swacey; the gruff booming of Laske, the *Miss Fire*'s left-waist man; and Bayer following after, whistling softly.

'What's the word?' Hagen called into the dark.

'Red,' shouted Cronin.

They surged in a tumbling bunch by Hagen, their feet crunching heavily down the gravel walk.

Hagen turned and, finding the door of the latrine, went in.

Inside, two bare lights hung over the green-rusted sinks. The place smelled sour and dank, tart with Lysol. He passed Vilano on one of the stools and went to the basins, turned on a tap and began to lather his hands. The water was icy, like splashing fire.

He heard Vilano pull the chain of the overhead box; then the thunderous whine of the flushing water.

Vilano came to the basins, buttoning up. He stood beside Hagen and started to wash with the grey, gritty bar of sand soap in the tray.

Hagen dried his face and hands and saw Vilano looking at him curiously. 'What's eating you?'

'I just remembered,' Vilano said, 'who you reminded me of. You remind me of Bellows.' Carefully he closed off the tap. 'He was a sonofabitch, too,' he said easily and went out, drying his hands on his fatigues.

*   *   *

Another record—'I'll Get By'—was playing as Hagen went back to the Shack. He could hear it, low and sweet across the blackout. Briskly he hurried inside, shivering, and with a breathless, 'Ch-rist!' spun in, slamming the door shut.

Moody was leaning raggedly by the table, watching him, his long, solemn face ashen and pained, his eyes smoldering with a dark, wild light.

On the floor lay the loaf of bread, squashed.

A rigid waiting tensed the air. In the quiet, the phonograph played gently,

> *'I'll get by*
> *As long as I*
> *Have you...'*

['*I'll Get By (As Long As I Have You).*' Used by permission; see p. iv.]

Slowly, almost casually, Hagen started for his bunk, his look centered on Moody as, steeled, Moody moved in toward him, step by slow, sure step, his mouth drawn tight, tensing as he neared. Suddenly with a gutted, 'Motherfucking sonofabitch!' he sprang, clutching for Hagen's throat. His knee shot up, driving in.

Swiftly Hagen blocked it with his thigh and, flinging his kit aside, smashed out with his right, cracking sharp across Moody's jaw.

The shock spun Moody, staggering back over the table. He twisted for balance and, stumbling, fell slithering to the floor. He shook his head groggily. Blood trickled from his lips.

Hagen crouched, waiting, his body swaying.

Vilano bent over Moody and helped him to his feet.

Moody shook him off and, without looking up, veered brokenly to his bunk.

Bayer shut the phonograph off.

Hagen glanced around and from across the hut caught Wyatt's steady, probing look; then turned, picked up his kit and, flinging it to the shelf over the bunk, started to undress, grim and taut.

Wearily Bayer reached up and flicked off his light.

CHAPTER FIVE

The hut was dark, silent. The pot-bellied stove rumbled, glowing a dull red. Wyatt lay watching the shadows flickering over the curved wall. Then softly, from Bayer below: 'Wyatt?'

'Yeah?'

'I almost forgot. ... Good luck tomorrow.'

'Thanks ... Bayer?'

'Yeah?'

'What do you think the target'll be? ... Bayer?'

'Good night, Wyatt.'

'. . . Good night.'

Wyatt lay back, his hands locked behind his head, watching the weird, red-tinged shadows, wondering.

From the line the high, coughing thunder of revving engines cracked across the darkness.

Part Two

MISSION ONE
March 2, 1944

CHAPTER SIX

From the back of the canvas-covered lorry, crowded to the tailgate with gunners and flight gear, Wyatt looked out, watching the slow unwinding of the road behind them as steadily they lumbered over the rise and down the perimeter track. The sky was silent, a crisp, sunlit blue. Distantly the hills gleamed, gentle with late morning. Near, the shacks and tents of the outer base spun by, the knolls and levels of new grass, the waiting Fortresses—most of them still olive drab—the low bushes, the sparse, budding trees; and everywhere the freshness of the clean day, the sweetness of chilled air ... and the hush ...

The target was Chartres, a minor run, a secondary target. From other fields, the major forces had been earlier directed to Deep Penetration targets within the Reich. But this, Wyatt thought, was the beginning.

Late takeoff, easy run. That had been what Bayer had said. And yet—on such a day as this, perhaps in a matter of only hours now, this lovely day—this lovely fragment of a day— could be the last of his life. And if not today, then perhaps tomorrow's flight would do it, or the next. And so it would be—like this—from now on in, whenever he went up. Always the possibly last, lovely time of life.

The lorry eased to a trembling pause.

'Okay,' called the driver, 'Number seven.'

A gunner from the rear muttered, 'That's me,' and stumbled his way through, dragging after him his flight bag. He bumped against Wyatt, heaving his bag over the tailgate, then clumsily crawled over and jumped to the ground. He swung his flight bag to his back, yelled, 'Let 'er go,' and started up the revetment to a waiting Fortress, the *Bombay*, Lyzak's ship.

The driver shifted gears and the lorry rumbled on, slowly.

Wyatt watched the *Bombay* gunner trudging like a tired old man, the bag heavy on his back, across the revetment to his crew; and as he watched, a chill, numbing dread seeped through his veins. He felt the tightness in his throat, the constriction through his body—the iron-tight resistance against all motion.

And if the end were today—Why was he here—now—today?

Desperately Wyatt forced his mind to focus through his fear. *Why* was he here now? Because, he knew, he had believed. He had believed once—once upon a time—in the reality of the human spirit, its dignity and rights. Because he had truly believed that Nazism was evil and a threat to that spirit, and had to be broken. That if these ideas were real to him, he had no choice but to take an active stand—or lose his own integrity, his own basic spirit, the reality of himself.

'Number eight,' yelled the driver. The lorry throbbed to a waiting halt; and another gunner, silent and stony-faced, threw his flight bag out, leaped after it and, shouldering the bag, shuffled up the revetment to Aronson's *Queen O' Reno*.

One of the gunners hollered, 'Okay!' And the lorry moved on again.

Wyatt's face was set, his eyes dark. He felt his palms sweaty in the cool air. A turbulent surge of dark wonder beat through his mind: *Were* these ideas *his* ideas? And *were* they real to him? Or were they real only to Uncle Seth, the family, his teachers—to the whole fabric of which they had been a part, of his education and life—but *not* to him? Were they only propaganda, a false ideology, and he the blind victim of a political state as evil and wrong in its way as Hitler's Third Reich? *Was* he more than this sweating body of fright—this reality of dread and fixed composure? *Was* this thing called spirit more real than this sure body of feeling and thought? Were ideas *real*? And even if they were, *could* a man—like himself—actually, willingly *die* for them?

'Number nine,' shouted the driver. The lorry drew to a pulsing wait. No one moved.

The gunner across from Wyatt nudged him on the knee. 'Yours,' he said.

Wyatt nodded and stiffly climbed out over the tailgate, dragging his flight bag after him.

The gunner helped him with it.

'Thanks,' said Wyatt.

The gunner flicked him a wave.

'All cleared,' yelled Wyatt.

The driver shifted. The lorry whined away, lumbering toward the next stop.

Wyatt swung the bag to his shoulder, turned and for a moment stood looking at the Fortress, his eyes uneasy. She seemed strangely new by daylight, even lovelier than by starlight; but still, silver and proud.

The rest of the crew had already assembled, preparing for the late takeoff.

Starrett was up in the flight deck, checking over the controls with Kirby, the co-pilot—a short, grumpy Yankee with a slow, cautious look and a droll, quizzical mouth. Starrett turned and, seeing Wyatt below, grinned.

Wyatt nodded, catching the quick glance, and signaled back without a word.

In the Plexiglas nose Gillis, the bombardier, sat crouching over his bombsight. Beside him Kramer, the navigator, bent over the nose turret, checking the guns. Gillis was a dark-eyed, bony Texan with a sly, tricky grin and a frisky catamount temper. Kramer was blond and boyish, his eyes shrewd and grey, his mouth laughter-lined. He waved down, beaming, as Wyatt ducked under the nose and cut to the other side.

Heavily Wyatt slid his bag through the side hatch and looked in. Nelson and Hagen were

64

anchoring their waist guns. Beyond, in the radio room, Golden was changing sets. In the tail Swacey was kneeling, a rag in hand, cleaning off his windows.

'Where the hell you been?' asked Hagen.

'Checking out with Bayer,' said Wyatt.

Hagen glanced to him sharply; then, reaching down, swung Wyatt's bag to the side. 'Your guns are in the tent.' He pointed to a square canvas tent beyond the revetment. 'Miller's checked your turret already.'

'Who's Miller?' asked Wyatt.

'Your ground armorer,' said Hagen. 'He said it's okay.'

Wyatt turned and started away.

'And tell Cronin to bring some oil!'

At the tent the flap swung back and a lean, angular tech sergeant came out, his sharp face grimy and streaked with grease, his heavy leather jacket torn and scratched, with yellow chevrons painted on the sleeves. He eyed Wyatt quickly, then grinned. 'Morning, Wyatt.'

Wyatt cocked a quizzical eye. 'Morning—'

'Greene,' said the sergeant. He gestured toward the tent. 'Your guns are in the bottom rack. Miller's gone for some coffee. He'll check in with you when he gets back.'

'Thanks,' said Wyatt.

'Don't mention it.'

*   *   *

65

The tent—like the armorers' shed on the line—was dark, cluttered, stale with a dank, musty odor. A small, bare bulb glowed dimly over the work counter. In the corner a squat iron stove smoked between two dirty cots piled with gritty pillows and torn, oily blankets. Plane parts, tool kits, boxes of ammo, moldering rags were strewn around.

Cronin was wiping down his gun barrels, his hands gleaming with oil. 'Thought you'd gotten lost,' he said.

'They moved the ship,' said Wyatt. 'I didn't know it.' He knelt by the gun rack under the workbench and from the bottom shelf, with a grunt, hoisted out the twin fifties. 'Hagen wants some oil.'

'He can get it himself,' snapped Cronin.

Silent, Wyatt slipped off the canvas sheaths and started to dismantle the guns for a check. Suddenly one of the bolts slipped from his hands and fell jolting to the floor.

Cronin glanced to him sideways, his eyes quick.

Wyatt picked up the bolt and, wiping the dirt off, examined it closely, then set it in the pan of oil.

'You see Moody this morning?' Cronin asked.

'Yeah,' said Wyatt. 'Him and Bayer. Their flak leave came through. They're leaving tomorrow, Bayer said—depending on today—'

'Lucky bastards,' Cronin muttered. He lifted his guns to his shoulder and, shoving aside the tent flap, ducked out.

Wyatt looked over the workbench. The bolt glistened in the oil pan. He picked it up and started to strip it down, his face set.

CHAPTER SEVEN

A dark, burly sergeant, bull-necked and unshaven, wearing a battered fleece-lined jacket, ambled up the revetment to Starrett with a paper cup steaming with coffee and handed it to him. 'Wyatt said you'd like a cup,' he mumbled, uncertain.

Starrett took it with an appreciative nod. 'Thanks, sergeant.'

'I'm Miller,' the sergeant grunted. 'Ground armorer.' His voice was rough, friendly. 'Good luck with 'em, sir.' He turned and shuffled heavily away, toward Wyatt at his turret.

Slowly Starrett sipped the coffee, his eyes scanning the men lying about, waiting, like him, the takeoff signal from Operations. And like him, he thought, feeling in the blood that quick excitement that wasn't all fear, though fear was a part of it. That curiosity—about combat, what it would really be, how they would meet it. And adventure—But that was a part of it, too. It had always been a part of

67

flying for him, but now it was edged—and sharply honed, too—with the chance of death.

Chance, Luck—again. That had been why his name for her had been *The Lady Luck*. A good name. But the crew had others—bright, shining names that made the most of her being silver. Only Hagen had wanted to smut her as *The Urgin' Virgin*, and had been stormed down (there was something in their attitudes toward Hagen today—something dark, angry—that he'd have to look into) until finally, as one, they had named her *The Silver Lady*.

It fitted her, Starrett thought, studying her now, glittering in the sunlight. His ship. The brightness of a clean, silvery pride welled within him. His ship ... and his men. Men he would be bearing into combat in less than half an hour.

Kirby, over there with Nelson and Golden, lazing on his back, his cap over his face, his hands behind his head, listening to their talk. Kramer and Gillis by the coffee tank on Miller's truck—high-spirited, hell-bent for fun, wherever they were. Swacey and Cronin sounding Greene out—most likely about the shack-up possibilities on base. (The base-fed girls smuggled in from London or Norwich. He had seen them about—starved, frail young things. He hoped they were safe lays, not clapped up or syphilised.) He saw Cronin throw back his head and laugh. And there, under the ship, Wyatt at his turret, with Miller squatting beside him, watching. (Quakers. That had thrown him last night. Wyatt's struggle had been deeper, more central, than he had guessed. Still, if he had come through so far—What were the chances now?) And Hagen—Starrett frowned, then relaxed, seeing him inside, by the open waist gate.

All present and accounted for. And, but for Hagen, a good, tight, well-formed crew he had shaped together for this moment, and the days ahead—a crew he was proud of and trusted, to lead into anything ... and men to die with if that was to be.

An ear-splitting rebel yell broke lustily across the quiet. A horn honked wildly as Starrett wheeled, seeing a jeep careening at full tilt, veering up to the revetment and, with slammed brakes screeching, jerking to a shocking halt beside *The Lady*.

Perched atop the back seat, Lieutenant Aronson swung his legs over the side, hopped down and lankily started around the ship, looking her over with an appraising eye.

Behind him, his co-pilot, O'Hara—a husky, apple-faced Californian—switched off the ignition and climbed out.

They were both in their flight coveralls, their leather jackets painted identically with the scarlet *Queen O' Reno* across the top, the card of the queen of diamonds in the center and the row of seven yellow bombs along the bottom.

Quickly Starrett went to meet them, flinging

69

aside his now empty paper cup.

'Come over to wish y'all luck,' Aronson said.

'Thanks,' said Starrett.

'Beats my ass, though,' Aronson drawled, shaking his head, his eyes still on *The Lady*. 'You getting this here job, and me—li'l ol' wonderful me—getting a beat-up box-kite—'

'If you can't fly it, don't knock it,' snorted O'Hara.

'Bucking for new molars, man?' Aronson asked, turning.

O'Hara grinned. 'Sorry, Pappy.'

Aronson nodded, satisfied; then, to Starrett, 'How'd you get it?' he asked, slapping *The Lady*'s side.

'Luck,' said Starrett. 'Pure luck.'

'Ol' Pappy here,' said O'Hara, 'he don't believe in luck.' He winked to Starrett. '*He*'s not superstitious.'

'This guy—' Aronson cocked his head at O'Hara disgustedly—'he's got everything but brains. Look at those coveralls!'

'What's wrong with 'em?' O'Hara wanted to know, frowning.

'They stink,' said Aronson. 'He's afraid to have 'em cleaned.'

'They're lucky,' O'Hara retorted, and looked at them lovingly. 'Don't want to wash the luck away.'

'For seven missions yet he's been wearing them.'

70

'And I'll keep on wearing them till we're done!'

'They'll rot first,' said Aronson. 'Already they stink up the ship—'

'It's the way you fly stinks up the ship—'

'If you don't like the way I fly,' snapped Aronson, 'walk.'

'*You* ain't superstitious, eh?'

'No!'

'Good!' said O'Hara, 'because you left your harmonica back at briefing.'

'Clementine?' Startled, Aronson felt his pockets; then, 'Jesus Christ!' Quickly he spun, yelling, 'I'll see you later,' to Starrett and leaped for the jeep. 'You coming?' he called to O'Hara.

O'Hara waved him on. 'Miller'll take me back.'

With a grinding of gears, the jeep jolted into life, bounced reeling across the field and sped wildly down the perimeter track.

Grinning, O'Hara looked after him, then turned and, with a wink to Starrett again, drew a harmonica out of his pocket and ambled toward Miller's truck, playing:

> '*O my darling . . .*
> *O my darling . . .*
> *O my darling Clementine . . .*'

Starrett only shook his head, watching O'Hara lazily on his way to Miller, and

71

grinned.

But the grin faded as his earlier thoughts returned, in the realization, the dark awareness that Chance was really a major part of that excitement, too: that every takeoff now would be a spin of the wheel—and their bet had been placed. He looked to *The Lady* again, wonderingly—as if to see beyond the sun-flashing glitter of her surface.

CHAPTER EIGHT

Crouching under the ship, Wyatt shoved his turret about, the guns pointing aft, reached in and locked it into position; then swung the curved iron door up and locked it shut.

Hagen leaped down from the side hatch and came up, wiping his hands. 'Okay,' he said. 'It's set.'

'Thanks,' said Wyatt and scooted to his feet as Starrett crossed under the wing—'Seven minutes to go'—and went to Kirby, dozing in the sun.

Uneasily Wyatt started slowly down the revetment, his look withdrawn.

Hagen frowned, following. 'Still pissed off about last night?'

Wyatt only shrugged.

They walked a few steps, silent; then Hagen grinned. 'Bet you wish you were pushing a pencil now.'

'I had my choice,' Wyatt said. 'Same as you.'

'Sure,' said Hagen. 'But I'm cut out for this stuff.'

'For flight pay and glory, right?'

'Sure beats slogging through mud,' said Hagen. 'What's your excuse?'

Wyatt frowned, wondering; then, seriously, 'To see how much of me is real,' he said.

Hagen cut him a sharp look. 'Like trying to prove something?'

Wyatt glanced at him, suddenly curious. 'That's the second time you said that—about proving something. Yesterday at the shed, and now. Why?'

'Why what?' snapped Hagen.

'What are *you* trying to prove?'

'Not a goddam thing,' Hagen said tightly. 'I've got eight inches that proves all I need to prove.'

Wyatt shrugged again.

They turned at the edge of the revetment and started back. Wyatt looked at *The Lady*, then down at the ground again. Their pace was slow and even.

Hagen eyed him sidelong. 'Ever hear of a guy called Bellows?'

'Yeah,' said Wyatt. 'Bayer told me about him. His ship blew up a couple of months back, just outside Paris. Why?'

'Did he get out?'

'Somebody did. They saw a chute.'

Hagen nodded, certain. 'Bet it was him.'

'Why?' asked Wyatt. 'What's with Bellows?'

Hagen shrugged. 'Vilano said something about him last night. Nothing important. Just—'

'There she goes!' cried Swacey.

Wyatt and Hagen turned.

Two green flares arced swiftly into the sky. Almost instantly the roar of revving engines started thundering across the field.

Quickly Wyatt and Hagen dashed for the ship.

Greene stood at the side hatch, checking with Starrett, then flicked him a quick salute and stepped back.

Starrett turned and hoisted himself in.

'One thing, sir,' Greene called.

Starrett looked back over his shoulder. 'What?'

'She's a sweet ship, sir.' He glanced up, his look steady. 'Always bring her back.'

'Yeah.' Starrett nodded, and grinned. 'Sure thing.'

Greene waved again and took position to guide her out.

Hurriedly Hagen boosted Wyatt in, swung in behind him and pulled the door shut with a hard, metallic slam.

A moment later the props started turning, blasting explosively. From the waist gate Wyatt saw the grass bent back, lashed by the prop wash. A paper cup spun into the air.

A tremor shivered through *The Lady*. Then gently she nosed about, eased down the revetment and slowly thundered forward.

CHAPTER NINE

Hagen watched Wyatt snap on his chute harness and plug his boots into his heated suit; then, arranging his chute pack in the corner, lie down by the turret well and, closing his eyes, curl up in rest, looking so cool, so damned calm. There was something about Wyatt that disturbed Hagen. But he couldn't figure it. That crack about finding how much of him was real—asking *him* if he had anything to prove. Shit!

Hagen's mouth tightened. He turned, leaning by the waist gate, and looked out over his gun mount.

The Lady moved slowly, moved and stopped, moved and stopped again, rocking gently, easing into line. The air was filled with the roar of engines, shrill with the squeal of brakes. Fortress followed Fortress, lumbering into position toward takeoff. The flashing of propellers whirled glittering in the sunlight. Then ... the waiting ...

Seconds ticked away ...

Ground-crew men stood about, watching, their eyes intent, silent. Suddenly a rising crescendo of engines gunning to high speed shocked the air. At the head of the track the lead Fortress hurled across the runway, faster, gathering speed, racing against the wind. The tail lifted. Headlong across the field it flashed, heavy and swift, shooting from earth.

The next followed, and the next, one by one rising sunward.

Finally *The Silver Lady* swung teetering into place, facing the runway, and halted, poised. The engines revved up, louder and louder, cracking the air. The thunder mounted. The ship reverberated, straining to break loose. Then slowly it started down the strip.

Hagen looked down, watching the rough grain of the runway easing under. Suddenly his eyes darkened. He glanced back toward the radio room, the bomb bays beyond, the racks loaded, heavy with bombs; and shot a look forward toward the trees at the edge of the field, then down again. The strip blurred into a whir of spinning earth. Slowly up came the tail. Quickly he looked to the trees again, tensed.

The Lady hurtled on. Then—abruptly—the thunder quieted to a steady, throbbing drone.

Below, he saw the shadow of the ship, swift along the runway, over the edge and beyond, rippling through the grass. The treetops whirled under, clustered like bushes, and dropped behind.

Quietly Hagen breathed and turned to Nelson beside him.

Nelson gave a long, low sigh and, uncrossing his fingers, signaled Okay. In the breast pocket of his shirt the corner of a leather-cased snapshot stuck out. He started to draw on his flight clothes.

Hagen looked to the tail wheel; then, putting on his helmeted headset, plugged in his intercom, clicked the hand switch and, pressing his throat mike, reported: 'Right waist to pilot. Tail wheel up and locked.'

'Roger.'

Hagen draped the switch cord over his gun and, reaching for his flight bag, tugged out his flight gear.

Nelson, bulky in his heavy, fleeced-lined flying clothes, sat on an ammo box, zipping up his boots, the boxes of radar-deflecting chaff beside him, the silver-glittering strips of foil spilling free.

Swacey crawled forward from the tunnel-like tail, edged around the tail wheel and, bracing himself to his feet, balanced as the ship banked slowly.

Hagen rode the turn, glancing from the waist gate, watching the earth veering in a slow circle below, the patchwork of field and forest dipping and reeling gently, then leveling again and sliding out of sight as the ship righted.

Swacey squeezed his way between Hagen and Nelson to where Wyatt lay; then carefully stepped around him, going into the radio room.

Wyatt stirred, grunting.

A moment later Swacey came back, a small canvas tool-kit in hand.

'Gun trouble?' asked Hagen.

Swacey shook his head. 'Just in case,' he said.

He started toward the tail; then suddenly stopped, turned and went back to Wyatt, and almost carelessly touched Wyatt's chute pack; then, grinning in passing Hagen, scrambled back toward his tail again.

Hagen shot Nelson a look, quizzical. 'What was that for?'

Nelson grinned. 'I don't know. But he always does it.'

Hagen looked to the chute pack, puzzled.

Nelson started to strap on his flak vest.

Wyatt moved, sighing, and huddled closer to the corner, his eyes still closed.

*   *   *

'Pilot to crew. We're at ten thousand. Go on oxygen. Over.'

Quickly Hagen unplugged his intercom and, going to Wyatt, shook him gently.

With a start, Wyatt spun and blinked up, clear-eyed.

Hagen thumbed to the turret. 'Time,' he said.

Wyatt nodded and, with an easy shrug, got to his knees and bent over the turret well. His actions were smooth, deliberate, his hands steady and sure.

Hagen watched him closely, wondering, as from the side of the turret Wyatt unsnapped the iron crank, engaged it in its socket and, releasing the brake, started to crank the ball into entry position. Slowly it revolved in its fixed ring. The door rolled up into the ship.

Tightly Wyatt held the crank in check, reached over, unlocked the curved door and, swinging it open, braked the turret from the inside. Then, testing it with his foot, he grunted, satisfied, and snapped the crank back into place.

Slowly he got to his feet—a strangely controlled casualness in his look—reached for the crossbar over the turret and, gripping it firmly, looked down into the open hatch.

Hagen glanced in. The guns, framing the sides, were pointing straight down. The narrow iron seat curved along the back. The computing-sight jutted from the control panel. The heavy round glass sighting-pane was directly under; then the earth—ten thousand feet below.

Wyatt's hands tightened on the crossbar. Suddenly, with a quick sigh, he started to lower himself gently down into the turret.

The wind thundered about it, whipping up through the well ring. The ball trembled in the vibrations of the ship.

Wyatt's hands eased from the bar as he

settled in his seat, his legs spread to the foot-rests on either side of the sighting-pane. He looked up, his face stilled with calm, and signaled with a lazy wave.

Hagen eased back as Wyatt, slipping his gauntlets on, reached back over his shoulder for the door and, leaning forward, drew it shut.

It closed with a dull iron sound. The lock handles turned, snapped into position. Hagen tested them, securing them tight; then crouched back on his haunches, waiting.

A moment later he heard the whining of the turret motor. Heavily the turret revolved, swinging up and around. The door slid slowly below the ship.

Hagen frowned, watching the turning ball, then glanced around, checking. In the corner behind him lay Wyatt's chute pack. He looked at it, then turned, raising his head to Nelson. 'He leaves it outside,' he said.

'That's right,' said Nelson.

Hagen's frown deepened. 'Supposing we get hit or something.'

'He'd get out.'

'He'd better,' muttered Hagen and rose, crossing back to his position. 'I've got to stick around till he does.'

Nelson looked at the turning turret. 'I've seen him,' he said. 'He's fast.'

'Supposing not fast enough. Supposing he gets stuck, or the turret jams—then what?'

Nelson glanced up, his eyes searching.

'So it's two of us then,' snapped Hagen. 'Right?'

'Wrong,' said Nelson and looked at him evenly. 'It'd be three of us then.'

There was only the drone of the ship.

Hagen turned, his jaw set hard, snapped on his oxygen mask and plugged into intercom again.

*　　*　　*

The air was thin, freezing. Over mid-Channel the waist gates had been shoved back for test firing. Now the wind lashed icily in, chilling them, despite their heavy clothing.

Hagen glanced to the two oxygen tanks outside the ball turret and checked the pressure gauge, then, pulling his collar tighter, looked to Nelson.

Nelson leaned against his gun, scanning the sky, his tall form stooped, bulky in his flight gear, his flak vest strapped on like an apron of steel, his hands thick with gauntlets, his face— half hidden under the heavy flak helmet— grotesque in the oxygen mask.

Hagen turned away again, checking his own oxygen.

The intercom crackled: suddenly—

'Navigator to crew. France, dead ahead.'

'Dead, hell!' snapped Cronin. 'Look at that flak!'

Ahead the forward group was passing the

81

coastal guns. The sky was daubed with flak bursting in black puffs of cloud.

Hagen clicked his intercom switch. 'Thought they said it'd be light.'

'Wait'll you see the target,' said Gillis.

'Ball turret to navigator.' Wyatt's voice was cold and slow. 'One ship going down. One o'clock low. Do you see it?'

'Christ!' muttered Kramer.

'No chutes,' said Wyatt. 'Flak accurate. Over.'

Hagen clicked in. 'Hagen to Wyatt. You okay?'

'Sure. Why?'

Hagen paused, frowning. 'Just checking.'

*   *   *

The sky was dirty with quick, startling clouds, explosive, dark, and stunted, drifting by. Fragments rained against *The Lady* in sharp, brittle bursts, like pebbles flung hard against tin. *The Lady* shifted gently in evasive action.

Quickly Hagen crouched down under his waist gate, huddling against the armor plate.

Nelson had spread a spare flak vest— Wyatt's—on the floorboard and was squatting down beside Hagen.

The ship swung, maneuvering. Suddenly it bucked, rose and fell quickly, and righted again with a jerk.

'Ball turret to navigator. There's a ship in

82

trouble. Three o'clock level. One of ours.'

'Roger.'

'One engine shot out.'

'Yeah. I see it. The *Bombay*.'

'Lyzak's ship,' Cronin cut in.

Hagen eased to his feet and peered out.

A ship was dropping behind, losing altitude. One of its engines was feathering.

'She turning back?' asked Kramer.

'No,' Hagen called in. 'She's trailing. Picking up again, I think... Yeah. She's pulling up Tail-End Charlie.'

He watched the Fortress winging in and rising slowly.

Behind, the sky was grey, haunted with spent flak clouds.

*   *   *

The mission droned on. France flowed below them, brown and greening. Rivers, sparkling like spilled silver, trickled glittering through the checkered fields. Towns and villages slid by like miniatures, roads and byways lacing the land together.

'Tail gunner to crew. Fighters. Six o'clock high. They look like bandits.'

'Navigator to tail. How many, Swacey?'

'Seven—so far.'

'What kind?'

'Can't tell yet.'

Swiftly Hagen swung his gun about, his

fingers easing back the slack on the trigger, his body keyed excitedly.

'Bombardier to pilot. Nearing target. Approaching IP.'

'Roger.'

They were reaching the Initial Point now, where the squadrons would start their direct, undeviating run on the target.

Hagen looked up searchingly, watching the fighters' high, thin vapor trails white against the deep blue sky. Suddenly the trails arced, sloping in a downward-dropping flight.

'Coming in,' called Swacey. 'Moving toward four o'clock. Hagen?'

'Messerschmitts,' said Hagen. 'Top turret?'

'Ready,' said Cronin.

The fighters swooped in, black-winged, darting like hornets.

Hagen caught one in his ring sight, tracked him, swerved his gun to an easy lead and pressed the trigger. The gun jarred him, thundering in his hands, the shells and links spuming free. He fired in short, abrupt bursts. The fighter zoomed by, rose in a high chandelle, then banked and swung back for another attack.

The sky was crisscrossed with tracer fire from the surrounding Forts. *The Lady* vibrated with the gunfire from all positions. Hagen swung again, firing as the fighters rolled past, always outside the group, and around, playing it cozy. He glanced to Nelson hunched over his sight, tracking, firing—the spurts of links and shells spewing into the waist; and at the ball behind him, spinning, shocking with the thunder of the twin fifties. And again—whirling—the fighters coming in—

Steadily the bomber formation closed tighter together. The *Bombay* dropped slowly behind.

'The *Bombay*,' Hagen called in. 'She's straggling.'

'They're after her,' yelled Swacey.

Hagen watched as the fighters dove in, one by one, plunging for the *Bombay*. They veered in from the sides, barreling under, careening back.

A quick flash—one of the fighters twisted, spiraling crazily, exploded.

'They got one!' shouted Swacey.

Smoking fragments drifted lazily earthward.

'Look!' cried Hagen.

The *Bombay* flung convulsively up on her left wing, shuddered awkwardly, then dipped, her wingtip broken, sheared half away and dragging behind. She slid sideways, struggling.

The fighters came in at her, faster, swinging nearer, their guns flashing.

'Can you get them?' Hagen called in.

'No,' said Swacey. 'They're out of range.'

'Navigator to crew. Flak. Twelve o'clock level.'

'Bombardier to pilot. IP. Hold her steady.'

The Lady settled, straight into the flak. 'Pilot

to bombardier. She's all yours, Gillis.'

'Roger.'

'They're getting her!' Hagen said. Tightly his hands clutched his gun grip.

Two of the Messerschmitts dove firing in on the *Bombay*.

Suddenly—a blazing ball of bursting fire, a smoldering puff—

'Christ!' shouted Hagen. He stared at the hovering cloud.

The intercom clicked. 'They got her,' Swacey muttered. 'Right in the bombload.'

'Any chutes?' asked Kramer.

'Nothing,' said Swacey. He sounded surprised. 'Nothing at all.'

Hagen turned. He saw the ball turret motionless. Bursts of flak boomed against *The Lady*, showering her with fragments of steel.

'Hagen to Wyatt.'

Silence.

'Hagen to Wyatt. Wyatt, check in.'

Slowly the turret started to turn from aft position. 'Ball turret ... okay.'

'They're turning off,' Swacey called in.

'Flak,' said Kramer. 'Getting heavy.'

'Bombardier to ball turret. Check below.'

'Roger.' The turret swung down, searching the under area; then quietly, 'Ball turret to bombardier. All clear below.'

'Roger ... Bomb-bay doors opening.'

Hagen looked out. They were on IP, with no maneuvering possible. They had to ride the bomb run now, their flight path level and straight for target and straight into the flak patterned before them.

'Radio to bombardier. Bomb-bay doors ... down and locked.'

The sky was thick with flak, the shells bursting in close, concentrated fire right over target. The formation was winging in through the barrage.

Suddenly *The Lady* jolted. Muffled concussive waves boomed, lashing around her. Black, dwarflike clouds exploded out of nowhere. The ship bucked and lurched, shivered and straightened again.

Hagen ducked, crouching against the armor plate, his hands tight on his gun mount. He glanced to Nelson beside him. Nelson nodded.

'Lead group getting it bad,' Wyatt called in.

'Bombs away!' shouted Gillis.

The Silver Lady quivered, then abruptly bobbed up, light and easy.

'Let's get the hell out of here!' Kramer snorted.

'Jesus Christ!' cried Golden.

'Ball turret to bombardier. Bombs falling jumbled.'

'One's stuck!' yelled Golden. 'The others bounced off it!'

Quickly Hagen looked up, then leaped to his feet, yanking his cords and oxygen tube free.

The ship bucked again.

Hagen grabbed the emergency oxygen bottle

from the side, snapped it onto his chute harness and, connecting it to his mask, darted for the bomb bay.

Golden startled, seeing him, then pointed to the bomb bay. Hagen made for the doorway.

Already Gillis was there, bracing himself on the narrow catwalk.

Hagen peered down through the open bay. The wind whipped buffeting up in quick-tearing blasts. Flak clouds drifted under. The earth glided twenty thousand feet below.

Carefully Hagen eased out onto the catwalk between the racks and, crouching down beside Gillis, examined the bomb. It hung dangling from the lower inner rack. Its lead lug had jammed in the shackle, bent and turned in by the weight of the bomb. The arming wire had been pulled from the tail fuse.

Gillis studied it, frowning, jolting the emergency release; then, signaling to Hagen, quickly got to his feet. Hagen rose with him. Gillis motioned him to kick at the bomb—their weights together to break it free.

Hagen nodded. The wind pushed against him. Tightly he clutched the racks and braced himself as Gillis was doing; then both together slammed at the bomb—again and again with hard, heavy, stomping kicks.

Suddenly the bomb slipped, broke free and fell.

Hagen leaned back, winded, watching it falling, dwindling, disappearing into the pattern of the drifting earth.

Slowly the bomb-bay doors started to whine, drawing up, closing together.

Gillis signaled him with a wave and turned back toward the nose section.

With a long, easing sigh Hagen turned and, gesturing Okay to Golden, went back to the waist. He stopped at the turret, checked Wyatt's oxygen, then reeled to his own position, slumped exhausted against his gun mount and, disconnecting his mask from the emergency bottle, reconnected with the mainline supply and switched it on High. A cold, swift blast of pure oxygen swelled his lungs. He breathed it in heavily, gasping; then, straightening up, shaking his head quickly, turned the control to Normal and plugged in his intercom.

'Hagen. Checking in. Over.'

'Good work,' Starrett called in.

'Thanks,' said Hagen, and clicked off.

Nelson tapped him on the shoulder and pointed out the window.

Behind them, dark-boiling towers of smoke rose billowing from the target.

*　　*　　*

The sky was quiet. Below them glittered the Channel. Behind them ebbed the coast of France. Wind-drifts of flak cloud hovered in the distant air. Before them lay England, the white cliffs of Dover gleaming in a narrow, sunlit line across the water.

'Pilot to crew. Down to ten thousand. Remove oxygen.'

'Bombardier to ball turret. Climb out, Wyatt.'

'Roger.'

'That wasn't so bad now,' Swacey called in.

'A snap,' said Hagen. He pulled off his oxygen mask. The sweat chilled instantly in the fresh air.

'A milk run,' said Cronin.

'Two ships down,' said Nelson.

'Any flak damage?' Gillis asked.

'A few holes, I bet,' Swacey said.

'Nothing bad,' said Cronin. 'The lead ships got it all, I think.'

Hagen saw the turret turning, unplugged and went to help Wyatt. The turret swung down.

Suddenly, 'Christ!' said Hagen as the iron door rolled into view, scarred by deep grooves, clawed by deflected flak fragments.

The motor cut as the turret hit its downward point. Quickly the locks snapped back and the door swung open.

Wyatt shoved it back, pulled off his oxygen mask and looked up, meeting Hagen's eyes. Then quietly he reached up and handed Hagen a piece of jagged metal. 'A souvenir.'

Hagen took it, examined it closely. 'Flak?'

Wyatt pointed. In the Plexiglas side pane to

90

the right, just inches from where he sat, was a small hole.

*   *   *

With a grunt Wyatt locked his turret into aft position, turned and signaled to Hagen.

Hagen crossed back to his position, plugged in his intercom. 'Hagen to Gillis. Ball turret up and locked.'

'Roger.'

Hagen watched as stiffly Wyatt got to his feet and, stretching, came down to stand beside him, his face marked with the imprint of the oxygen mask, his hair matted. He leaned against the gun mount, tired, drawn, and looked out—with a look that seemed to Hagen as dark and as rigid as ever. Even more so.

*   *   *

The formation was lowering, circling the field. Two ships had veered away, easing down for emergency landings. The first ship banked slowly, her nose insignia the blazing nude of the *Miss Fire*.

Hagen caught Wyatt's startled look.

A red flare shot skyward from her waist.

Hagen felt a tension, a feeling of uneasiness new to him as he watched the *Miss Fire* gliding in below, an ambulance racing across the field to meet her.

91

CHAPTER TEN

The waiting room of the Infirmary had a clean, ethery smell that bothered Wyatt. It reminded him of that long, far summer of Uncle Seth's dying. And the silence.

Across the pale green corridor, the night nurse sat at the corner desk, checking over a sheaf of reports. She glanced up once and, meeting Wyatt's look, smiled efficiently and turned another page. It crackled in the drowsy, antiseptic stillness. The clock above the ward doors ticked slowly: seven thirty.

Wyatt checked his watch, with the sudden, odd awareness that he hadn't looked at it since briefing this morning. How long, long ago that had been—as if the Wyatt that had set the watch this morning was another, distant being from this that sat here now waiting for Vilano, and remembering the grey, stricken face of Bayer at interrogation, his tight, abbreviated gestures (as if he'd shatter at a touch), and—Wyatt's whole body tensed within—feeling, himself, now so blindly lost (spiraling down through a dark, diminishing will into nothing).

Tensely Wyatt got to his feet and started to walk restlessly about.

The nurse looked up again; then, gently, 'Your crewmate?'

'Moody?' Wyatt shook his head. 'No. Just a

friend.'

The nurse nodded, watching him, turning her pen in hand.

Uneasily Wyatt sat down again.

The nurse went back to her reports, silent. Suddenly, with an abrupt shake of her head, she began to write again.

Minutes clicked away.

How many years ago was it he awoke this morning, young and clean? He remembered himself then, and the hope he had had that somehow—today—the doubts within would clear, the insight would come—that never came. And since that waking he had seen Lyzak blown up in a burst of flame; he himself had fired to kill another human being—not once, but time and time again as the MEs had swung firing in; and he had felt the swift, near-touch of death as flak and gunfire had burst about his turret.

Still, he had prayed. In the lone intimacy of his turret, he had strained for that inner gleam, that insight that would be his courage, the conviction that even here in his war-thundering turret still there could, and would, be an answering, strengthening touch from God, some realization—only to find his stillness within drying into emptiness, into nothing.

Perhaps his people had been right: that in the midst of war and violence God was a stranger. And he had been wrong: that his actions were

93

not, as he had once so surely felt, his answer, and his only one, to the Will that must be done, even as Christ had, Himself, in the temple struck out against evil—physically, angrily—

'Wyatt?'

He looked up as Vilano came down the corridor, the ward doors swinging gently behind him. His face was drawn, sad.

The nurse set her reports down. 'Sergeant Vilano?'

He turned.

'Your pass slip, please.' She reached out her hand.

Vilano went back to her, reaching into his jacket pocket, and, taking out a crumpled slip, handed it to her.

The nurse nodded a smiling 'Thanks.'

Wyatt rose as Vilano, returning, zipped up his jacket and, meeting Wyatt's questioning look, only shook his head, his hands a gesture of helpless unknowing.

*   *   *

The night was a hushed, windless dark, damp with a fine, chilling mist.

The road from the Infirmary was steep and winding, cutting through a wooded field at the far west end of the base to the main road leading back to quarters. The sound of their footfalls was slow and hard in the silence.

Then, quietly, 'He doesn't give a damn,'

Vilano said tightly. 'He just laid there, staring all the time.' His voice was husky. Quickly he cleared his throat. 'I told him they saved his leg. But he—he just—laid there.'

'Perhaps it's the shock.'

'Who're you kidding?'

Wyatt said nothing.

'What did Hagen say?'

'He went to tell Phyllis.'

'Boy,' muttered Vilano, 'that bastard doesn't miss a trick. Heard he played hero today.'

'He helped kick a bomb out.'

'Too bad he didn't go with it. Watch it. There's a hole here somewhere.' Vilano flicked on his flashlight, beam downward, and flashed it about. There was a rocky pit to the right. 'Yeah. There—that bomb-crater—'

They skirted the hole.

He snapped the light off again.

'The trouble is, Moody's a bastard,' Vilano said. 'I mean, one of them real kind. Y'know—never knew who he was or where he come from. He just grew up—in one of them institutions. He never had nobody—till Phyllis.'

'Did Hagen know?'

'Nobody. Just me and Laske—and the skipper, I guess. Just like—' Vilano broke off, uneasy, uncertain.

Wyatt waited.

'Wyatt?'

'Yeah?'

'Mind if I tell you somethin'—I mean, just us?'

'No,' said Wyatt. 'What?'

Silence. Only the footfalls in the darkness. Then:

'It wasn't like we said it was. I mean, like we said it on the reports. It wasn't no gun accident. Moody done it himself, with his own forty-five. He was trying to make it for good, but Laske saw him. They started to fight. That's when I heard them from the radio room. I saw Laske get the gun down, but it went off in Moody's leg.'

'When did it happen?'

'Just before coming in.'

'Anybody else know?'

'No. Just me and Laske—and Moody.'

'Leave it at that,' Wyatt said.

'Yeah... Thanks.'

Across the dark, the shriek-whining of an engine cracked across the sky.

Wyatt hunched his shoulders, pushed his hands deeper into his pockets. 'What time's your flak leave start?'

'Seven tomorrow. Maybe eight. And, then, *paisan*—' Vilano sighed a low, easing sigh— 'sleep,' he breathed. 'For two whole weeks, nothing but sleep, without—' He broke off again, caught with surprise. 'You know—I just thought,' he said, 'about Moody back there.'

'What about him?'

96

'He can sleep now,' Vilano said curiously. 'From now on he can sleep without worrying about tomorrow.'

'Yeah,' said Wyatt softly. 'He's lucky.'

*   *   *

Wiggam was alone in the Shack when they came in. He was squatting on the floor before Moody's open footlocker. The bunk was stripped down: the three sectional mats, forming the mattress, had been piled at the foot, the dark, dingy blankets folded and stacked on top, with the striped, yellowing pillow. Only a rusted hanger hung from the clothes rack. The shelf above had been cleared. The light glared starkly down on Wiggam, a bulging canvas barracks bag propped to one side. His fat hands pawed, picking among the things in the chest. A small clutter of postcards, a lighter, chevrons, a half carton of cigarettes, a candy bar, a gold-capped pen lay in a heap beside him.

Questioningly Wyatt looked to Vilano beside him.

Vilano's eyes were sharp and dark. Without a sound he crossed the hut and stood behind Wiggam, watching.

Roughly Wiggam jerked out a pair of shorts and an undershirt and, with only a glance to them, stuffed them into the barracks bag; then, dubiously picking up a pair of wings—silver embroidered on blue—he turned them between his fingers, thumbed them over lightly and laid them on the pile beside him.

'What the fuck do you think you're doing?' Vilano snapped.

Wiggam spun, startled.

Swiftly Vilano shoved him aside, swooped up the things and jammed them into the barracks bag. The wings fell to the floor.

Wiggam stared, his face red and quivering. 'He told me—Moody himself—'

'These are his!'

'He said I could take anything—'

'Just try it!'

Wiggam faltered, meeting Vilano's look. 'But he ain't gonna be needing those no more.' He pointed to the wings.

Vilano looked at him a long, steady moment; then, 'Why don't you take a good healthy shit for yourself,' he said quietly. 'It'll clear your head.'

Uncertainly Wiggam watched him.

Vilano's eyes were piercing.

Sluggishly Wiggam got to his feet, pouting down at the footlocker; then, with an angry snap, flicked an envelope from his back pocket and, tossing it down, stomped away.

Frowning, Vilano picked it up. There was a heavy penciled scrawl across the back. He read it and glanced to Wyatt. 'It's for Phyllis. To be opened if he went down.' He flipped it over, then sharply to Wiggam, 'You read it!'

Wiggam slouched at the table. 'So what? It's only his insurance.' He shrugged. 'He made it out to her.'

Tightly Vilano's lips pressed together.

Wiggam only glowered at him.

Vilano turned, folding the envelope, and tucked it into his pocket. He pulled off his jacket and cap and eased, grunting, to the floor. Quietly he picked up the wings, looked over Moody's things, then started to pack the barracks bag.

Wyatt came up, slipping off his windbreaker. 'Need some help?'

Vilano shook his head. 'There's not much.'

Wyatt nodded, leaning against the bunk.

'TEN-HUT!'

'Cut the shit,' Vilano snorted, looked up and abruptly froze.

Wyatt turned, and stiffened.

In the doorway, Finch, a husky, six-foot master sergeant, stood at rigid attention, a pencil and a clipboard in hand.

Before him, a short, pinch-faced first lieutenant glanced quickly about the hut, his eyes ferreting, his mouth small, thin-lipped, his nose long and pointed. His uniform glittered, his bars flashing, his creases sharp and precise, a narrow strip of ribbons above his left breast pocket—the American Theatre, the European Theatre and a red-and-white Good Conduct.

His look hardened on Vilano. 'Stand to attention there!'

Slowly Vilano rose.

'And you there—' to Wyatt—'attention!'

Wyatt dropped his windbreaker and stood looking straight ahead.

Wiggam jumped up, knocking back his chair, and thrust out his chest.

The lieutenant surveyed them, dark-eyed; then started quietly down the hut, his head turning from side to side, checking the bunks and floor, his face cold with disgust.

Finch followed him, expressionless.

The lieutenant turned back and, stopping before Wyatt, 'Who's barracks chief here?'

Wyatt frowned, confused. 'I don't know, sir.'

'You live here?'

'Yes, sir.'

'And you don't know?'

'No, sir.'

'We haven't any,' Vilano cut in.

The lieutenant wheeled, his face tightening. 'Your name, sergeant?'

'Tony Vilano.'

'"Sir," when addressing an officer.'

'Sir!'

'Who's responsible for conditions here?'

'No one—sir.'

'No one?'

'We all are—but we haven't had time, sir.'

'No?' The lieutenant glanced to his chronometer. 'It's eight o'—twenty hundred, sergeant.'

'Yes, sir. But we didn't land till after five.'

The lieutenant's mouth twitched. 'That still leaves *three* hours.'

'We had interrogation.'

'For *three* hours, sergeant?'

'And we had to eat.'

'You've been *eating* all this time?'

Vilano tensed, silent.

The lieutenant smiled. 'Take his name, Sergeant Finch.'

'For what?' snapped Vilano.

'You're restricted.'

'We're on orders for flak leave,' Vilano said tightly. 'Signed by Colonel Davisson.'

The lieutenant's eyes sharpened, then swung to Wiggam.

'Me, too, sir.'

'And you?' he asked Wyatt.

'No, sir.'

The lieutenant looked at him. 'Take his name, sergeant.'

'But—'

'He's not in charge, sir,' Vilano said.

'I know,' the lieutenant snapped. 'No one is.'

'I was mistaken, sir.'

The lieutenant glanced up, quizzical. 'Mistaken?'

'Yes, sir.'

The lieutenant's lips curled in a thin smile. 'Then, sergeant, who *is* responsible?'

Vilano took a deep breath. 'Sergeant Moody, sir.'

'Take the name, Sergeant Finch.'

'Sergeant James Moody,' Vilano said. 'Staff sergeant.'

Suddenly the lieutenant frowned. 'On flak leave?'

Vilano shook his head. 'No, sir.'

The lieutenant turned. 'Do you have the name, Sergeant Finch?'

The master sergeant nodded, jotting it down on the clipboard.

The lieutenant grinned, satisfied. 'Now, then—' he looked around slowly—'I've warned you all before. I'll warn you all again— for the last time.' He cleared his throat. 'So long as I'm in charge of—'

The door clicked open and Bayer came in. His face was white and tired. He saw the lieutenant and stood to a steeled attention.

The lieutenant glared at him questioningly. 'Sergeant Moody?'

'No, sir.'

'Speak up!'

'Sergeant Bayer.'

'Sir!'

'Sir!'

The lieutenant looked him over, then turned abruptly and eyed Vilano sharply. 'Now—as I was saying: So long as I'm in charge of this area, it'll be kept neat and clean, the floors swept, the beds made tight and according to regulations.' He paused, letting his words settle with dramatic timing. 'From now on, I shall make it a *daily* practice, men, to inspect this area, barracks by barracks. I'll come by again—you may be sure of that—and I warn you, men—' he cast a glance to each of them—'if it's in any way the same, this dirt and this clutter here, I'll have every man here gigged until conditions are rectified. Is that clear?'

Vilano nodded. 'Yes, sir.'

'Very well.' Briskly the lieutenant turned and started out, the master sergeant behind him.

At the door the lieutenant looked back, his tone crisp. 'And just because we're in a combat zone, men, is no reason for any of us to forget we're still soldiers—all of us. Remember that. That's all.'

The master sergeant turned—'As you were'—and followed the lieutenant out, his middle finger raised stiff behind his back, signaling Up His Butt!

Quietly the door closed.

'Someday,' Vilano muttered, 'that sonofabitch is going to get it.'

'Who is he?' Wyatt asked. He picked up his windbreaker.

Vilano went back to packing Moody's things. 'Waverly,' he said. '*Lieutenant* Waverly.'

* * *

103

Wyatt crossed the hut and flung his windbreaker across the bunk. 'You eat yet?' he asked Bayer.

Bayer shook his head, glancing away. He reached for his knapsack and began packing his toilet kit.

'Getting ready for tomorrow?'

'Tonight,' Bayer said. His voice was low, uncertain. 'The skipper fixed it up.' He turned. The ancient blue-grey look in his eyes was a bright, fierce glitter. Only his lips smiled—a thin, rigid smile. 'Dory'll be waiting,' he said. 'I called her—about Lyzak.' Quickly he looked to his packing again. 'Know what she said?... She just said, Hurry over—she'd be waiting.' He shrugged, taking a deep breath. 'Two to one she'll be wearing that damned blue dress. Guess I'll have to buy her another one now.'

'Yeah,' said Wyatt quietly. 'I guess so.'

'Skipper's been offered lead ship,' Bayer said. He opened his footlocker and started to pack his B-4 bag.

'Think he'll take it?'

'He's taken it,' Bayer said. 'Him and the navigator. It means captaincy for them.'

'When?'

'Right after flak leave,' Bayer said. He shrugged again. 'Everything changes then,' he muttered, tugging off his jacket. 'For two whole weeks you get away from it, with nothing to do but rest—and think. Like Lyzak said, that'll do it—the thinking. You see things different then. And they change—I've seen it. Everything changes—too much.'

'And bust goes the crew?' said Wyatt.

'What crew?' Wryly Bayer looked at him, then started to fold his jacket. The leather gleamed warm in the light. 'This is all that'll be left of it,' he said, and for a moment stood looking at the insignia, the flaming nude with the *Miss Fire* across the top and the row of fifteen yellow bombs crowding along the bottom. 'And one for today,' Bayer said tensely. 'One for today and nine to go—unless they push it to thirty.' Quickly he tossed it into his bag and reached for some shirts.

'What now?' asked Wyatt. 'The Pool?'

'I guess so,' Bayer murmured. He glanced to the jacket again. 'But we almost made it,' he said.

Wyatt frowned. 'How many have?' he asked. 'As a crew, I mean?'

'None from here,' Bayer said. 'None I remember. But I've been told some do.' His face suddenly clouded. He stood wordless, studying Wyatt, the old, inscrutable sadness haunting his eyes; then quietly he turned. 'But with you—your bunch,' he said, 'there's a difference.'

'A difference?' Wyatt asked. 'How?'

'You believe,' Bayer said. 'You think you'll make it.'

'Doesn't everyone?' asked Wyatt. 'Don't you?'

Bayer's hands paused. 'No.' He shook his head gently. 'I never believed in anything, I guess. But you—' He looked up, almost smiling. 'You believe in your crew. I think you believe in a lot of things. And that's the difference... That's all the difference there is.'

*   *   *

The door slammed open and banged shut, hard, as stormily Hagen snapped off his jacket and strode grimly to his bunk, his mouth drawn tight, the left side of his face scarred with blood-clotted scratches. He flicked off his cap and flung it down on the side table, swung up on his bunk and lay back, silent.

Wyatt looked to Bayer, puzzled.

Bayer only reached for some socks.

Vilano went on with Moody's things.

Wiggam, playing solitaire at the table, glanced toward Hagen with a faint smile.

Wyatt watched, wonderingly, as Hagen pulled out his cigarettes—empty. With a muttered 'Sonofabitch!' he crumpled the pack and flung it to the floor, glancing around. 'Hey, Wyatt, got a cigarette?'

Wyatt shook his head. 'No. I don't smoke.'

Hagen turned. 'Vilano?'

Vilano said nothing.

'Wiggam?'

Wiggam frowned over his game, his face glistening with sweat.

Wyatt held out his hand to Bayer. 'Give me a cigarette.'

Bayer hesitated, then, taking his pack from his bunk, shook one free and gave it to him.

'Thanks, Bayer.'

Wyatt turned and went to Hagen, tossing the cigarette up to him. 'You got a match?'

Hagen nodded, taking a book of matches from his pocket, and, striking the last match, lit up. 'Thanks.'

The dusky tones of a record sifted through the silence:

I'm going to buy a paper doll
That I can call my own...
A doll that other fellows cannot steal...
['Paper Doll,' by Johnny Black, © Copyright
by E. B. Marks Music Corporation.]

Wyatt shot a glance down toward Bayer, slowly winding the phonograph, not looking up.

Vilano smiled.

Wiggam twitched in his seat, grinning.

Hagen's eyes narrowed, staring at the overhead light. He blew a thin, whorling wreath of smoke at the ceiling, his voice a low, steeled whisper. 'Tell him to shut it off before I bust it over his fuckin' head.'

Quietly Wyatt went to the phonograph, picked up another record and changed the tune.

Bayer looked up from his packing. 'Sorry,' he said and shoved some handkerchiefs into his knapsack.

'How's it going?' Wyatt asked.

'Nearly done,' Bayer said. He zipped up his B-4 bag, then, suddenly, 'While I'm gone,' he said, 'it's yours.' He nodded toward the phonograph. 'I'll bring you back some new records.'

'Thanks.'

There was an awkward pause.

'You'll probably get some rough runs,' Bayer said. 'Berlin maybe.'

'Yeah. Lyzak said—'

'Keep turning your turret,' Bayer cut in. 'It helps to deflect the flak.' He started to buckle his knapsack. 'And about that jacket—I've got one for you.' He glanced up sideways. 'I'll give it to you when I get back.'

Wyatt grinned. 'My size?'

'It'll fit,' Bayer said softly. 'All the way.'

He started to undress, to change into full uniform, as Cronin and Swacey barged in, flushed.

'What's the word?' asked Wyatt.

'Green,' said Cronin.

Wyatt felt a sudden relief, a lightness within.

'And look,' said Cronin. He had a glow on, his jacket unzipped, his cap on crooked, perched at the back of his head. He reached inside his jacket and pulled out a sketch of a Petty girl in a bathing suit, sitting with one leg stretched out, and holding a raised knee; and above her, in yellow, *The Silver Lady*. 'Well?' said Cronin.

Wyatt's eyes laughed. 'Fine,' he said.

Cronin eyed him, uncertain, then grinned; and turning to Hagen, went down the hut. 'How about you?'

Hagen studied the sketch, his mouth sagging. 'It stinks.'

Cronin frowned, taking the sketch back.

'Starrett thought it was okay,' said Swacey.

'So what's to say?' Hagen muttered. 'If Big Daddy Starrett says it's okay, so why ask?'

'The others liked it,' Cronin said.

Hagen only shrugged and butted his cigarette into the butt can by his bunk. 'So it'll do.'

The glow went from Cronin's face. 'Thanks,' he said and swung back to Swacey and Wyatt.

'We've got a guy to paint it,' Swacey drawled. 'Four pounds a jacket. Okay?'

Wyatt grinned. 'Half price for a windbreaker?'

'Hey, Bayer—' Cronin came up, taking off his jacket—'let's have the bomb stencil.'

'Sure thing.'

Cronin spread his jacket out on the table and, taking the stenciling kit from Bayer, went to work on the jacket. Swacey ambled after. Wiggam swept up his cards and sat back, watching.

Hagen dropped to his feet, slung on his

jacket and, seeing Wyatt down the hut, said, 'How about the club?'

Wyatt shook his head.

Hagen only shrugged again and sauntered out. The door closed after him, hard.

Wyatt turned and caught Bayer's look. 'He'll learn,' Wyatt said.

'Don't bet on it,' Bayer muttered. 'You'd lose.'

*　　　*　　　*

Tiredly Bayer swung his overcoat across his arm and turned from his bunk. He was in full uniform, his gas-mask across his shoulder, his knapsack and B-4 in hand. 'Well?'

'You look fine,' Wyatt said, and went down the hut with him.

Wiggam flicked a listless wave.

Vilano got to his feet, his hand outstretched. 'Don't forget—see you in two weeks.'

Bayer set down his B-4 and took Vilano's hand. 'In two weeks,' Bayer said; then, turning to Wyatt, 'Take care of yourself.' He grinned.

'Sure thing,' said Wyatt.

Bayer shook his hand, a firm, sure grip, and for a moment the grin went from his eyes and the clear, true look of his strange, unutterable sadness returned. He nodded and turned and, picking up his bag, walked out with a forced, jaunty stride.

Uneasily Wyatt watched him go and, as the

110

door closed behind him, looked to Vilano.

Vilano was tensely, angrily stuffing in the last of Moody's things.

Wiggam shifted his eyes, watching Vilano, his face blank, vaguely bewildered.

'Hey, Wyatt,' yelled Cronin, 'look!'

Proudly, with a sweep of his hand, he held up his jacket.

On the bottom was a single yellow bomb.

PART THREE

'BLOODY MONDAY'
March 6, 1944

CHAPTER ELEVEN

The briefing room was locked. Hagen turned and shouldered his way back through the crews crowding the corridor. Cigarette smoke hung acrid and heavy in the air. A rising undercurrent of anxiety eddied through the seething restlessness, the low-droning talk. Gunners and officers mingled tightly together, their glances quick, uneasy, darting to the locked doors.

He saw Wyatt standing against the wall— alone in all the crowd—his face the usual cold mask. Suddenly Hagen grinned. Behind Wyatt was a bright Army poster: *Is this trip necessary?* Jesus, what a joke!

A gunner jostled him—'Sorry, Mac'—and pushed through.

Hagen turned. The back of his jacket was now gaudy with the Petty girl, *The Silver Lady* and a row of three yellow bombs.

A surge went through the crowd, pressing Hagen hard against Wyatt, then eased again. He glanced to his watch. 'It's almost four,' he said.

Wyatt nodded. 'There's Nelson.'

Hagen looked up and saw Nelson forcing his way through to them. His face was nipped red. The chilled, clean smell of cold air was still fresh on him. 'What's the bad word?' he asked.

'Berlin,' said Wyatt.

'Again?'

'Maybe we'll get there this time,' Hagen said. 'Everybody's invited.'

Nelson's face tightened. 'Maybe we'll hit bad weather again—'

Two lieutenants pushed by, their faces drawn.

Nelson shoved against Hagen to make room for them.

Their jackets bore the insignia of *The Princess Pam* and seven bombs.

Nelson stood back again. 'What a hell of a way to start a week,' he muttered, and turned, looking over the crowd again. 'Wonder what the wife would say.' He smiled to Wyatt. 'I told her I'd gotten sinus and couldn't go up any more.'

'Think she'll believe you?' asked Wyatt.

Nelson shrugged.

'How's she coming?' asked Hagen.

'Fine, I guess.' He stood back to let a bombardier pass. 'Says she's glad I can't see her now. Says she's like a cow.'

'Let's get the show off the ground!' somebody yelled.

A gunner banged thunderously on the door, shouting, 'We ain't got all day, you know!'

'*I* have!' a gunner bellowed.

A tensed laughter broke over the crowd.

Abruptly the doors clicked open.

The crowd surged forward, pressing, shoving, pushing into the briefing room—a Nissen hut with its curved walls covered with yellowing beaverboard, the lights bright, harsh and cold. In front, rows of straight-backed chairs faced a dais. The crew benches crowded to the rear. Along the side walls were silhouette charts of enemy aircraft. The windows were blacked out with heavy blue-black curtains tacked in at all four corners.

Uneasily Hagen glanced to the wide map of Europe that stretched between two easel blackboards across the front wall. A drawn projector screen blocked out the area from the Channel to the Russian border, but lines of red yarn stretched from England eastward to— somewhere behind the screen. He eased by the projector stand midway down the center aisle and slid in at the nearest bench with Wyatt and Nelson. Cronin, Swacey and Golden shoved into the bench in front of them.

Noisily the officers swung into the front seats. The gunners filled the benches. The fine leather smell of jackets warmed the air. The drone heightened. The flow of men swelled to the walls. They stood restless, lined against the back. A tingling nervousness quickened the rising uproar.

Then slowly the Old Man stepped to the dais—a husky, curly-headed colonel, thirty-five, with prankish eyes and an easy grin. He stood waiting, his face lined now and serious, his flight jacket half zipped, his battered 'go-to-hell' cap set back at an angle. He watched the men before him, his hands in his hip pockets, his shoulders straight back.

A tensing quiet stilled the room.

He eyed them all, his face grim. Then slowly, without a word, he turned, crossed to the wall and raised the screen.

Groans cut from the men.

Hagen glanced to Wyatt and saw him tighten, silent.

'Sonofabitch!' Nelson muttered.

'What'd you expect?' Hagen asked. 'Pas-de-Calais?'

In the bench in front of them, Swacey reached out his palm, grinning to Cronin.

Cronin frowned, fumbled in his pocket and flipped a shilling to Swacey. 'Shit!'

Hagen caught Golden's explosive 'Oy vey!' then looked up as the Old Man stepped forward again, his hands back on his hips.

'Well, there's our target—the Big Town— Berlin. Only, this time it looks like we're really going to see it.' He paused, looking around. Then quietly he started to pace back and forth, frowning. 'Most of you know what the score is... This is our third try. Friday we hit bad weather. We had to go in for secondary stuff. The same thing Saturday—except that one wing did go over. But today—it's all the way—

for all of us...

'Today the targets are all in the Berlin area. The Erkner Bearing Plant. The electrical factories at Klein Machnow. And for some, the Daimler-Benz works at Genshagen.

'But, as you've probably guessed, it's more than just Berlin today. More than just factories...'

He stopped and studied their faces.

'Today we're after the Luftwaffe. And what's more, they know it. They've been waiting for this day. For the past few raids they've been keeping down. Saturday, over sixty of them were sighted, and not one of the whole group came in for an attack. I guess you know why. They're playing it cozy. They're holding off for the big one—today...'

Slowly he started to pace again, thinking.

'"No bombs will ever fall on Berlin.' That's what Goering said... He's wondering now... But even so, so long as there's a Luftwaffe, he said, there'll always be a Germany... That means one thing—the Luftwaffe has to go.

'But it's more than that, too. The Luftwaffe's the pride of the Nazis, and the Nazis are an extremely proud people. Knock out the Luftwaffe—as we've started to do over Schweinfurt and Regensburg—and you knock out their pride. And where their pride is great—and goes—the heart—the fighting heart—goes with it.'

He grinned. 'Simple, isn't it?'

A low, uneasy laughter rippled over the hut.

'But there's something else—something—the one thing that Goering hadn't counted on: the fact of the long-range fighter. Today's the test. Our Mustangs and Lightnings, carrying wing tanks, will have full flying range. That means we'll have full fighter coverage clear to Berlin and back—it says here.'

He turned, grave-eyed. 'So that's the picture: to get the Luftwaffe into the sky—and knock them out of it—the best we can.'

Then suddenly he shrugged, smiling. 'I'm not used to spieling off like this.' He looked around; then, abruptly, 'Now, for the details...'

*   *   *

Carefully, acutely Hagen listened as, one by one, plans for the raid were given. He felt the tension of controlled excitement within him rise with every mounting detail. Takeoff. Rendezvous. Landfall. IP. Time over Target. Estimated Time of Arrival. A litany of time and place.

The route was traced along the red yarn: from England eastward over the Zuider Zee, straight across Germany and in to Berlin, over the target and out again; then westward back over Germany, and home to England.

Ship positions were assigned, the box formations diagrammed on the blackboards.

The Flak Officer blocked in the estimated barrages, the possible mobile units, the strength of the overall batteries.

The Weather Officer gave his report of good visibility over target.

The screen was lowered again. The lights cut. The white, steady shaft of the projector beam slit the darkness. Slides of Berlin, in clear, detailed aerial photographs, were flashed on. The approach, the landmarks, the targets were pointed out, explained.

Next, the enlarged maps were shown. Here would be escorts—Spitfires. There, P-51s. Here, possibly an attack—'the Abbeville Kids'—the sharpest of Goering's forces, the yellow-nosed FW190s. There, outside Berlin, P-51s and P-38s—maybe. Here, a flak installation. There, another. And there ... and here ...

The slow voice of the Intelligence Officer droned on in the darkness.

All the way in, the red line was marked across Europe, and all the way out again. Cryptic patches of color, crosses and lines, circles and dots were noted, interpreted, guessed at.

Finally, the close-up map of Berlin glowed on the screen, the railroads, the roads, streets and parks symmetrically beautiful— surrounded by a solid wall of flak guns.

The droning voice stopped. The projector clicked off, and the lights snapped on again, quick and blinding.

Hagen blinked his eyes, stung with the bright, sudden glare.

Quietly questions were asked, the words hesitant, wonderingly considered.

The answers came back thoughtfully, gravely certain.

Then, silence...

The Old Man stepped to the dais again. 'Okay. That's it,' he said. 'Check time.' He raised his wrist, sliding back his sleeve, and called the hour.

The men studied their watches, waiting.

Slowly the second hand swept around ... ticking ... ticking ... five ... four ... three ... two...

'Hack!'

The room buzzed with talk.

Outside, the sharp, explosive coughing of an engine thundered across the field.

The briefing-room doors were unlocked and pushed open. The men got up, stretching, horsing uneasily, crowding as they milled out.

Hurriedly Cronin and Swacey shoved into the crowd. Golden stayed for the radio briefing. Hagen eased into the mob, with Wyatt and Nelson behind him.

*　　　*　　　*

Lockers clanged in the drying room. Benches scraped back and forth. Doors slammed open, banged shut again. Deftly Hagen kicked his locker door, then jolted it hard with his hand. The bent metal door shivered. The lock clicked open. He tugged off his jacket and, reaching in for his flight bag, started to undress.

Gunners in long-johns crowded the aisles, taking off their ground clothes, climbing into their heated suits and heavy flying gear. The air was warm, soured with stale body smells and sweat, pungent with the fusty odors of unwashed clothes, leather and camphored fleece.

Nelson glanced up from the bench beside Hagen. 'What do you think?'

Hagen shrugged. 'Let's face it,' he said. 'We're bait.'

Nelson kicked off his shoes. 'That's what I figured, too,' he muttered. 'We'll probably get the whole frigging Luftwaffe today—everything—'

Hagen nodded. 'In spades.'

Quietly Nelson pulled on his heavy woolen socks.

Hagen glanced down the aisle.

In the corner, Wyatt stood zipping up his heated flying suit, his face thoughtful, his actions stiff, deliberate.

Hagen watched him darkly; then turning, saw Nelson looking up at him, his eyes curious.

Quickly Hagen emptied out his pockets, saying nothing.

The chute room was jammed. Gunners pressed in on Hagen from all sides, elbowing by, wedging in at the counter, shouldering out again.

Over the chute racks hung a neatly lettered sign: YOUR DOG-TAGS ARE ALL YOU NEED. TURN IN ALL OTHER IDENTIFICATION.

Hurriedly the thin-faced corporal behind the counter scrawled Hagen's name on a slip of paper, swept the wallet and change into a narrow tin box and looked up again, his voice routine, his brown, squinty eyes blinking tiredly behind thick lenses. 'Anything else? No letters, cards, personal papers?'

'Nothing,' said Hagen.

The corporal nodded. 'Back chute?'

'That's right. Right-handed.'

The corporal swung about, glancing over the stacks behind him. The shelves were orderly, lined with numbered chute packs.

Three other corporals and a staff sergeant hustled about, calling out numbers, pulling down chutes, signing the gunners out. 'Next?'

The corporal came back, tossing a tightly bound chute across the counter.

Hagen looked it over, checked the pull of the rip-cord, the sealing wire, packing date and snapping lugs, signed the slip and turned away.

The corporal blinked up. 'Next?'

124

Nelson shoved his wallet across the counter. 'Nelson.'

* * *

Outside in the yard, Hagen, chilled through, waited in the black cold. The gunners loaded into the trucks. Flashlights snapped on and off. The slitted beams of the lorries slanted through the whorling mists, motors idling, pulsing with a low, rumbling throb. Tailgates clanged up, chains grating through the iron lock bars. Calls and shouts rang through the blackout. *'Load 'er up... Take off!... All set!... Next!'* Gears shifted, grinding into high as the trucks swerved joltingly out of the yard. Wheels crunched heavily over the graveled road, brakes whining. Another truck swung into line, its narrowed beams sliding across the fog.

'Hagen?'

'Over here.'

A light clicked on, then cut.

Nelson started across the yard.

The loading sergeant yelled, 'Take 'er away!'

A truck drove on, lumbering into the dark, its lights like glowing antennae probing the way.

'That's it!' the sergeant bellowed. 'You guys'll have to wait for the next one.'

Nelson set down his bag. 'Where's Wyatt?'

'He's left already.'

Hagen struck a light. The spurt of flame flickered over his face, his eyes squinting, his

125

cheeks hollow with shadow. He drew on his cigarette, his hands cupping the match, then suddenly whipped it out. Only the dull red tip of the cigarette glowed in the darkness.

'He worries me,' Hagen said, low.

'Because he's a loner?'

'Nobody's that alone without a reason.'

'Maybe he's got a reason.'

'He's got a problem,' said Hagen.

Nelson eased down to wait, sitting on his bag. 'Then it's *his* problem.'

'Not when *my* fucking life depends on it.' Hagen's cigarette glowed bright and dimmed again. 'His folks living?'

'Yeah. Why?'

'He doesn't talk about them.'

'So? Neither do I—or you.'

'He never gets any mail.'

'Maybe he doesn't write.'

'Why not?'

The muted lights of a truck swept the yard. Nelson got up. 'Maybe for the same reason he took the ball turret.' Deftly he swung his bag to his shoulder and fell in with the other gunners.

Hagen flicked his cigarette down, squashed it underfoot and, picking up his bag, wedged in line behind Nelson. 'He had to, didn't he?'

'He could've been right-waist.'

'Okay, you guys. Load 'er up,' the sergeant yelled.

The gunners crowded into the truck. Nelson

126

tossed his bag in and hoisted himself up over the tailgate. Hagen was the last one in. He yanked himself up by the chains and squeezed in beside Nelson.

'Let 'er roll!' the sergeant shouted.

The truck started off, veering around the yard.

'Then why?' asked Hagen. 'Why the ball?'

'Why not?' said Nelson. 'I figure he's used to fighting things out alone.'

*　　*　　*

A still, uneasy calm lay over the field. Eastward, the first grey light of morning filtered low and ghostly through the rising mist. The high silver rise of *The Lady*'s dorsal fin glimmered in the new light as Hagen swung out of the side hatch and stood glancing around.

The crew, restless, lazed about the ship. Starrett and Kirby stood under the nose guns, talking quietly. Cronin and Swacey sprawled under the wings, dozing, their caps over their faces. Gillis and Kramer sat beside them, playing tic-tac-toe on the back of a log sheet doodled with swastikas. Golden sat crosslegged in the grass, tugging at his boot zipper. Nelson handed him a cup of coffee, then squatted down beside him, silent. Wyatt lay in the grass alone, his fingers tracing in the dark, gritty earth, his face somber with a still,

127

wondering look.

Hagen frowned; then, unzipping his jacket, strode across to Wyatt and, with a grunt, dropped to his knees and stretched out. 'Not much longer.'

Wyatt glanced to his watch. 'No. Not much.'

Hagen rolled over on his back, his hands under his head, and stared at the clearing sky. 'It's the waiting does it,' he said.

Wyatt looked up. 'You, too?'

'I've felt better,' Hagen said and yawned, closing his eyes. Then, 'Remember that guy Bellows—went down near Paris?'

'Yeah?'

'Miller just told me—he's back in England.'

'He's sure?'

Hagen nodded. 'Some guy at Intelligence saw the report. Miller heard it yesterday.' He opened an eye and grinned to Wyatt. 'Some dame got him out—Kiki something. Walked all the way out with him.' His grin broadened. 'Miller says he probably shacked up with her all the way. Real shrewd.'

Wyatt shrugged. 'Bayer said he was a crud.'

'He just played it cozy,' Hagen said. 'Like me.' He lay back smiling, closing his eyes again. 'I wonder if it's hard—learning French...'

CHAPTER TWELVE

Wyatt tugged at the grass, then suddenly got to his feet.

Hagen cocked an eye at him. 'Where you going?'

Wyatt said nothing, but crossed to *The Lady*. Quietly he hoisted himself up into the ship, his face taut, his eyes deep, dark, as if with hurt.

The waist was hollow, shadowy with half-light, and cold. Sunlight eased in through the closed waist gates. The curved aluminum sides glittered duskily in the caught light. Flight bags and ammo boxes and flak suits lay piled about. Cords dangled from the intercom switches. The clean, cold smell of metal and grease, ammo and oil chilled the air.

Slowly Wyatt moved and stood by the left waist, looking out across the silvering field. His hand rested cold on the machine gun. His eyes scanned the sky, his face tensed, drawn in sharpening lines. Tightly the fingers gripped the gun casing, the nails clutching hard. The veins in his hand swelled, ridging the narrow wrist.

Suddenly his lips broke with a ragged groan. He raised his head. '*Help me!*' he whispered desperately. '*Help me!*'

His breath caught with a dry, harsh gasp;

then eased in a deep, quavering sigh. He slumped against the gun, his eyes closed, his forehead resting on his arm.

Then, from outside, Starrett's voice: 'Hagen—where's Wyatt?'

Wyatt looked up quickly.

'In the ship,' Hagen said.

Wyatt took a deep, long breath, then slowly let it out again and leaned against the gun, waiting, looking out the waist gate.

'Wyatt?'

He turned.

Starrett stood at the hatchway, his grey eyes sharp; then, lightly swinging himself in, crossed the waist. 'You all right?'

'Yes, sir.'

Starrett studied him, then glanced about, curious.

'I was looking for something,' Wyatt explained.

Starrett turned. 'Anything important?'

Wyatt nodded. 'Yes, sir—to me.'

Starrett met his look. 'Did you find it?'

'No, sir.' Wyatt glanced out toward a bird gyring over the field.

'What was it?' Starrett asked.

'It's personal, sir.'

Starrett followed his look, silent; then, quietly, 'We'll be getting passes soon,' he said. 'This week-end maybe.' He looked to Wyatt. 'You've never been to London.'

'No, sir.'

'You'll like it, I think ... in the spring—'

'Yes, sir.'

Starrett frowned at him, sidelong. 'Wyatt? What was it—the thing you lost?'

Wyatt shrugged; then looking at Starrett, slowly smiled. 'If it's around, I'll find it,' he said. 'If not—'

A sharp report cracked across the field. The signal flares shot skyward and dropped, trailing smoke.

'That's it,' said Starrett. He turned and started for the radio room, then stopped and looked back. 'If you find it, Wyatt—when you do ... let me know.'

Wyatt nodded again. 'Yes, sir. You'll know.'

'Sir?' Golden sprang in through the hatch. 'Greene wants to see you.'

Hurriedly Starrett strode to the hatch as Nelson and Hagen swung in. 'Greene?' He crouched down, his hand on the door.

'I just wanted to give you the word,' Greene said.

Starrett nodded. 'Always bring her back.'

'Yeah,' said Greene. 'That's it.'

Starrett grinned. 'Will do,' he said and rose as Greene flicked him a wave.

Quickly Starrett pulled the door shut with a slam, locked it; then turned, sprinting toward the flight deck.

Wyatt watched as Hagen, by the right waist, plugged into intercom. He saw Nelson slip the leather-cased snapshot into his breast pocket and, catching Nelson's look, grinned. Then quietly he went to his turret and curled up on the step around it, his head resting on his chute pack, his eyes closed.

Abruptly the air cracked with an explosive, whining shriek.

The Lady shook, quivering with the jagged, deafening roar.

Wyatt shifted about, his arms folded under him, his fists tightening, hard.

*   *   *

'Ten thousand!'

Wyatt felt the sharp nudge and glanced around to see Hagen thumbing to the turret. He nodded and swung up on his knees, his motions deft, precise, as he engaged the crank, released the brake and wound the turret into entry position.

Hagen stood back, watching.

The drone of the ship thundered around them. Swiftly, in slapping gusts, the wind blasted up through the turret well. The thinning air stung with a brisk, dry cold.

Wyatt turned to Hagen and, securing the turret, signaled with a nod and carefully lowered himself into the ball.

His heavily booted feet slid into the foot-rests on either side the sighting-pane. He settled on the narrow, armored seat and, with a glance up to Hagen, drew his oxygen mask across his face and hooked the strap tight to his helmet. Then, reaching up, he caught the door locks, leaned forward and pulled the door shut over him.

The turret shivered, loud with the wind buffeting against it. He fastened the locks, pushed his safety belt aside and plugged in his oxygen tube and intercom. Chills needled his body. Quickly he plugged in his heated suit, flicked the control switches at the left of his gunsight and drew back on the controls.

A low, whining tremor filled the turret as slowly the ball slipped around, turning upward. Wyatt rode with the turn, settling back against the curved iron door. He shifted his right foot, pressing the intercom button by the foot-rest. The headphones in his helmet crackled.

'Ball turret to skipper. Checking in. Over.'

'Roger.'

He leaned back, his legs up, and eased the turret around, checking the underside of *The Lady*. The sleek silver belly gleamed, tinged with a sparkling blue glitter.

The rest was sky—the blue, stark immensity of morning, pure with original light.

He swung the turret downward.

Clouds, etched with radiance, hovered glowing below. They stretched out, scattered across the earth. Their shadows drifted, dimming the shallow hills, the checkered fields in tidy, hedged patches and squares like an

133

inlay of green and brown mosaic.

'Left waist to pilot. Formation. Nine o'clock level. Ours, I think.'

Wyatt pulled back the controls. The ball whirled up and around.

Distantly, bombers dotted the sky, clustered like motes in the sunlit air. Swarms of nearer formations streaked the sky with high, thin vapor trails.

Slowly *The Lady* banked.

The horizon wheeled, slanting across the sighting-pane. The turret filled with a flashing of sunlight. Abruptly the earth swung down and away; then, teetering, leveled into view again.

Fortresses closed in, winging around them: some rising nearer, others falling behind, jockeying for position. Most were olive drab; a few were silver.

Steadily a ship eased in low, from behind. Aft of its nose was the insignia of a crowned, pistol-toting blonde, with the name *Duchess of Denver* and a row of twenty red bombs below it. A score of twelve swastikas—one for every plane downed—underlined the bombs. The *Duchess* started to rise.

Wyatt clicked intercom. 'Ball turret to pilot. Better pull her up a bit. Ship's coming through. Closing in.'

'Roger. What's the ship?'

'*Duchess of Denver*. Tail number four-five-two.'

'Roger.'

Gently *The Lady* dipped upward.

The *Duchess* passed under, gliding toward the right, then slowly climbed.

Suddenly a swift, bucking shock knocked *The Lady* aside. The turret jolted. The ship lurched, pitching sideways.

'Prop wash!' yelled Cronin.

Tumultuous air flows buffeted against *The Lady*. The wings shook, straining against the blasts. She rocked and skidded, slipping across the air.

'They're pulling in too soon!' called Hagen.

'Starrett!' Kirby's voice was desperate.

Quickly Wyatt shoved his controls. The turret spun down, jarring against the stops. He swung, reaching up—

Sharply *The Lady* dropped. The weight of the motion slammed Wyatt hard against the turret door, pinning him back as the pressure mounted, forcing in, crushing against him.

'Got it!' snapped Starrett. 'Now hold it!'

Slowly *The Lady* veered, taut with strain; then suddenly bucked and fell again, lightly.

Abruptly the pressure cut, and Wyatt lurched forward, slumped over his gunsight.

The Lady caught—and evenly leveled out.

'Jesus Christ!' sighed Kirby. 'Wow!'

'One more flip like that,' said Cronin, 'and we've had it.'

'That sonofabitch!' muttered Hagen.

'Y'all ought to see Kramer here,' Gillis

135

drawled in. 'He's white as a polar bear's ass.'

' 'Course,' said Kramer. He laughed quickly. 'Look, Ma—no guts.'

'Pilot to crew. Check in.'

Swacey clicked in. 'Tail. Okay.'

'Hagen. Okay.'

'Nelson. Okay.'

Trembling, Wyatt slipped his foot to the switch. He took a quivering, deep breath; then, curtly, 'Ball turret. Okay.'

'Radio. Okay.'

'Top turret. Okay.'

'Bombardier. Still here.'

'Navigator. That's it, Dad. Nobody's jumped yet.'

'Pilot to crew. Roger. Over.'

Starrett's voice was crisp and sure. A grin came through it—even after the switch had clicked out.

Wyatt raised his head and, with a caught sigh, leaned back, curved against the door, his face brittly calm and cold—as if nothing had happened.

*   *   *

The North Sea glittered below. The wrinkled light of the water flashed gold with morning. Clouds, caught by dayfire, drifted miles under. The thin, freezing air numbed Wyatt's forehead. His legs, raised on the foot-rests, were stiff with a dull, dry ache. A still, strange

136

look haunted his eyes as he watched the shores of England dimming behind them, fading under the shimmering morning haze.

Then abruptly, with only a glance behind, he swung his controls about and held the turret eastward. The sky was a fierce blue splendor of distance flecked with bombers—wings and whole divisions bearing east, towering in high formations.

Steadily *The Silver Lady* droned on.

*   *   *

'Bombardier to crew. Over North Sea. Test-fire your guns. Over.'

Wyatt reached to his gun switches and flicked them on. He checked his line of fire, then, pointing his turret downward, pressed the firing-buttons on his control handles. The turret jarred with the rapid fire of his guns.

From every position *The Lady* thundered with quick, sharp bursts.

The crew checked in.

Wyatt clicked his intercom. 'Ball turret. Okay.'

'Roger.'

'Navigator to crew. There's the coast.'

'Get ready for anything,' Gillis called in. 'Here we go.'

Wyatt slid the turret sweeping around and up, his grip tight on the controls.

*　　*　　*

Below, the land flowed under—a patchwork of lines and squares, colors and miniatures. The flashing of ground guns flickered like pin-pricks of instant light. The flak broke around them, the sudden black puffs exploding, drifting by.

The formation veered, shifting and swaying in evasive action.

The turret spun lightly.

Concussions boomed against *The Silver Lady*.

'Navigator to pilot. Ship ahead—hit. Number-three engine out... She's aborting.'

'The *Duchess of Denver*,' said Gillis.

Gently *The Lady* rose.

Wyatt swung his turret forward.

Ahead, the *Duchess of Denver* banked through the bursting flak, her dead engine billowing with dark, erupting smoke. Her wingtip was jagged. She nosed about, clearing the squadrons, and circled back.

The Silver Lady climbed, edging forward.

The intercom clicked. 'Beyond flak range,' Gillis called in. 'Clear ahead.'

Wyatt swept his turret pointing aft as the *Duchess of Denver*, flying low and alone, wove through the flak bursts, the smoke trailing thick from her engine. She rose and fell, gliding from side to side, heading west.

138

'The *Duchess* is on her way,' Swacey called in.

'Roger,' said Kramer.

'Number three still smoking,' said Wyatt.

'Badly?'

'Yeah.'

'Hope to Christ she makes it,' Kramer muttered.

'Co-pilot to crew. In new position. Over.'

Wyatt eased his turret around. A ship nosed into left position—the *High Tail*, her insignia a pair of legs sticking out from a circle of clouds.

Another ship, the *Princess Pam*, maneuvered toward right wing, the gun turrets revolving slowly as if sizing up *The Lady*.

Wyatt counted the red-painted bombs on her side—twelve so far.

Rigidly he turned his turret forward.

*　　*　　*

The intercom crackled. 'Co-pilot to crew. Fighters. One o'clock high.'

'Ours?' Kramer called in.

'Could be. I can't tell yet.'

'Escorts, maybe,' said Kramer. 'They're due about now.'

'Maybe,' said Kirby. His voice was slow. He was chewing gum. 'Maybe not.'

'They look—*Christ*! Bombardier to crew. Messerschmitts coming in—one o'clock high.'

'Tail to crew. More coming in—six o'clock level.'

139

'How many?' snapped Kramer.

'A whole shitload,' said Swacey. 'Fifty, maybe.'

'Twenty here,' shouted Gillis. 'They're hitting the high group!'

'They're leveling in,' yelled Swacey.

Wyatt whirled his turret aft.

Fighters bore in, flying in close formation, their vapor trails white against the blue.

Wyatt eased down on his range pedal, framing them in his sight, waiting.

The vapor trails arced. Slowly, squadron by squadron, the fighters broke away, graceful as an aerial ballet. They peeled off, turning high, and spiraled down.

The Forts pulled tighter together.

'Watch it!' Swacey bellowed. 'Here they come!'

Swiftly the Messerschmitts winged in, hurtling through like crosses flung through space. Bursts of 20 mm. shells puffed in sudden, bright explosions.

'They're coming right through the formations!' yelled Swacey.

The Lady thundered, her guns firing, tracers streaking the sky.

The fighters dove through, their cannons blinking, then veered and banked, whirling away, high and back.

One came rolling under, turning up its armored belly, as Wyatt fired, the turret swinging, tracking its flight, the guns

140

hammering explosions.

The fighter looped downward, plunging away.

Swiftly Wyatt swung back again as three planes, winging as one, dove in for them, split and darted by.

'Got him!' cried Hagen.

An orange burst of flame spurted from one of the fighters. A black cloud of smoke skidded across the sky. The ship broke like a brittle toy and fell, dropping in smoldering pieces.

'Watch it!' called Wyatt.

Another swung up, bearing in high, the wings sparking with cannon fire.

'Christ!' shouted Hagen.

Wyatt spun to the left as the *Princess Pam*, arching up in half a rising loop, buckled under the strain. The wings quivered. Slowly the ship cracked in two.

A cry caught in Wyatt's throat as he stared, watching the men tumbling brokenly out of the halved ship.

The wreckage spiraled down, its wings feathery with flame, the ball guns still blazing—wildly, at nothing.

Two chutes opened up.

A third caught tangling in the spinning tail wreckage.

Wyatt watched the man struggling, tearing at the chute, kicking free, falling, clutching at the sky. Over and down and down he spun, twisting like a convulsive ant—dwindling to a speck—and then ... only the patterned earth...

Stunned, Wyatt followed the fall. Suddenly, uncontrollably, his legs started to shake. They slipped from the foot-rests and fell under him, useless. He felt sick. Like a vortex whorling around him, the instant of the tumbling men screaming through space (soundless in the turret noise) shrieked in his brain, searing the memory in—the lasting scars—

'Look!' shouted Swacey. 'The bastards are strafing the chutes. Wyatt! Can you get them? Tail to ball—can you get them, Wyatt?'

A tremor shivered through Wyatt. Swiftly he looked up. His legs swung back into position, his left foot jamming down on the range pedal. Through the sight he saw two Messerschmitts wheeling in, their wing guns firing, diving toward the floating chutes.

One of the fighters veered into his sight grill. He fired, tracking with short, deliberate bursts. The fighter staggered. A piece of its wing flew off. The plane banked dizzily and turned, gliding low and away. The other rose in a half-roll and headed back.

The chutes drifted slowly earthward.

Wyatt watched, his breathing deep and even, his tight rigidity gone; but his eyes—cold, empty of all light—were dark with a clear, unfathomable sadness.

'More fighters!' called Swacey. 'Seven o'clock level.'

'Look!' Nelson shouted. 'Escorts! Nine o'clock high.'

'You sure?' asked Kramer.

'P-51s!' said Golden. 'Nine o'clock high.'

The Messerschmitts had regrouped. But high and beyond them, to the right, another formation—of Mustangs—dotted the sky, then broke—plane by plane peeling off in a swooping dive toward the MEs.

The Messerschmitts split up. Half the formation rose, gyring back to draw off the attack. The other half bore in, plunging for the Forts again.

Wyatt leaned forward, his leg tensed guiding the range pedal, his hands firm on the controls, waiting. Then as the Messerschmitts cut through, he fired.

* * *

'Flak!' Kramer cut in. 'Straight ahead. Heavy.'

'Christ!' muttered Hagen. 'If it isn't one thing, it's another.' Strain edged his voice.

'How's the ammo holding?' Gillis called in.

'Low,' said Hagen. 'How about you?'

'Down to spitballs,' said Kramer.

'Cut the chatter,' Kirby snapped. 'We're nearing target.'

Searchingly Wyatt eased his turret about. One ... two ... three ... four ... five. Five ships left of the nine he had counted that morning. Four lost from his range alone, with how many more from the high squadrons beyond his range? And from the squadrons and wings beyond them?

He raised his eyes beyond his squadron, beyond his group—his look deepening at the spectacle before him, widening as his awareness took it breathlessly in—of groups beyond his own, and wings stretching across the miles of clear blue sky to the farthest rims of sight. Beyond, on every side, formation on towering formation glittered far across the noon, in high, thundering armadas bearing steadily toward Berlin.

And as he watched, an awe dawned in him, aware that never before had he seen such a sight, that no man ever had but these here—this moment out of all time when thousands of free men rose in a single day as one, as a retaliative Spirit geared to the destruction not of Berlin but of the central Evil that had swept across Europe, crushing wherever it fell the singing, soaring, free soul of Man.

And slowly, as he watched, Wyatt felt again, stronger than it had ever been before, that fierce, inner glow warming and restoring him; the peace of conviction; the certainty that he was here at the right time and in the right place—for him. This day's run, the armadas winging about him, was Mankind's statement against Evil; and all these men—these thousands of men, here possibly to die for that belief—were part of him, and he of them; and this was—out of all time and place—his time and place to signature that statement, even if it be in blood.

A surge of life and renewed strength swelled through Wyatt. He felt the skin of his face prickle and his spine tingle with a feeling of quiet victory—the victory over himself, the agony redeemed.

Around them the squadron winged, tightening together.

* * *

'Navigator to pilot. Approaching IP. Over.'

'Roger.'

'Christ!' shouted Gillis. 'Look!'

'That's it,' said Kramer. 'Berlin.'

'Where?' called Hagen.

'Out toward two.'

'Holy jumping Jesus!'

Wyatt swung about.

The sky toward two was thick with flak. Thunderheads of swirling smoke towered, billowing from the earth. Flight after flight of advancing bombers swept over the burning city—hundreds of them, crowding in dark, precise formations through the flak. Fragments of planes spun flaming earthward. Men plummeted down, their chutes snapping open, drifting slowly through the bursting barrages. Swarms of Luftwaffe fighters dove through the invading bombers, their wing guns blazing, their rockets flashing. Tracers crisscrossed the darkening air. Lightnings and Mustangs veered rising and diving in, in swift curving maneuvers, dogging the Luftwaffe among the crossing bombers.

Suddenly—

'Bombardier to pilot. Turning on IP. Over.'

'Roger. It's all yours. Over.'

Gently *The Silver Lady* banked, rising, then slowly leveled and lowered again.

'Flak,' said Kramer. 'Heavy. Accurate.'

The Lady bucked.

Quick black puffs exploded around them. Fragments showered the sides, rattling like a hail of shot.

Wyatt spun his turret downward, turning it steadily. Clouds spread out below in a thin, hazy cover. Openings drifted by. Glimpses of earth glided under, shadowy with smoke.

'Nelson to crew. Fighters. Nine o'clock high. Bandits.'

'Sonofabitch!' yelled Swacey. 'The jackpot!'

Swarms of fighters swept like wasps down the sky.

'More,' snapped Hagen. 'Three o'clock level.'

'Two o'clock high,' said Kirby.

'Night fighters!' Cronin shouted. 'They're sending in night fighters—'

A thundering concussion rocked *The Lady*. Flak raked her sides. *The Lady* jolted, skidded sideways, then righted again.

'Messerschmitts—110s—coming in level,' said Swacey.

Recklessly the fighters dove in, rockets arrowing from their wings. Smoke snaked, swift and white, across the sky.

Guns thundered from *The Lady*.

'Watch it!' snapped Swacey. 'They're barrel-assing through!'

'Hold your fire!' shouted Hagen. 'You'll hit a Fort!'

A twin-engined fighter snap-rolled through the formation, the black-and-white crosses clear on the black wings.

'Three o'clock high,' Hagen called in. 'Focke-Wulfs. They're swinging in low, Wyatt.'

Wyatt slammed down his range pedal, swinging his turret toward three.

An FW-190 rose into his sight.

Quickly he thumbed his firing-switches. His guns blasted in sharp, short bursts.

Steadily the 190 bore in, stubby, blunt-nosed, its wings flashing.

The turret shook with the hammering repercussions of its guns.

The 190 shivered, then suddenly twisted, spiraling down. A long black cloud of smoke trailed from its engine.

Wyatt spun, tracking the second 190.

It banked. A burst of flak caught it square in the cockpit. The wings sheered off. The plane plunged like a blazing comet.

The intercom crackled. 'Bombardier to ball. Check below, Wyatt.'

'Roger.'

Wyatt swung his turret down, checking below.

A low group of Liberators eased into position under them.

Quickly Wyatt clicked intercom. 'Ball to bombardier. B-24s below. Repeat: Liberators below. Keep bomb-bay doors closed. Over.'

'We're making the run!' said Kramer.

'Liberators below,' Wyatt repeated.

'Hold it!' said Starrett.

Wyatt kept his turret down, watching the low group making its bomb run.

The sky was filled with bombers, group after group of them gliding and crossing the smoke and flak.

'Somebody's fucked up!' Gillis called in. 'We're nearly on target.'

The low group bore steadily through the flak. Suddenly the lead ship flung up and over, flames flapping from its right wing.

The Lady jolted and pitched, tossing from side to side. Wave after concussive wave broke buffeting against her.

The intercom clicked again. 'Pilot to crew. We're making a second run. Over.'

'Through this?' Kramer shouted.

Wyatt tensed.

Suddenly *The Lady* shivered. A hard, thudding shock knocked her aside.

148

'Jesus!' yelled Cronin.

Another blast caught.

The Lady reeled, struggling for balance.

Fragments pelted against her.

The Lady floundered, straining in a tight bank, as the whole formation veered for a second run.

'Bombardier to crew. Making second run. Over.'

Slowly the squadron wheeled through the churning flak.

The turret shook, throbbing with the jagged vibrations. Wisps of black clouds drifted across the sighting-pane.

Ahead, clouds obscured the city. Smoke billowed in somber, tumultuous towers swelling through the low haze. A dirty, fiery glow swept like a deluge of flame across the earth.

A still look of sadness deepened in Wyatt's eyes, the overwhelming pity, and the biting anger that this should have to be. If Christ had wept over Jerusalem, what would He have done now over Berlin?

'Bombardier to ball. Check below.'

Wyatt tore his gaze from the flaming city. 'Roger.' Swiftly he spun his turret about; then briskly, 'All clear below.'

'Roger... Bomb-bay doors opening.'

Wyatt raised his turret.

Flak puffed about them.

Slowly the belly of *The Lady* opened, the

149

sleek silver doors steadily parting.

Golden cut in from the radio room. 'Bomb-bay doors down and locked.'

'Roger.'

A sharp, caroming crash jolted against the ship. The turret jarred, stopped. Startled, Wyatt joggled his controls. The motor whined, shrill. The turret held, stuck.

Sharply Wyatt flicked off his power switches, snatched his hand cranks free and, engaging them in the overhead sockets, tried turning them. They tightened, fixed.

The gears were jammed.

The Lady tossed, lurching and bucking about. The flak thundered, thick and flailing against her.

Quickly Wyatt shifted his foot to intercom—then, abruptly, caught himself, his eyes on the bomb-bay doors wide for the bomb run. With a tight grimace, he drew his foot away, snapped the cranks back into place and, with a tensed, quick prayer, sat back and waited.

The Lady rocked through the bursting flak, her wings—

Wyatt started. Through the side pane he saw the jagged edges of a hole glittering near the right tip.

'Bombs away!' shouted Gillis.

Swiftly, train by train, the bombs dropped from the belly. *The Lady* shivered, suddenly rising, light.

'Okay!' called Golden. 'Bombs away.'

'Now,' snapped Kramer, 'let's get the fuck out of here!'

The Lady veered, wheeling from the target in formation. The bomb-bay doors started slowly to close.

Wyatt clicked his intercom, his voice tight, quick. 'Ball to Hagen. Turret jammed. Check ring.'

'Fighters!' Swacey cut in. 'Seven o'clock level.'

'Wyatt—try it,' said Hagen. 'Slow.'

Wyatt switched on again. The turret motor started up. Gently the turret moved.

'Hold it!' snapped Hagen. 'Now—back.'

Wyatt eased the turret backing around.

'Cut. Now—try it. All the way.'

Carefully Wyatt swung full about. 'That does it,' he said. 'What was it?'

'Shells,' said Hagen. 'Caught in the ring.'

'Pilot to ball. Okay, Wyatt?'

'Roger.' He whirled the ball around swiftly toward seven, bracing himself as through his sight he framed a gaggle of black twin-engine fighters firing in.

*   *   *

'Navigator to crew. Nearing coast. Over.'

The bombing of flak thundered around them. The quick wash of fragments clattered against the sides. *The Lady* swayed and rolled, shagging from side to side. The black smudges

151

of flak cloud broke, drifting through the formation.

'Thick enough to waltz on,' Swacey called in.

'Show me,' said Hagen.

'Bombardier to crew. Beyond flak range. Over.'

The Lady leveled out.

With a heavy grunt Wyatt eased up his turret and leaned, limp, against the curved door. His back ached. His legs were numbed with cold. Slowly he turned the ball, sweeping the sky.

Thunderheads swirled, towering about them like the ramparts of Valhalla. Huge, windy caverns whirled into their depths, turbulent, glowing with the late afternoon sun.

A low wing of Liberators flew toward the left, far and out.

Steadily, through the steep sun-golden canyons of clouds, the group winged on, droning like a formation of dragon flies. Behind them the flak clouds hovered, grey and fading in the wind. Wyatt swung the turret aft again and counted: one ... two ... Two were left of the nine.

'Nelson to crew. Fighters. Eight o'clock high.'

'190s!' Swacey cut in. 'Yellow-nosed—'

'The Abbeville Kids!' said Hagen.

Swiftly Wyatt swung about. Toward eight, he saw the fighters—Focke-Wulfs, their blunt noses a clear, bright yellow.

152

They winged, leveling in, in tight formation; then suddenly veered apart and dove, their wing guns flashing.

'Watch it!' yelled Swacey. 'Watch it!'

'What the fuck do you think I'm doing!' snapped Nelson.

'They're coming through!'

'Easy, boy. Easy,' said Wyatt. His words were slow, quiet. 'We see them.'

'Roger,' said Swacey. His voice evened off. 'Coming in toward seven.'

The Lady shook with the rapid thundering of guns.

The fighters swung through, barreling between the Forts.

Wyatt wheeled, firing. A Fort crossed his sighting-pane. He cut his fire.

The 190 went through—the pilot, helmeted, bent forward. He dove, rolling his ship, the armored underside turned up.

'Tail ship. Knocked out,' called Swacey. 'Straggling.'

Wyatt whirled toward six.

The tail ship dropped behind, its starboard engine shot out, the prop feathering slowly, glinting.

Three of the fighters plunged for it, firing, then swooped about and dove in again.

Fire burst from the dead engine. The ship fell farther behind, swaying. The side hatch swung open, snapped off and spun crazily back. One by one the men leaped, tumbling out. Chutes

153

mushroomed over the checkered earth. The plane pitched on its side, circling in a slow, downward sweep. Flames tipped the wings. Quick fires exploded through its body. Pieces shot off, dropping in jagged debris.

'Christ!' yelled Kirby. 'The top group—*Starrett! Pull up!*'

'Not yet!'

'They've crashed—they're falling—you're heading for them!'

'God-dammit, shut up!... *Now!*'

The Lady shot up, whipping in a steep, straining climb. The pressure crushed down, swift and stunning, on Wyatt. His body seemed iron, heavy with unbearable weight. The Fort behind them followed them up, taut with the sharp ascent.

Wreckage swept under the sighting-pane. Two Fortresses, locked twisted together, spiraled under—and suddenly a blinding ball of flame erupted. A black, billowing cloud bowled through the sky, flames bursting through it. The shock flung *The Lady* high on her wing.

The pressure on Wyatt cut.

'Jesus H. Christ!' muttered Kirby.

'What happened?' called Swacey.

'The high flight,' said Cronin. 'One of the planes got hit, fell on the one below it.'

The intercom clicked. 'Starrett.' It was Kirby, his voice subdued. 'Aronson just called in. He says Thanks.'

154

Wyatt smiled. If Starrett had pulled up too soon, Aronson—the ship behind—would have crashed into the exploding Forts. In God we trust, and Starrett.

'190s. Four o'clock high,' said Hagen.

'Fighters!' Gillis called in. 'Twelve o'clock level.'

'Focke-Wulfs!' said Kramer.

'Like hell!' shouted Gillis. 'They're ours—Thunderbolts!'

'P-47s!' Cronin called in. 'Little Buddies. Escorts.'

*　　*　　*

The Thunderbolts darted over and about them, herding the ragged group west. Below, the whitecaps swept in broken waves across the grey-green waters. Two Thunderbolts swung low, buzzing the crests. Wyatt watched them, a warm, smiling wonder in his eyes.

'Hagen to ball. Oxygen tanks nearly empty. Climb out. Over.'

Wyatt clicked the intercom. 'Ball to Hagen. Wait'll we hit England. Over.'

'Pilot to crew. We're letting down now. Over.'

'Navigator to Wyatt. Look—toward twelve.'

Wyatt spun his turret up and forward. A low, thin line rose darkly along the horizon.

'England!' said Wyatt.

155

'It's not Coney Island,' said Kramer.

'With you navigating,' Gillis drawled in, 'I wouldn't bet on it.'

'Pilot to crew. Down to ten thousand. Off oxygen. Over.'

'Bombardier to ball. Climb out, Wyatt. Over.'

'Roger.'

Awkwardly, his fingers tight with cold, Wyatt unsnapped his oxygen mask and let it hang to one side. He breathed a slow, full breath, feeling the fresh, chilling air cold on his face, sweated and lined with strain. But the light in his eyes—his look was etched with a difference—a strange, set intensity, a steadiness lit from within.

The fields of England rolled under them, the sunlit hills, the pastures dotted with cows.

An almost breathless instant of release struck through *The Lady*.

A rutted dirt road wound through a greening lea. A girl with a blue kerchief about her head guided a flock of white geese down the way. She stopped and looked up, her hand shading her eyes, then waved.

A smile broke on Wyatt's face. As if she could see him, he waved back, grinning.

'Hagen to ball. Nearing base. Over.'

'Roger.'

Wyatt spun his turret down, switched off and, gearing the off-power clutches, unlatched the locks and swung back the door.

156

Hagen was kneeling by the turret, waiting, his look a question.

Wyatt grinned and nodded Fine; then, unplugging his cords and tube, hoisted himself up and out of the turret. He tugged off his helmet and tossed it across to his flight bag; then stretched, flexing his arms and legs— 'God!'—and, with a sudden grunt, knelt again, engaged his crank handle and, releasing the brake, locked down the hatch and started to roll the turret into stowed position.

'Hey, Wyatt.'

He secured the turret tightly, replaced the crank and rose, turning to Golden in the radio room. 'Yeah?'

Grinning, Golden handed him a slice of cheese and a hardtack biscuit from the K rations.

'Thanks,' said Wyatt. He took the cheese and, leaning tiredly against the bulkhead frame, started to munch it.

The waist was littered ankle deep with cartridge shells and ammo links. The burnt, acrid smell of gun smoke stung the air.

Nelson leaned by his gun, eating a Milky Way, his face streaked dirty and haggard, drawn with tension. But as his look met Wyatt's, he smiled and nodded Okay.

*   *   *

Wyatt watched from the waist gate as *The*

Lady lowered for landing, the field flashing under. The wheels suddenly touched, the brakes screeching. Roughly the ship bounced up, jolting, then settled again, hurtling down the runway, checking its speed, easing to a taxiing glide.

A moment later she nosed to her revetment.

Greene, his hands raised guiding her in, backed away, grinning.

Gently she swung about in a teetering pirouette. The engines revved, gunning up in an explosive roar, then abruptly cut. A shiver trembled through her, then stillness.

Quickly Hagen brushed by Wyatt, unlocked the side hatch and, slamming it open, tossed out his flight bag and leaped down.

Nelson followed.

Wyatt jumped out and, turning, reached for his flight bag.

A hard, heavy cuff knocked him aside. He spun.

'You made it!' shouted Miller, his arms flung wide. His bearded, burly face was shining. His thick hands caught Wyatt's in a crushing grip. 'Congratulations!'

'Thanks.'

'Land!' yelled Golden, tumbling out. 'Land!' Clowning, he fell on his knees and kissed the earth, salaaming to it.

Nelson stood looking about the field, then quietly, 'I never knew a day could be so long,' he said.

'How'd the ball go?' said Miller.

'Swell,' said Wyatt. He started for the turret.

Miller caught him by the shoulder. 'I'll take care of the guns,' he said. 'You take it easy.' His eyes, red and tired, twinkled with irony. 'Like me.'

Wyatt grinned and turned.

'A picnic,' said Hagen. 'All we needed was a dame.'

Greene laughed.

'Christ!' said Swacey. 'Look at that tail!'

Streamers of jagged metal twisted from the tailfin. Half the group letter had been blown away.

'We'll patch it up,' said Greene. He studied it. 'A nice big patch—'

'You saw the right wing?' said Cronin.

'I saw it,' Greene said. 'You guys just ain't got no respect for government property.'

CHAPTER THIRTEEN

Tiredly Starrett dropped from the nose hatch, his body taut. He stretched, rubbing the kinks from his muscles.

Hurriedly Greene crossed under the wing. His hand shot up in an abrupt salute.

Starrett looked up, grinning, and motioned to *The Lady.* 'Always bring her back,' he said.

'Yeah,' said Greene. 'But just look at 'er, sir.

159

Flak holes all over the place.' He looked at Starrett; then, meaningfully, 'We ought to armor the flight deck, sir.'

Starrett shook his head. 'No. No changes.'

'But, dammit, sir—'

'Truck for interrogation!' Kramer called out.

Starrett glanced up.

A canvas-covered lorry swerved in from the perimeter track.

Greene frowned. 'You superstitious, sir—about her?'

'What gave you that idea?' said Starrett, and suddenly winked as he turned and started toward the truck.

*   *   *

The truck drove slowly back to the briefing yard. The crew sat on the side-board seats, their flight gear piled in the center. Starrett sat at the end by the tailgate, looking across the field and the passing, empty revetments—the ground crews standing around, idle against the emptiness.

The sun was low, westering in a vivid, fiery glow. Clouds massing high and far gleamed with the stark light of the ebbing day. Shadows deepened, blue and purple, across the field. The grass rippled with a shimmering quiet, gentle with wind, a warm welcome back to earth.

He turned, searchingly glancing at his men.

160

They sat silent, still in their flying clothes, their faces smudged with sweat, the red marks of their oxygen masks still sharp across their cheeks, their hair matted, their looks haggard, grey with fatigue. One by one he looked at them, his eyes quiet and proud.

These were his men, and they had had a rough one today. War had whirled and exploded death around them, and they had come through—beautifully. Even Wyatt. He had worried about Wyatt this morning, seeing him alone in the ship. But now—He looked across to Wyatt, the face tired, marked, and yet—the deep, still look in his eyes now. He wondered what had caused it. What had happened up there today in the turret? And how long actually had Wyatt been hanging there, jammed, before calling in? He had waited until after bomb run. Then—just the call-in, simple, direct, as if asking the time. One of these days he would have to talk with Wyatt, get to know what made him tick, as a person, not just as a crewman—

A strange jolt of thought struck him. *As a crewman*. That had been how he had seen them all. Not as people, deep in life, with feelings and thoughts rooted in years long before he had crossed their ways. Oh, he knew the surface facts—their hometowns, their women, some of their adventures, their natures. But what did he know of them as human beings, what they believed, why they were here—their motives, their drives? Their lives were tangled with his in this mess. Why? Chance? Luck? Or was there something more behind it all, which something in *their* lives might explain. Why these nine men now?

All he knew was that suddenly they were men with lives he wanted to know, to understand, as he had never understood them—now, while still there was time. These nine had shared death with him, closer this day than ever before—*and* life. He was proud of them with a welling surge of pride, yet all he could do now was sit here in a strain-weary silence and look at them as if separate from their lives, as if nothing at all had happened upstairs—these, *his* men, closer than brothers in facing death, and in life, distant as strangers.

Abruptly, with a shifting of gears, the truck swung quickly into the briefing yard and jolted to a sharp halt.

Stiffly the crew climbed down, dragging their flight bags after them, and filed raggedly into the briefing hut for interrogation.

*   *   *

At the interrogation table, Starrett raised his cup of hot cocoa and drank, his eyes on Wyatt.

'Nothing but clouds and smoke,' Wyatt told the Interrogation Officer. 'Like the whole city was up.'

'But nothing you could pin-point?'

'Nothing.'

The Interrogation Officer pursed his lips, jotted down a line and glanced to Swacey again.

Swacey downed his jigger ration of Scotch and, crumpling the paper cup, shook his head. 'I wasn't even sure it was Berlin,' he muttered.

The officer glanced around. 'Anything else?' His look swept the table.

Starrett set down his cup. 'That's it, I guess.'

The officer nodded. 'Okay,' he said. 'That's it.' Briskly he gathered up his report notes and, laying them aside, called, 'Next!'

Tiredly the crew shuffled to their feet and, turning, pushing back their chairs, started from the room.

Starrett followed, easing his way slowly between the tables and the crewmen toward the door. From all sides he caught snatches of questions, quiet and direct, from the Interrogation Officers; and the replies, low and laconic, rising to excitement, from the crewmen:

How many chutes?

Three. Maybe more. I couldn't tell. I was busy...

They were 410s. Right?

He was near enough to spit at. Barrel-assing right through.

What altitude?

Wait'll I check my log... Yeah. Twenty-five thousand feet...

Like this, see? He comes right through, so I shoots...

How many yards, about?

You'd say it was accurate?

You ought to see my bombsight—what's left of it...

About what time? Where?

Sure, they went down. Christ! I saw them, didn't I!

Mobile installations? You're sure they were mobile?

The last of the crews waited by the door, scuffing about in their heavy flying boots.

Starrett edged through to the corridor.

A thin, pale-faced mess corporal stood by the doughnut-and-cocoa stand just outside, a full cup in hand. He held it out to Starrett. 'More, sir? There's plenty left today.'

Starrett shook his head and started down the hall to leave.

At the entrance the Old Man stood leaning by the open door, silent, his face stubbled with a day-old beard and streaked with grime, his hair tousled, stirring in the light wind. He was looking out across the field, his eyes dark with loss.

*　　　*　　　*

'To the crew,' said Starrett. He raised his glass and drank.

Aronson, sullen-eyed and frowning, looked

164

across at him, his own glass held motionless. Suddenly, with a snap of his hand, he downed his drink. A trickle glistened down his chin. Broodingly he wiped it away and from the bottle on the table beside him poured himself another and sat heavily back, silent, glancing vaguely around the empty lounge.

It was nearly twelve. The lounge—a converted Nissen hut adjoining the Officers' Bar—was shadowy with firelight from the grated hearth before them. The firelight gleamed on the leather sofas and polished furnishings, and tinged the deep, patterned rug with an erratic glow. Over the fireplace was an enlarged Kodachrome mural of raiding Fortresses stilled in the calm blue sky.

Aronson's mouth twisted, his eyes on the mural.

Starrett watched him, wondering.

Slowly Aronson turned and, meeting Starrett's look, shook his head. The firelight flickered across his face, shadows sketching it in deep, somber lines.

'I'm drunk,' he said softly. 'You know?' His words were clipped, distinct. 'But we don't go up tomorrow, do we?' He shook his head again. 'Of course not... We get a break—some break...'

Starrett settled back, studying his drink.

Aronson shrugged. 'Another guy gone,' he muttered. 'I told you, didn't I?'

Starrett nodded. 'Moore.'

165

'Got his arm shot up,' Aronson mumbled. 'That's five so far. Five out of nine. Leaves four... Diggs. O'Hara—O'Hara with his stinking coveralls. Lever. And—Stone. That's all that's left of—It used to be a good crew, you know.' He looked up, almost smiling. 'And we've only fourteen more to go, man— fourteen more trips and—we'll be done, then. All done... How many you got now?'

Slowly Starrett turned his glass, thinking. Then, 'Twenty-one,' he said. 'If they don't boost it.'

'Twenty-one,' Aronson murmured. 'Maybe twenty-six.' He snapped the glass down. 'And you drink to them!' He squinted at Starrett. 'Because you're proud of them. Because they're your crew. Your crew ...' Tiredly he shook his head again. 'But don't, Starrett. Believe me, don't think of them. Don't ever give them more than you have to—because if you do ... Just don't. That's all.' He frowned, pouring himself another drink. 'I'm drinking too much, man. Do you mind?'

Starrett only looked at him evenly.

Aronson nodded. 'I know how it is,' he said quietly. He turned, looking at the mural. 'The way it starts—being a skipper. Keeping the men in line. Knowing them. Working, living, flying with them, And then, somewhere along the line—somehow—it happens.'

Slowly he got to his feet and started forward, his glass in hand, his eyes on the Fortresses.

'You wake up in the morning—or maybe it's in the middle of the night—and you're suddenly scared. You're wondering ... will O'Hara's cold get better ... or will Stone's wife get that divorce ... or is Lever okay in town. He's always getting lost. Even in Denver, with a map we'd drawn for him. We had to go looking for him. The whole crew... And London, the bombings there—will they be safe? Happy? ... And you wonder about Travers, afraid something might happen to his hands. Wants to be a pianist... He could've been, too. But he was the first. Flak. Right in the back... And his hands—weren't even scratched.'

He paused, looking into his drink. 'But that's how it happens—that moment you wake up—and wonder. And suddenly you realize— you're not yourself anymore. You're nine other guys. You're O'Hara and Lever and Travers and all the others. You're a part of them—and you're nothing to yourself. You've found out—you've given so much of yourself to them, there's nothing left in you. And it's all too late—

'And every time they get hurt—or die— something goes of you. You know that, Starrett? And for what? Why?'

He turned, leaning against the wall. 'I don't know,' he muttered. 'I only know—that's the beginning of it.' Silently he stared at his jacket on the floor; then quietly, 'Look at the record,' he said. 'The bombs there—the nice even rows of them … crowding out your luck. They get heavier—you'll see—heavier with every one you put on. And then, the more that go on, the more you can feel your men getting tight—and you find yourself waiting … waiting for the snap of their nerves. And it's then your fight really begins—if you're to hold them together—or what's left of them.'

He shook his head and, downing his drink, crossed to the table and poured another. The Scotch splashed about. He turned. 'Another?'

'No. Not now.' Starrett looked at him, his eyes searching.

Aronson shrugged, fumbling with the bottle cap; then tossed it clattering aside. He glanced up, grinning. 'But the funniest part—now get this, Starrett—the funniest part is the end… So you get them through—or what's left of them—and it's over. It's over, Starrett, and the crew breaks up. And you—you're all split up, and empty—and never the same again … because in every man of your crew there's a part of you that you can never find again… Never.'

He bowed his head, turning his drink slowly; then, glancing up, met Starrett's look and raised his glass. 'To the crew,' he said.

PART FOUR

LONDON
March 9–12, 1944

CHAPTER FOURTEEN

Grimly, with Aronson beside him, Starrett strode toward the Officers' Club, his whole tired body still taut with the tensions of the day's nine-and-a-half-hour raid—the second major assault on Berlin this week, and as rough as 'Bloody Monday' (as *The Stars and Stripes* had called it) three days ago. But his fatigue burned up in the anger seething through him.

For a week now he had been wrangling for London passes for his crew. Today the passes had come through. Already Gillis and Kramer were on their way with Kirby, and even he himself had had a room set by at the Regent's. But just as he had been about to leave, Cronin had come to the BOQ uniformed for London: The enlisted passes had been held up. The crew had been gigged until further orders.

'Whose orders?' Starrett demanded.

'Waverly's,' said Cronin. He sat on Starrett's bunk, waiting.

The dim, lazy tune of Clementine drifted through the tension. Aronson leaned back in his bunk, his harmonica held lightly, his eyes on Starrett.

Starrett's mouth tightened with anger. 'For what reason?'

Cronin looked up, sharp. 'We didn't pass inspection.'

'Inspection!?' Starrett stared, stunned and unbelieving. 'Didn't you tell him we didn't land till after four? We didn't clear till nearly six!'

Cronin shrugged. 'He says we should have swept up this morning—before we took off.'

Starrett nodded. Then swiftly he took up his jacket and cap. 'You go ahead,' he said. 'Give me half an hour. Then go to the Orderly Room and pick up your passes.' He looked at his watch: seven thirty. 'He's probably at the club now.' He looked to Aronson. 'Thirsty?'

Aronson grinned, swung his legs about and got to his feet. 'Who's buying?' he asked.

Starrett snapped his cap on, his look cold steel. 'Waverly,' he said, and started out.

*   *   *

The Officers' Bar was quiet, the lights dim. Smoke drifted vaguely about, eddying through sounds of talk, glasses clicking, a radio playing low.

Starrett saw him at a corner table, alone, and crossed the room to him, Aronson closely behind.

'Lieutenant Waverly?'

Startled, Lieutenant Waverly looked up. His eyes were black and small. He glanced to the silver bar on Starrett's collar, and slowly set down his drink. 'Yes?'

'Mind if we join you?' Starrett said, pulling up a chair on Waverly's left.

172

Waverly frowned. His glance flashed from Starrett to Aronson and back again. 'By all means.'

'Thanks,' said Aronson and, drawing up a seat at Waverly's right, edged close, crowding Waverly in.

The non-com behind the bar caught Starrett's signal and drew two brews.

Waverly studied the highball before him, his hands moving uneasily about the half-filled glass.

Aronson leaned back, looking over the room. 'Not much of a crowd tonight,' he said, and shook his head ruefully. 'Not many left, I guess, now.'

Waverly shot a questioning look to Starrett.

Starrett looked about the bar.

'New men, though,' Aronson went on and, turning, sighed to Starrett. 'Too bad Carter's not here.'

'Yeah,' muttered Starrett. 'That poor sonofabitch.'

'And just last night,' Aronson said gently, 'joking the way he did.' He looked at Waverly. 'You knew Carter, didn't you?'

Waverly pursed his lips, thinking.

'An observer,' said Aronson. 'A flight observer. Used to be a supply officer.'

Waverly shook his head. 'Can't say that I did,' he said lamely.

A mess boy brought the two brews from the bar and set them down on the table. Aronson tossed a florin onto the wet tray.

Starrett unzipped his flight jacket and, frowning, reached for his brew, raised it to Aronson. 'To Carter,' he said sadly.

Slowly Aronson held up his glass and nodded. 'To Carter.'

Waverly looked to them both, disturbed; then hesitantly, vaguely uneasy, raised his glass and finished off his drink.

Angrily, as if tensely overcome, Aronson snapped down his glass.

'Forget it,' muttered Starrett. 'He never knew what hit him.'

'Bad?' ventured Waverly, uncertain.

Starrett nudged Waverly to silence, frowning a warning.

Waverly's eyes widened. He nodded as if he understood and, turning to Aronson, 'I'm sor—' He broke off, puzzled by Aronson's look.

Aronson was eyeing him searchingly; then quietly, with a shrug, he lifted his drink to Waverly. 'You're no Carter,' he drawled, dubious, 'but—we'll make a go of it. You'll see.'

Waverly jerked about, staring at Starrett.

Starrett only nodded reassuringly. 'He means it,' he said encouragingly. 'He'll do the best he can.'

'F-for what?' Waverly stammered, his neck muscles ridging sharply.

Quietly Starrett studied the brew stains on

174

the table. 'You're being recommended,' he said, 'as Carter's replacement, for active flight duty as observer, next run.'

Waverly's face twisted, grey. 'Me?! But—but who'd recommend *me*?'

Starrett eyed him straight. 'My crew,' he said simply.

Waverly stared at him unbelievingly. 'B-but they can't!'

'They're going to the colonel tomorrow,' said Starrett.

'But I—I don't qualify,' Waverly said.

'*Every* officer—flying or non-flying—qualifies,' Aronson said calmly. 'There's a shortage, see? I mean, after two runs on Berlin in one week, we've lost the assigned ones.'

'And from what I hear,' Starrett said coldly, 'you do qualify—*lieutenant*. From what I hear, you see everything ... dust on a high shelf ... a cigarette butt under a corner bunk...' He looked at Waverly wryly. 'You'd make a perfect observer ... from what I hear.'

Waverly drew himself together. His breath came hard. 'It's—it's my duty to—see—things.'

'Precisely.' Starrett nodded, and smiled. 'So now you're graduating. Tomorrow they'll go to the colonel—with the recommendation—'

'He won't listen to them. They're *enlisted* men—' He broke off, catching Starrett's granite look.

'Come to think on it,' Aronson drawled,

'guess who recommended Carter.' He looked at Waverly meaningfully.

Waverly stared at his glass, dead still.

Slowly Starrett leaned back. 'Of course,' he went on, not looking up, 'they were to have been in London tonight.' He glanced up. 'But somebody held up their passes.' He smiled again. 'And if they can't go to London, they'll be on base ... all day ... with nothing to do ... nowhere to go ... except—visiting maybe...'

Waverly's face was sickly white.

'Or they could leave tonight,' Starrett said. 'It's up to you.'

Waverly stared, stilled and taut, his face gleaming damp in the dim light, his eyes fixed on his empty glass. Then slowly, 'If you'll excuse me—' He got up and, turning, tightly erect, started out through the room, his head held high and rigid, as if the way he walked were important.

Starrett looked after him.

'Think he'll do it?' asked Aronson.

Starrett nodded, his mouth tight with anger and disgust. 'He'll do it.'

Aronson looked at Starrett; then quietly, 'You had to do it,' he said kindly. 'It was him or the crew. That was the choice.'

Starrett shook his head. 'There wasn't any choice,' he muttered and, frowning, downed his brew.

CHAPTER FIFTEEN

From the table by the restaurant window, Wyatt watched the late afternoon sunlight mellowing Leicester Square. He felt tired now, quiet and reflective. His earlier exuberance at being finally in London, at visiting at last the places so long familiar to him in his reading, and the sheer joy of having been released for two whole days together from the threat of death now ebbed from him as the day waned in a golden glow from the sky.

The weather had been warm, spirited, blessed with spring, and nothing he had seen had fallen below his excited expectations. But now as the second and final evening of his leave was easing into the shadows about the square, a vague sorrow muted his thoughts, a sense of loneliness, almost of loss, as of time squandered—frivolously—as if he could be spendthrift with time.

He had seen London—as he had always dreamed it would be—from Picadilly to Tower Hill, from Soho to Buckingham Palace; he had missed nothing he had wanted to see. But now he realized that what he had seen had been the London of his child-young daydreams, a London recalled of a lost, romantic past; and all the time about him had been the vibrant, vital London of Now: a scarred, bustling

London that for all these precious hours he had wandered through, untouching and untouched.

The myriad people passing, flowing around him, in and out of uniform; the crowds milling, thronging about the daylight streets and into the blackout hours—of all these hurried thousands, not one had he known. Not one face had he seen, not one pair of eyes met with meaning. And now the air was golden with light, and soon the shadows would deepen—too, too soon.

'I *am* sorry, sergeant, but would you mind sharing your table? We are that crowded, you know.' The waitress stood looking down at him, smiling. Wyatt glanced beyond her to the doorway, queued already with waiting people.

'No, of course not.'

The waitress turned, signaling to a figure in the line, and, motioning her to the chair opposite Wyatt, deftly set down a glass of water, cutlery and a menu.

A young girl crossed slowly, uneasily through the table-crowded room and, looking at Wyatt curiously, sat in the offered chair.

'What'll it be, miss?'

The girl took up the menu, scanned it quickly, then ordered in a soft, hesitant voice.

She was pale and plain in a tweed suit and a light blue sweater, a single strand of pearls about her neck. Her hair was brown, soft, carelessly lovely. Her eyes were a clear, pure

178

blue, her lips—only lightly touched with color—gentle-seeming. There was an almost translucent fragility about her that reminded Wyatt of the pearly glow of early morning at twenty thousand feet.

'—and tea, please,' she added, looking up.

The waitress jotted it down, took up the menu and, glancing across to Wyatt, hurried off, grinning.

The girl looked across to him uncertainly. 'Do you mind,' she asked, 'sharing your table this way?' Her voice was thin and shy.

Wyatt smiled up. 'Of course not. Why?'

'I just wondered,' the girl said quietly. She looked at him curiously, then, self-consciously, glanced about.

From around them an easy, casual chatter droned under the clicking of plates and trays, the ringing of the cash register by the door, the busy hurryings of the waitresses.

'Do you live in London?' Wyatt asked, friendly.

'No. Not now. We used to.'

'Where do you live now?'

The girl eyed him wonderingly; then, 'In Kent,' she said. 'The Combes—a village just outside Sevenoaks.'

Wyatt smiled. 'I don't know where that is,' he said.

'Southeast England,' the girl said. 'But I'm staying a few days with a friend in Ilford.'

'And that's—?'

'In Essex,' the girl said. 'Just outside London.'

Wyatt nodded; then, with a grin, 'My name's Wyatt,' he said. 'Tom Wyatt.'

The girl frowned, her eyes searching his. 'Joyce Cheyne here,' she said quietly. 'Joy, to my friends.'

'Why not Joy to the world?' asked Wyatt.

Joy smiled, a warm, lovely smile, and nodded. 'Joy to the world then, sergeant.'

'I'll drink to that,' Wyatt said lightly and raised his water glass to her.

Joy studied him wonderingly again, then shyly grinned, her eyes puzzled, and raised her glass.

Dinner with Joy was a delight. Never before had Wyatt felt so at one with a person, so free to be himself, and she—He saw in her a fresh, alive spirit that matched his own, the same quiet shyness that covered so much of fun and response to life. And she was lovely to him with a loveliness that was more a glow in the eyes and a lilt in the voice than any beauty of face or line. In fact, her teeth, though tiny and bright, were crooked, and she had a jagged red scar by her left ear. But it was a face of strength and gentleness, and the eyes were deep enough for compassion and understanding.

Time and again he had found himself glancing at her during their meal, and wondering about himself, too—about the strange, new freedom he had found in himself this hour. It was as if he were suddenly, with all his being, ready for this moment—He caught himself in thought, reaching for an awareness. This moment—as if this were a moment special, out of all time and place, like that moment over Berlin—and when slowly he focused into the Now again, he found himself staring into her eyes, and she into his, without a word. Then for a long, still while they turned back to their eating.

*   *   *

The waitress hummed, serving them their puddings, and, with a wink to Wyatt, turned away with a flair in her step.

Wyatt grinned.

'There goes my reputation,' Joy said wryly.

'All the way,' said Wyatt; then suddenly, 'Do me a favor?'

'If I can,' she said.

'Show me London.'

She laughed. 'All of it?'

'All we've time for,' he said.

'But I've got to go back.'

'Where?'

'Ilford,' she said. 'I'd promised Kay—'

'Who's Kay?'

'My friend. I'd promised I'd meet her at Liverpool Street Station at nine.'

Wyatt looked to his watch. 'That gives us four hours.'

181

'But wouldn't you rather—well, find somebody else?' she asked.

'No.'

'But I'm—' She looked down, embarrassed. 'I'm—'

'If you really don't want to—'

'But I do.'

'Well, then?'

Joy looked at him, uncertain; then, lowering her eyes, 'I don't know,' she said softly. 'I— Does this sort of thing happen often? To you, I mean?'

'What sort of thing?'

She raised her look slowly. 'Picking up girls.'

Wyatt eyed her evenly. 'No,' he said. 'Never before.'

Joy met his look, frowning; then, gently, with a shadow of a smile, 'But why me?' she asked.

Wyatt smiled. 'Because it's London, and I'm alone, and suddenly, out of nowhere, I'm asked to share my table with you.' He looked at her simply. 'Providence,' he said.

'Do you really believe that?' she asked. 'Really?'

'Among other things,' he said, 'yes.'

Joy said nothing. She only studied him with a long, questioning look; then slowly, beautifully, she smiled and nodded. 'Your servant, m'lord.'

*   *   *

A hurdy-gurdy played in the twilight in Trafalgar Square. The man was blind, his cap torn, his jacket spotted with dropped-food stains. His face was wizened and tough-skinned, stubbled with a prickly white beard. He stood by the curb, winding out a creaky 'Londonderry Air.'

Beside him an old woman sat on a folding chair, a battered flowered hat atilt on her head, a full tray of violets in her lap. Her face was wrinkled and quiet, her eyes quick. She smiled toothlessly and held out a bunch of violets to Wyatt. Her hand shook, bony and loose-skinned.

Wyatt glanced to her and smiled. He dropped a ten-shilling note into the tray beside the hurdy-gurdy; then, taking the violets, paid the old woman a florin and handed the flowers to Joy.

Joy looked to him, surprised. 'Thanks, Tom. Thanks very much,' and with a wondering glow, pinned the violets carefully to her lapel.

The old woman grinned at them, nodded, 'God bless ye' and, turning to the man, tugged his sleeve. The old man smiled and cranked the hurdy-gurdy faster. The tune seemed suddenly to leap glinting with sound, alive.

Wyatt tipped his cap to them and continued the walk.

With a shy, sidelong look, Joy drew nearer, holding his arm tightly.

From London Bridge they watched the night darkening over the city. A strong, steady wind blew chill from the river.

Joy turned uneasily. 'Shall we go now, Tom?'

'If you wish.'

She frowned, shivering. 'Please.'

He glanced at her. 'Are you all right?'

She forced a smile. 'There's a club I want you to see.'

He looked at her. 'Is that it?'

She met his eyes, then slowly turned away. 'No.'

He waited.

She stared into the Thames. The wind from the river stirred her hair gently. Then quietly, 'We used to live over there,' she said; she nodded downriver. 'I was fourteen then and— it's just that I've never liked that part of town. That's all.'

She turned to him uncertainly.

Wyatt caught her look and smiled; taking her arm, he glanced beyond her down the Thames. His face tightened. Jagged, bombed-out buildings jutted into the sky.

*   *   *

The club was a small second-floor hall, smoky and crowded, noisy with a dimly lit band playing in the corner. Men and women milled jostling about, talking, laughing, drinking.

Joy found them a spot by the stairs. 'Here,' she said. She motioned to two free steps and sat down, her drink—a gin and orange—in hand. Wyatt sat below her, a Coke in his.

'Is it always this crowded?' he asked.

'I don't know,' Joy said. 'It's my first time here. Kay told me about it.'

'She gets around, doesn't she?'

'I guess so.' She took a slow sip.

Wyatt looked about, silent.

'You really don't like clubs, do you?' Joy asked, watching him, and smiled. 'You're more the fields and hills and sea type, I'd say.'

Wyatt grinned and drank his Coke. 'How do you know?'

Joy nodded, her eyes bright. 'I know,' she said; then, leaning back, 'I think you'd love Kent, Tom. Mine's a small cottage near The Combes—it's called The Linnet. I love linnets. And there are fields and hills on every side. You'd love it, I think.'

'You live there alone?'

'Yes.' She held her drink in hand, thinking. 'My parents were killed in the bombing—back there. I—I'd been lucky. When they found me, I was still alive. I've an annuity now, and the cottage. It belonged to my Aunt Edith once. My mother's sister. When I got out of the hospital, I had to go there. I work—as a chemist's clerk—part time. It's enough.'

'And Kay?'

'She'd been married to my brother Brian. He'd had it, though. He'd been a pilot—Spitfires—one of the few to whom so much was owed.' Her voice was cold; then, 'It's all so senseless.'

'What is?' He set down his glass and took her hand in his.

Her hand tightened in his. 'It's just that I want to see you again,' she said softly.

'And I you.'

'But we can't make plans, can we? I mean—with you going off. We can't say, I'll see you tomorrow. Or next week. We can't ring each other up. We can't—'

'We can write, and we can think of each other. We can—think of each other every day. And the next time in—'

'But that's just it, Tom. Next time? It's like Kay and Brian. We haven't the time, Tom.'

'We don't know that, do we? We don't know that for certain.'

She only looked at him, her eyes dark with doubt, troubled.

He leaned up and kissed her gently on the lips.

*   *   *

They sat listening to the girl singing from the bandstand. The song drifted, soft and clear, over the listening, dimly lit club.

186

'I'll be seeing you
In every lovely Summer's day,
In everything that's light and gay,
I'll always think of you that way...'

'I love that song,' Joy whispered.

'Do you like dancing?' asked Wyatt.

'Very much,' said Joy.

He got to his feet and held out his hand to her.

Joy reached up, then suddenly caught herself and pulled back. Her face tensed. 'Not now, Tom. Please.' She glanced to her watch. 'It's— it's nearly time,' she said. 'And it *is* a way to Liverpool Street Station.'

Wyatt frowned, puzzled.

She only watched him, with concern. 'I told you, Tom—you should have found someone else.'

He looked at her searchingly; then gently, 'I don't think there could have been anyone else,' he said and again held out his hand to her.

She met his look and, taking his hand, slowly got to her feet.

*　　　*　　　*

The whining roar of the underground thundered through the vaulted corridors. A rushing draft of wind whirled down the arced, brightly lit tunnel. Commuters streamed by them, hurrying to and fro, up and down the stairs.

'This way, Tom.' She guided him down the sloping ramp to the waiting platform.

With a start, Wyatt stared about him—his first time in the underground so late.

The platform teemed with men, women and children hustling about, readying for the night. Bunks and cots and mattresses were lined against the curved walls. Piles of blankets and bedding lay heaped among boxes and make-shift tables and chairs. Suitcases and cartons of clothes lay scattered about. Curtains were strung up by some of the cots. The air was a din of calls, baby cries, laughter and quiet talk.

'...every night,' Joy said. 'Some, ever since the blitz.'

'Like this?'

'They've nowhere else,' Joy said. 'Once you've been bombed out, it rather limits things.'

Slowly they started down the narrow edge of the platform, Wyatt silent, looking about them...

to the portly, spectacled, white-haired gentleman, with his coat buttoned up, a scarf about his neck and hatless, sitting stiffly erect in a battered chair, a book in one hand, a pipe in the other. Beside him a blanketed mattress and a box crate, like a night table, were neatly set up. Books lined the inner shelves of the crate. He drew on his pipe contentedly and, with all the aloof dignity of a man before his

188

own hearth, turned another page...

'...so as 'ow I'm so tidy and all, with me 'ouse, ye see. And a lovely place it was, too.' The woman was thin, haggard-looking, with quick, wrenlike gestures, her hair streaked with silver. But her face—with the wide brown eyes, the thin, sharp nose and pointed chin—shone as, perched at the edge of a cot, she leaned forward, gossiping with the fat, small-eyed woman lying in the bunk beside her. 'Oh, a lovely place it was, too. All blue and white, like. A cheer to come 'ome to, 'e used to say. So 'e says, 'Ere ye be, love. And just like that, 'e 'ands me the 'ole thing done up lovely. Fifty-six pieces it was. All blue and white like me parlor. So I says, Berty, ye shouldn't've done it, love. 'E was always doin' things like that, me Berty was. So all about me parlor I sets 'em up, plates an' cups an' saucers—the 'ole set so's everybody could see 'em, I was that proud...' Between them was a rickety end table, with a small framed wedding picture and a single blue-and-white cup cracked down the side...

'...Will-yum! William! Where the 'ell's William got to? 'Ey, William?' A gaunt, disheveled, anger-eyed woman glanced around the platform, searching, a squalling baby in one arm and three dirty-faced, shaggy urchins scampering about her. Suddenly her eyes widened in terror. '*Will-yum!*' Quickly she swung the baby to the nearest urchin, a boy about ten, and ran down the platform. A tot of

189

five or so was just slipping off to explore the rails below. The woman screamed. A waiting soldier grabbed the child and held him back. The mother came up, thanked the soldier kindly and, holding the tot at arm's length, swatted him hard across the head. 'Ye wants to get 'urt?' the woman grumphed, and clipped him again. 'Playin' out there! Gawd!' and dragged him, wailing and kicking, back to the others...

'...'ell, says I.' The young man grinned. 'I don't mind startin' from the ground up, I says. But, blimey, mate, from the *under*-ground up—well, that's goin' it some.' The girl beside him laughed. The man was pale, hollow-cheeked, bony; his hair black and uncombed. He lay on the floor with only a blanket under him and smiled at the girl. She rested on a thin mattress, pale and pregnant. She grinned back at him, and slowly her hand stole from her blanket and, catching his, squeezed it hard. His other hand closed tightly over hers...

...carefully the young woman in tweeds tucked the child in and, drawing a sheet from the upper bunk, curtained off the light from the boy's eyes. Then, smiling, she sat beside him, brushed back his hair and, caressing him gently, began in a low, cultured voice, 'Now, once upon a time—oh, long, long ago...'

'Anyone 'ere knows 'ow to bandage a foot?' A fat, slovenly woman limped down the platform, one foot bare and swollen, a bandage

190

in her hand. She looked about. Quietly the aloof gentleman laid aside his book and pipe and, getting up with a grunt, went to the woman. She stared at him, surprised, as he took the bandage from her hand, knelt down creakily and, placing her foot on his knee, began silently, with a few clumsy starts, to wrap it tenderly for her...

Wyatt turned, scanning the length of the platform, his eyes deep with wonder.

Joy looked to him, frowning. 'You'd never seen this before?'

Wyatt shook his head.

'It's quite common, really,' Joy said.

Wyatt's lips tightened, his whole body rigid, as he looked down at a little girl sitting on a cot, staring dull-eyed at the floor. She was about six, a tiny, thin girl with long yellow hair. Her dress was old, a drab grey. A rag doll sat propped up beside her. Wyatt stared.

'Tom?'

He turned.

Joy searched his face questioningly. 'What is it?'

Wyatt nodded toward the tiny girl. 'I was thinking about Berlin,' he said. 'I was wondering—in Berlin now—how many—just like her. Like all these here. Because of us. Innocent, helpless people—with a right to live, to enjoy life—to laugh. But instead they're driven underground—by fear and danger—'
He shook his head, and shrugged.

'I keep trying to find a reason,' Joy said. 'Only—there isn't any. Not here. Not anywhere.'

'It may be here, Joy.' He glanced along the platform beyond them. 'Suffering, hope, the will to live—the common denominators of humanity. And—in the long run—maybe this is necessary.'

'How?'

Wyatt frowned, trying to find the words in the darkness of his feelings. 'I don't know. Maybe if Man suffers enough, he'll grow sick of that suffering. And out of that—maybe— the wisdom might come—that all men are brothers, that this world isn't the All of life.'

Joy shook her head. 'But how much, Tom? How much suffering will it take?'

Wyatt shrugged again. 'That, only God knows. But maybe it's in the wind now. I don't know. But I do know we've got to believe it. The belief comes first—always.'

'And you believe.'

'Don't you?'

Joy only looked at him, then slowly smiled. 'Would you settle for hope?'

*   *   *

The clock at Liverpool Street Station glowed at ten to nine.

'There's Kay,' Joy laughed and pointed beyond the crowd to a tall, blonde girl, smartly trim in the uniform of a WAAF sergeant, pacing nervously back and forth beside the waiting train.

'Come, Tom. Do meet her.'

Wyatt nodded, and hurriedly they forced their way through the swarming crowd.

'Hurry,' Joy called. She turned, beckoning to Wyatt, as a heavy, burly man, carrying a large suitcase, shoved roughly against her. She spun, with a low cry.

'Joy!' Swiftly Wyatt caught her, holding her up.

Startled, the bull-necked man dropped his valise. He bent over her anxiously.

Her breath came in tight gasps. 'I'm—all right,' she murmured. She leaned against Wyatt, quivering for air. 'Silly of me,' she stammered. 'So sorry, sir.'

The man frowned. 'You're sure you're all right?'

'Quite,' she said. She braced herself, smiling. 'Quite all right, thank you.'

The man gave her a last quick look, then grabbed up his bag and hurried off, frowning.

She straightened her shoulders and, brushing back her hair, smiled again. 'Clumsy of me, wasn't it?'

Wyatt looked at her. 'Joy?'

She grinned. 'There's Kay.' She walked slowly, as if uncertainly. 'Kay?'

Kay turned and, with a sudden grin of relief, 'I thought you'd gone without me—or something.' Her eyes searched Joy.

Joy gestured to Wyatt. 'Kay, I'd like you to meet Tom. Sergeant Tom Wyatt. Tom, Kay Cheyne.'

Kay's grip was firm and friendly. 'A pleasure, sergeant.'

Wyatt grinned. 'For me,' he said.

Kay smiled at him with sharp, shrewd eyes. Her eyebrows were beautifully arched, and her hair, drawn tightly back, gleamed with a soft golden sheen.

'Look,' Joy said gaily. 'Viol—' She broke off. Only the pin was left. She glanced to Wyatt, dismayed. 'I've lost them.'

'Maybe when you fell,' he said.

'Fell?' Sharply Kay looked to Joy.

Joy forced a smile. 'An accident. I—I tripped just now. Right into a man.'

Kay frowned, silent.

'But they were such lovely violets, Kay.' She looked to Wyatt. 'I'd never had violets before,' she said. 'I'm sorry, Tom.'

'There'll be more,' he said. 'Next time.'

Kay stiffened, looking at them.

'The next time,' Joy said. 'Just—write me. You've the address. And if I can, I'll come.'

'And I'll tag along,' Kay said. 'Would you mind?'

'A double date?' asked Wyatt.

'Know anyone for me?' asked Kay; then wryly, 'Nothing special, of course. Just tall, dark, handsome and rich.'

Wyatt grinned. 'Hagen, maybe.' He looked at her. 'Except he's not rich.'

Kay shrugged. 'Novelty,' she said. 'Keeps one from growing old, they say.'

The train whistle sounded, a high, deafening shriek through the station.

Kay started for the train. 'Come on, Joy.'

The light darkened in Joy's eyes. She glanced to Wyatt's wings, then to his face. 'Take care of yourself.'

Wyatt nodded. 'You, too.'

She smiled and held out her hand.

He held out his arms and she went to him. They held each other tightly, their lips meeting with a fierce, welcoming kiss.

'Come, Joy,' Kay called.

Tenderly Joy drew away, her eyes on Wyatt—deep and misted. She smiled, shy again; then abruptly turned and hurried toward the train.

The whistle blasted shrill again, and the station roared with the pistoning thunder of the engines forcing the heavy wheels along as slowly the train moved out.

*　　*　　*

Wyatt stood there, staring down the empty track. Slowly a warm, wondering smile kindled in his eyes. His whole being felt buoyant with a sudden, unbridled elation. He turned and, whistling brightly, wanting to sing, to shout even, ambled jauntily down the platform. Suddenly he started—broke off.

At his feet, ground into the pavement, lay a crushed bunch of violets.

CHAPTER SIXTEEN

Starrett lay back in the chair, staring out the window across the sleeping city. The blackout curtains had been drawn back. The room was dark, the floor dusky with moonlight. The scarred outline of London lay silvery under the moon, the ruins shadowy, hushed in the deep night quiet. Slowly he raised his drink again and finished it off.

The sheets rustled on the corner bed.

He turned, waiting, listening.

The springs creaked. Then the woman's voice, sleepy and warm. 'Bill?'

'Over here, Rita.' He set down his glass.

'What time is it?'

'Late enough.'

The springs creaked again. He heard the blankets being turned aside, then the soft, barefooted steps across the carpeted floor.

'Couldn't you sleep?' she asked gently.

'No. Want a drink?'

'A cigarette, please.' She came into the slanting moonlight, slim and pale in her slip: a dark, tall woman, her hair black and long, her face heart-shaped, with wide, intelligent eyes and a smiling, sensitive mouth. She had his blouse draped over her shoulders for warmth. The wings caught flickering in the moonlight.

He lit a cigarette and handed it to her.

'Thanks,' she said.

She sat on the arm of his chair, silent, looking at him. The nearness of her was delicate with perfume.

Quietly he rested his arm along her thigh.

She leaned over and kissed his forehead. 'Tell me,' she whispered. 'I'll understand. And if I don't, I'll listen.'

Starrett shrugged. 'I was thinking of *The Lady*,' he said. 'Our ship. I was wondering who took her up today.'

'Others can take her up?' she asked.

'If there's a run,' he said.

Gently she drew away. 'So now,' she said, 'you're wondering: Is she all right? Did she come back?'

'Yeah. That's it.'

'I wish I were a bomber,' she said. 'To be loved like that. To be—needed.'

Starrett patted her knee, smiling. 'You're needed,' he said.

Rita laughed. 'By whom?'

'Me,' said Starrett.

Rita frowned, then quickly she shook her head. 'No. Not really,' she said. 'I'm just somebody for a week-end. Remember? Convenient, but not needed.' She glanced to him questioningly.

Starrett picked up his glass and handed it to her.

She took it and, rising, went to the bureau. The bottle and glasses glistened in the moonlight. She poured a refill and, returning, sat beside him again, giving him the drink.

Starrett shifted uneasily. Suddenly, almost angrily, he took another swallow, then got to his feet. 'It's just like Aronson said,' he muttered. 'In the middle of the night, he said, you'll start thinking, wondering—' He broke off, staring out the window.

'About what?' asked Rita.

'Right now, about Hagen,' he said.

'Your gunner?'

'Yeah.' He tugged at the curtain, frowning. 'I keep getting the feeling that he's going to act up someday. And before that, I was wondering about Kirby. And then Wyatt—' He shook his head. 'The things they never tell you.'

'Who?'

'They just give you nine men—nine men you'd never seen before—and you start from there, cold. Like putting a machine together— the duties, the men. You match them up, and they click, so you think all you've got to do to bring them through is to keep them clicking. All nice and cold. But then—later— somewhere along the line—like Aronson says, it changes. There's only one thing you think about: to get them through. But you can't.

198

There're so many things beyond what you can do—flak, fighters, sickness, crack-ups—things you *can't* control. But it doesn't make any difference because you're still thinking *you've* got to get them through. They're your men. You're responsible for them. You end up fighting—what is it? Luck? Chance? Fate?' He shook his head again and downed his drink.

Rita watched him, her eyes dark with understanding. Then, rising, she went to him, her hand gentle on his arm, her face lifted, her eyes searching his. 'Do you forget with me?' she asked. 'For a few minutes, maybe?'

He nodded, silent.

She smiled at him. 'Thanks,' she said softly.

'For what?'

'For needing me,' she said. 'Just a little.' And standing on tiptoe, she kissed him.

Slowly the blouse slipped from her shoulders. It lay on the floor, the wings glittering in the moonlight.

CHAPTER SEVENTEEN

It was early Sunday noon when Wyatt, chilled by the brisk, gusty wind, strode down the gravel walk to the Sad Shack. The door was open, the hut dark within. The stove had gone out, and the air was thinly cold.

Quickly Wyatt shoved the door shut behind

him and, slipping his gas-mask from his shoulder, crossed to his bunk, unbuttoning his blouse. Suddenly he stopped.

Bayer lay sprawled out, sleeping, his arms flung over his head, his hands clenched tight. His face was sallow, stubbled with a grizzly beard. His clothes were wrinkled, dirty. Cigarette stubs strewed the floor, the butt can overfilled. An empty fifth of Scotch lay under the bunk.

Frowning, Wyatt laid his gas-mask, cap and blouse on his bunk; then, undressing, changed from his uniform into his fatigues.

Bayer grunted, writhing in his sleep, his mouth drawn tensed.

Wyatt waited, motionless.

With a grimace, Bayer quieted, his hands still clenched.

Silently Wyatt folded his uniform, hung it up on a hanger and, turning, went to the stove. Deftly he started building a fire.

The wood crackled in sudden flames. The pungent tang of smoke filled the hut. Slowly he shoveled in coal from the scuttle, set the lid back again with a light iron clang and waited, feeling the heat warming his body.

The bunk behind him creaked.

He turned.

Bayer was looking at him, silent; then weakly, 'Back early,' he smiled.

'How're you feeling?' asked Wyatt.

Bayer shrugged, reaching into his jacket

pocket. 'Have a good time?' he asked. He drew out a crumpled cigarette.

'Fine,' said Wyatt. He lifted the stove lid again. The fire was coming strong. He reached for the poker and stirred the coals. 'Where are your bunch?' he asked.

'On pass,' Bayer muttered. 'Till Monday. The skipper's last official act—a bonus—for busting up the crew.'

'And after Monday?'

'Christ knows,' said Bayer. 'I don't. Maybe hang around till reassignment.'

Wyatt glanced at him. 'You on pass now?'

Bayer rolled over on his back, smoking, his eyes half closed. 'I came back last night,' he said, and looked up. 'Why?'

Wyatt frowned. 'Just wondered,' he said.

'Yeah,' said Bayer. 'Last night.' Suddenly, with a grunt, he swung up and sat wavering at the edge of his bunk, his head lowered.

'How about some coffee?' said Wyatt.

'Good idea,' said Bayer.

Wyatt glanced to his watch. 'The club's open.'

Bayer shook his head. 'Let's try the canteen,' he said. 'I'll clean up first.'

He got to his feet uncertainly and, with a shudder, picked up his toilet kit and started out. At the door he turned and looked back. 'I heard you had the Big One,' he said. 'Berlin.'

'Yeah,' said Wyatt. 'Twice.'

Bayer nodded; then, 'Glad you made it,' he

201

said quietly. 'Real glad.'

Abruptly he opened the door and went out.

For a moment Wyatt stared at the closed door, disturbed.

*   *   *

'Ready?' said Bayer. He left the door open, and a silvery sunlight slanted in.

Wyatt dropped from his bunk. 'Feeling better?'

Bayer shrugged, tossing his toilet kit on the side table. His face was clean-shaven, nicked about the chin, lined with a gaunt, haggard look. His hair was wet, combed down; his eyes sunken and haunted. Silent, he hung up his towel, his hands quivering.

Wyatt said nothing. Quietly he picked up his windbreaker and started to pull it on.

'Wait,' said Bayer. He turned and, going to his footlocker, shoved back the lid and pulled out a leather flying jacket. 'Here,' he said. He held it out, smiling. 'Just like I said.'

Wyatt looked at it, surprised. It seemed almost new.

'I told you I'd get you one,' Bayer said and, watching Wyatt, grinned.

Slowly Wyatt dropped his windbreaker and, taking the jacket, 'Where'd you get it?' he asked.

Bayer closed his footlocker. 'It's a spare,' he said quietly. 'We all have spares. Try it on.'

Wonderingly Wyatt slipped into the jacket, feeling the warm heaviness of it snug about his shoulders. The sleeves were too long. He tugged them back and, zipping up the front, turned about. 'How's it look?'

Bayer's eyes sharpened. He studied the jacket, silent; then he nodded. 'It fits. All the way.' He met Wyatt's look and smiled. 'Like it?'

'Sure,' said Wyatt. He grinned broadly. 'Thanks a lot.'

'Don't mention it,' said Bayer. He turned nervously. 'Let's go,' he said. His voice was almost sharp.

*　　　*　　　*

The canteen was quiet, smelling of hot coffee: a long, straight building of two Nissen huts joined, bordering a patch of meadowland at the southeast corner of the base. The curved, corrugated walls were painted a drab, dark green. Tables and chairs were set about, a row of narrow windows lining the right side. The sunlight glowed in.

On the left of the entrance were the counter-line, the service kitchen and, by the door, the cash desk.

A squat, white-haired woman in a tight Red Cross uniform sat at the desk, a roll of red tickets on one side, a tin cashbox on the other. She smiled at Bayer, a matronly smile. 'How many, sergeant?'

Bayer gave her a florin.

The woman counted off a florin's worth of tickets and slid them to Bayer. 'And you?' She looked to Wyatt, pleasant.

'The same, please.'

The woman nodded, gave him his tickets and slipped the money into the cashbox.

'Coffee,' said Bayer. 'Black.'

The red-faced woman behind the counter smiled and drew him a cup of black coffee.

Bayer paid her a three penny ticket, passed on to the sandwich section and, looking it over, turned away. He crossed to the corner table and tiredly sat down, staring into his steaming cup.

Wyatt followed, a Coke and a sardine sandwich in hand. 'Not hungry?' he asked. He pulled up a chair opposite.

Bayer shook his head and, raising his coffee in both hands, sipped it slowly.

Wyatt slipped his jacket off and draped it over the back of his chair, then turned and started to eat.

Through an open window, the wind eased in, milder now than earlier and smelling of new green and spring. The trees and bushes glistened with a fresh, sparkling clearness as clouds, bright with afternoon, drifted slowly westward.

Wyatt finished his sandwich and, brushing his hands on his fatigues, leaned back. His eyes met Bayer's.

Quickly Bayer dropped his look to his coffee again.

Wyatt studied his Coke; then, 'Want to talk about it?' he asked.

Bayer's hands arched his cup, the fingers pressing it hard. A low, trembling sigh shook his shoulders. He shrugged.

'I saw the doc yesterday,' he said quietly. His hands gripped the cup tightly. 'I ain't gonna fly no more.'

Slowly Wyatt turned his glass about.

'That's it,' said Bayer. He grinned, stiff as a mask. 'I'm grounded.'

Wyatt looked at him. 'For good?'

'What difference?' said Bayer. 'The crew's busted up—'

Suddenly the mask broke. His face twisted. He snapped down his cup and looked away, desperate, shaking with tension.

'Easy,' said Wyatt softly. 'Easy.'

Bayer bit his lips, brushing his hand across his chin. A broken smile quivered about his mouth. 'It isn't easy,' he said, 'telling a guy you've lost your guts.'

Wyatt looked down at his drink, then slowly raised the glass. The rim was hard and cold against his lips. He tasted nothing.

Bayer shivered. 'That's what I told the doc,' he said. His hands rubbed the table's edge. 'I guess seeing it all did it,' he said, low. 'Lyzak— the ship blowing up—and me—just sitting there, watching. I couldn't do anything else.'

'I know,' said Wyatt.

Bayer looked up again. 'But later—there was this Messerschmitt, see? Coming in, straight for us. I had him right in my gunsight. But—' He lowered his head, staring into his cup. 'I—I couldn't fire.'

Wyatt glanced to his Coke. 'We all freeze, one time or another, I guess.'

'Sure,' said Bayer. 'But most of the guys snap out of it.'

'Just as you will,' Wyatt said.

'No,' said Bayer. 'Not me. I know.' Suddenly he grimaced. 'If it hadn't been for Laske getting that guy, we'd-a all had it. The whole crew, Wyatt. *Nine other guys,*—all because of me.' His eyes were hard, glinting on Wyatt.

'Yeah,' said Wyatt. 'I see.' Then, gently, 'But maybe, with more flak leave—'

'That's what the doc said,' Bayer said. 'Only—' he gestured emptily—'I couldn't even take this one.' He glanced up again, his face drawn. 'Every time I heard a plane going over, I'd wonder. I sweated out every day, every raid I heard—' He broke off with a shrug. 'That's another reason I came back,' he said. 'I couldn't face Dory any more.'

Wyatt looked at him. 'Dory?'

Bayer frowned, studying his hands locked together tight. 'She knew,' he muttered. 'Oh, she kept laughing all the time, making like

206

nothing'd happened. But—she knew, all right.' He cracked his knuckles hard. 'She wouldn't let on, though... And then one night—about two, I guess—I woke up and there she was, looking at me.' He glanced to Wyatt. 'Crying.'

Wyatt said nothing.

Suddenly, angrily, Bayer shoved his cup away. 'Believe me,' he said, his voice cutting deep, 'it just doesn't pay having buddies.' He looked up wryly and tried to force his old grin. 'But—that's the way the song goes, I guess.'

Wyatt stared into his Coke; then abruptly he cleared his throat and, raising his drink, finished it off.

'Come on,' said Bayer. He slapped the table hard. 'Let's go for a walk.' He got up and started away.

Wyatt pushed back his chair and got to his feet. He picked up his jacket and, drawing it on, frowned. Just under the inner collar was an inked-in name: *Lyzak*.

CHAPTER EIGHTEEN

Hagen studied the chessboard; then slowly, uncertainly moved his queen across and captured Wyatt's red bishop. The hut was still but for the rumblings from the stove. Hagen leaned back under the stark overhead light. 'Your move.'

207

Wyatt edged forward, pursing his lips, and replotted the gambit.

Hagen glanced to Nelson, still in uniform, standing by his bunk, a letter in hand, his face disturbed as he read.

'What's the news?' asked Hagen. 'She okay?'

Nelson nodded. 'She misses me,' he said. He went on reading, then suddenly crushed the letter and flung it aside. He looked about. 'The others back yet?'

'Down at the club,' said Hagen. 'You're last man in.'

Nelson slipped his cap on and started out. At the door he turned again and came back, picked up the crumpled letter and, shoving it into his pocket, strode out. The door closed hard behind him.

Wyatt looked up and frowned. 'Wonder what the letter said.'

'She misses him,' said Hagen, and grinned. 'You don't think he's been alone, do you?'

Silent, Wyatt moved. He crossed his knight to challenge Hagen's queen.

Hagen studied the new threat. 'How'd you make out? See all the museums and stuff?' He backed his queen to safety.

'Some,' said Wyatt. 'Then I met a girl—two, in fact.'

'Two?' Hagen frowned up, curious.

'They'd like to double-date next time,' Wyatt said. He captured a pawn with the knight, again challenging the queen. 'I said

208

I'd ask.'

Hagen eyed him, puzzled. 'I find my own broads,' he said.

'Then that's it,' Wyatt said simply. He motioned to the queen.

Hagen's frown deepened. 'What are they like? How much?'

Wyatt glanced up. 'No price,' he said.

Hagen shrugged. 'I'd like to see her first,' he said. 'Can you get a picture?'

'Maybe. I don't know.'

'Try,' said Hagen and, smiling, 'I'll let you know *after* I've seen her.'

Wyatt nodded. 'We'll see.'

Quietly the door opened.

Hagen glanced up as Bayer came in. Furtively Bayer's eyes swept the hut; then, bracing himself, he smiled rigidly and came down the aisle. Hagen looked back to the board, studying it.

'How's it going?' Bayer asked. His step was quick, light. He stood smiling by the table.

'Fine,' said Wyatt.

'That's what you think,' said Hagen. He moved his bishop and took Wyatt's knight; then slowly glanced up, his eyes searching Bayer's. 'Back early,' he said.

Bayer's grin tightened. 'I got sick,' he said.

Hagen's eyes were hard. 'Of what?'

The grin cracked.

'Your queen's in danger,' Wyatt said. Evenly he held Hagen's gaze with a steady, commanding look. He nodded to the board.

Hagen retraced the move. His queen was again threatened, this time by a pawn backed by a bishop. He glanced up to Wyatt probingly. 'You're full of surprises tonight.'

'You just forget,' Wyatt said. 'The pawn. Remember?'

Hagen's look bore in. 'I'll watch it,' he said. 'From now on.'

Wyatt nodded. 'Then move.'

Hagen grinned and, with a flip of his finger, tipped the board over, spilling off the men. 'How's that?' he said.

Wyatt only smiled. 'You're improving,' he said lightly. 'You know when you're getting licked.'

Hagen's eyes sharpened, then cut before Wyatt's steady look.

Uneasily Bayer turned and, going to his bunk, stretched tiredly out. He lay on his back, staring up at nothing.

Wyatt started to pick up the scattered men.

Hagen sat back, pulling a cigarette from his shirt pocket. 'You heard about Bellows?' he asked Bayer. 'He's back in England, you know.'

Bayer frowned. 'It figures,' he muttered. 'Cruds like that—they always make out.' He turned to Hagen, then slowly, 'Know what kind of a guy he was? Like you, Hagen.'

Hagen's look narrowed. 'What's that supposed to mean?'

'It means—we had him figured.' He met Hagen's look squarely; then slowly rose, swinging to his feet. 'The tail gunner got fed up with him one night.' He crossed to the door wall where the pin-ups were and snapped down a Betty Grable. Behind the picture was a splintered hole in the wood. 'Here's where the bullet went through.'

'Bellows'?'

'No. The tail gunner's.'

Hagen frowned; then, looking to Bayer, 'He must've been a lousy shot.'

'Moody broke his aim,' said Bayer. He pinned the photo back again. 'The next day was Paris...' He turned back to the table. 'Good thing, too,' he said. 'If they'd-a gone on, somebody would've been up for murder.' He almost smiled. 'We even had a story ready— just in case.'

Hagen snorted. 'Some crew.'

'It could've been the best,' said Bayer, 'except for him. Kept screwing them up. All he thought about was Bellows.'

Hagen shook his head. 'I'd have killed that bastard if I'd been Bellows.'

Bayer looked at him wonderingly. 'Maybe that's what he did do,' he said, 'in his own way.'

Hagen frowned again. 'I thought the ship blew up.'

'It did,' said Bayer. 'But not suddenly.'

Wyatt turned. 'You mean there was time?'

'We thought so,' said Bayer.

211

Hagen cocked his head. 'Then how come only Bellows got out?'

'Yeah,' said Bayer, and looked at Hagen. 'How come?'

*　　　*　　　*

The hut was dark. The fire had long gone out. Hagen turned, restless in his bunk, and glanced at his watch, the dial luminous at two fifteen; then, reaching over to his shelf, felt for his cigarettes and matches and lit up. The flame spurted a shock of light into the darkness, then died in the slow red glow of the cigarette. He snapped the match out and dropped it to the floor, tossed the pack and matches to the shelf and lay resting, his free arm under his head. In the quiet he heard Bayer tossing in his sleep, and took a long, deep drag, then slowly exhaled.

More and more now he was finding it hard to sleep. In London he had lain awake through most of his second night, even with the girl beside him: he had let her sleep. He had lain there as he was lying here, looking up into the darkness, drifting in it, lost in it, until all there was of him and Now was darkness and the Nothing it was. Trapped in it.

All his life he had been trapped this way, nights like this ... as far back as he could remember ... as a kid back in Boston during the Depression, lying on a dirty, sprung sofa in

212

a sour-smelling two-room flat, hearing the scratching noises of the dark—the rats in the walls, the two whores in the creaking bed next door, the numbers man limping crippled to the john down the hall (like the night he went there for the last time and slashed his wrists); or the fighting and screaming of the Callahans down in the corner flat, the whole seven of them (until the day Callahan himself found his wife in bed paying the insurance man: she ran screaming naked down the hall, and he shot her in the back—with all the kids watching); and in the other room, his thick father snoring and his mother's thin whimpering—like a mouse dying softly in a trap...

And when she was gone, his father had turned the screws on him, for ten bleeding years until that night two years ago when strong and big enough to slam back

he crashed his father into the corner by the kitchen sink and stood there sweating, exploding inside, as the old man crouched low, breathing hard. '*You think you're a man. Just because you've got a pair of hot nuts, you think you're a man. Well, listen to me, me boy-o—*'

'*Why?!*' Suddenly, fierce, shouted with guts busting. '*To be like you?! You sonofabitch, you never did a fucking thing in your life to get us out of this trap. You just dug it deeper!*'

'*Then get the fuck out!*'

He remembered staring at him, then quietly turning and walking out ... only to find that,

213

no matter where he went or what he did, it was still the same trap—just new and different corners of it—with no way out...

except, now and then, those moments—flying—looking out over the world from clean miles of wind above it: moments he knew he needed to keep him going, the way he needed space and light and motion, the excitement—even the fear—that made him *know* he was alive: moments he felt—and almost knew—that there was a way out, if only he could find it—if only he had time—

Time—

He felt a slow twisting tension building inside him as if, from beyond the Nothing, he heard a dark, low laughter. Here he was in a trap to end all traps—a war he felt no part of—up to his ass in death, and any day now it could be quits for him...

with every mission, time running out. Time he needed—to find his way out. Time before death cut in—because that would be the end of it. The real Nothing beyond Nothing. But before it came—to live for once before he died. In time to know. In time to *live*!

His fingers flexed, snapping his cigarette in two. His whole body tensed. His throat was tight, barbed with the anger tearing to cut through—

'Christ!' he muttered, and jarred at the sound.

He listened, taut—(silence)—then eased,

turning to jab out the cigarette against his bunk. He dropped the dead, broken butt and lay back again, calmer, knowing he'd been kidding himself; knowing at the center of his being there wasn't any way out because this was it—Life—as it was and as it would be, and none of it made any sense: it never had and it never would. So fuck it!

He tossed, pulling his blanket tighter about him, and closed his eyes. Tomorrow it was back to the war again. He frowned uneasily, wondering how many tomorrows he had.

PART FIVE

TOMORROW AND TOMORROW
March 16–23, 1944

CHAPTER NINETEEN

Wyatt leaned in the doorway at the rear of the Shack, watching the sky, a crimson glow dying in twilight. Hagen had gone to the canteen for his cigarette rations, and the rest of the crew were already at the club, earlier than usual, for tonight the hut was depressing. Bayer was out in the latrine, washing up, scrubbing away the grease from his armament work; so Wyatt was alone.

He still felt keyed up with the tensions of the day's raid, a ten-hour run on Augsburg—their second mission since coming back from leave four days ago. But the sense of uneasiness he felt—it was more than the tightness he had known on the other raids. Usually by now he would start to unwind, almost to relax; but not today. It was as if he were still up there, as if there had been up there an unfinished reaction, delayed, suspended—but to what?

He turned and looked down the dark, empty hut—emptier now than he had ever known it.

The *Miss Fire* crew had moved out that morning, except for Bayer and Wiggam: Bayer because he had been assigned to temporary ground duty with *The Lady*; and Wiggam because he had conned Finch into letting him stay on as area orderly. Vilano and Reed had been reassigned to fill up split crews, Fletcher's and Aronson's. The rest had gone to the Pool (crowded now with spares) to wait their time and their chance.

Down the bare left side of the hut, the bunks had been stripped, the mattress pads piled with folded blankets, except for Wiggam's at the end, across from Hagen's. Another double bunk had been moved in to make room for the next crew to come.

And as Wyatt looked over the hut, he knew it would never again be the same. Perhaps that was the reason for his uneasiness. Perhaps not.

It wasn't so definite as fear—like the fear of death that he could face and deal with now—but rather a feeling that seeped through his veins darkly and cold. Flak, fighters, losses—these were routine now. But something had disturbed him, something like a thought that had crossed his mind, ungrasped, unfocused. Something—

It had come over intercom, in the way Kirby and Gillis had called in. There was something he felt in their voices, some tension coming through the strain.

Wyatt frowned, recalling the tones they had used—the same they had had on the Brunswick run yesterday. He had thought it only a bristly mood then, one that would pass. But now he knew there was something gone from them— the lightness of banter, the easy camaraderie. That was it! There had been something too crisp, too cold in their orders and reports,

220

something duty-demanded but—the warmth, the *heart* hadn't been there. And recalling it, Wyatt felt again the dark foreboding and the chill he had earlier known.

The spirit was such a tenuous thing—tenuous and vital; and if it were gone from *The Lady*—Even to imagine *The Lady* without her spirit, that spirit of brotherhood that had made them one, that was (as he saw it) their real strength and their armor—not against flak and fighters, but against themselves, their own separate intensities: to imagine her without that heart was to see, in effect, the end of *The Lady*—the crack-up that would destroy her, not from without, but from within. As it was, some of them might die, *could* die, and still she could go on, proud and as shining as victory, *if* her heart held; but without her spirit—

The paradox of the spirit—tenuous, yet when it held, how strong: and when it went, the way it could go—in a snap of nerves, or slowly, in little, uneasy ways slipping loose, like today...

Wyatt shook his head, clearing away the thought. No: he was tired, and when he was tired, he knew he brooded. Perhaps it was only in the way he felt now, deflected by other things ... like the letters from Joy...

The first one had come Tuesday, and one each day since, with the strange love-sadness in them, real now... And he had answered them, each for each.

Ever since that day in London with her he had suspected that for him, at least, it was love. He had known the joy of her sharing, the laughter, the oneness; but he had thought it too sudden perhaps, too miraculous, too like a romantic variation of the proverbial soldier lonely in an alien city. Yet as the days since had gone, and the nights, he had found himself thinking of her, seeing her vividly in all he did, and wanting, with strange desperation, to share with her—as with no other person he had ever known—so much of himself, of his thoughts, of his exciting wonder of living; and to know her, in every ray of being, to touch her, to kiss...

He had held himself in check, believing it only his response to the meeting. But then her letters came, with their delicate, yet open and clear echo of what he himself was going through, the glowing wonder and the shy doubt; and he knew that between them now there did exist an understanding and response, each to the other and to life, that was indeed touched with Providential splendor.

The feelings he had known of longing and incompletion in himself were being answered, fulfilled and completed in her, as hers were in him. And it was love, simply so, and stark as the ache it brought in the fierce desire now to live.

To want so urgently to live when almost daily he had to be where death touched wings—

But his decision had been made. And now, with someone to live for—as Nelson had, and all the millions of other soldiers with wives and sweethearts waiting—he knew he was no different from them; that now this, too, was part, not of the original price, but of the current going rate for his decision. And as such, it would be met, in full, sparing nothing.

He glanced up as the far door opened and a strange gunner, in full dress uniform, stood shadowed against the doorframe, a barracks bag slung over his shoulder. The gunner stood for a moment silent and still, staring across the hut, then entered and, crossing as if by habit to the table light, switched it on.

He was a huskily built staff sergeant, his face strong, his hair light, curly. He dumped his barracks bag to the floor and, taking off his cap, tossed it to the table. He caught Wyatt's look and stood a moment, sizing him up.

Wyatt came down the aisle, curious, noting under the gunner wings the Air Medal ribbon with two oak-leaf clusters. His eyes searched the gunner's. 'You looking for someone?'

'Maybe.' The gunner grinned. 'The *Miss Fire* still here?'

'No. They've just checked out.' Wyatt motioned to the empty bunks.

The sergeant's face darkened. 'They get it?' he asked.

'No. Split up.'

'What the fuck are you doing here!' muttered Bayer. He strode straight to where they stood, his toilet kit gripped in one hand, his towel across his shoulder.

The gunner turned, his look sweeping over Bayer; then, with a quick, uncertain grin, 'Bayer!' he said, and held out his hand.

Bayer only looked at it; then, glancing up, sharp-eyed, 'What's that for?'

The gunner held his look. 'For auld lang syne.'

'Then shove it up your ass,' said Bayer.

The gunner lowered his hand, glancing quickly to Wyatt, then back to Bayer again. 'Sorry,' he muttered. 'My mistake.' He turned, picking up his barracks bag, and swung it to his shoulder again, scanning the empty bunks.

Bayer studied him darkly. 'You staying here?'

The gunner nodded. 'Till further orders.'

'How come?' said Bayer, frowning. He tossed his kit to his bunk.

The gunner eyed him evenly. 'I asked to,' he said.

Bayer probed his look. 'Why?'

The gunner shrugged. 'I wanted to see my friends.'

'You never had any friends,' said Bayer.

The gunner tensed. 'Then call it the homing instinct,' he said quietly, and passed on.

Bayer watched him, wonderingly; then, 'Wait.'

The gunner turned.

Bayer went to him, his look uncertain, and stood a moment, his eyes searching. Then quietly, 'Something happened, didn't it?'

The gunner met Bayer's look. 'Something,' he said. 'Why?'

'I just wondered,' said Bayer, and held out his hand. 'Glad to see you.'

The gunner frowned, hesitant; then slowly, broadly grinning, gripped Bayer's hand strong in his own. 'Thanks,' he said. He looked to Wyatt. 'One of yours?'

Bayer turned, surprised. 'You haven't met?' He smiled at Wyatt. 'Wyatt, meet Bellows.'

*   *   *

Wyatt rested back, watching as Hagen pulled a chair up and sat closer by Bellows. He had never seen quite that look in Hagen before, almost of vindication, as if in Bellows Hagen had found the final proof to justify himself; a reflection he could not only understand but admire.

Bellows moved over to make room for him at the table where Bayer had already settled himself in for a long night of talk and reminiscences, a fifth of Scotch before them glistening under the still light.

Quietly Bellows edged back in his chair, his glass half empty before him. '... they were in the radio room,' he went on, low. 'That's where

225

the fire was. Even Reynolds with his arm bleeding—beating the fire with everything they had. But me—I figured they didn't have a chance.' He shook his head. 'No. That's a lie. I didn't figure anything. All I thought about was, Brother, here's where you get out. So—' He looked to Bayer, his eyes grey with thought. 'I got out—I jumped. And left them.'

Hagen nodded. 'Good thing, too.'

Bellows glanced up. 'Was it?' he asked, then shrugged, looking into his glass again. 'I've asked myself that a hundred times,' he muttered. 'And all I can think of is: If I'd stayed, if I'd helped—maybe they'd all have made it. Maybe we could have put out the fire.'

'Too much of a chance,' said Hagen.

'The chance they took,' Bellows said evenly. 'The chance I ran out on.' He sighed, his mouth drawn tight. 'Well, anyway—I landed in a woods and—I don't know—I didn't judge right and snapped my chute free. I fell and sprained my ankles—I couldn't move, and I knew the Jerries'd be on my tail. But just then this old Frenchman, Monsieur P—Picard—he comes up with a few guys behind him and they carried me down the road. They didn't make a sound. One guy climbed the tree and took the chute. Buried it, I guess.

'They took me to a graveyard near a church and—' He grinned. 'There was a hearse there, so they shoved me inside. There'd been a funeral, I think. Or maybe that was just part of their set-up. I never found out. And all the time my feet felt like they'd been broken clean off. They carried me most of the way through the bushes. But anyway—

'They drove the hearse back to the village and put it away. Then that night Picard came for me, him and some of his men, and brought me to this farm. Mme Corbert's.—I never thought I'd get through that night. It took us about six hours, it seemed, to go four miles—ducking, dodging, and me crawling that way. But—we made it all right.

'I stayed at Mme Corbert's for two, three weeks—in the loft, in the cellar, but most of the time right in her parlor, with nothing to do but learn French and talk with her, until I could walk again—and all the time the Jerries all over the place.'

He looked at Bayer. 'And that's when I began thinking,' he said quietly. 'Thinking about a lot of things. Me—remember? Suckers, I used to say. Everybody was a sucker except me. But here I was—with suckers risking their necks for me. I even laughed about it once.' He glanced down, silent; then, gently, 'But one night I saw this Mme Corbert alone. She was kneeling in the corner and turned, hearing me come in. And she just looked at me. She'd been crying. I think she even tried to get to her feet. But she couldn't.

'I stood there, waiting. And all she said was, "Picard's dead."'

'Later the others came—Jean and Philippe—and told us. Picard had been caught in Paris, trying to get a guy out. "We must get you from here at once," she said. "You are no longer safe here." She looked to Philippe. "Take him to Baudelaire's," she said, "and quickly." "But what about you?" said Jean. "It is my home here," she said, "I will stay." So we left... I remember the way she closed the door—so quietly...'

'But what about Kiki?' said Hagen. 'When'd you get to meet her?'

Bellows smiled strangely. 'After Baudelaire's,' he said. 'In Paris.'

Hagen grinned, sly.

Bellows' smiled broadened. 'Baudelaire's was a hotel,' he said. 'A cheap dive next door to a whorehouse.'

'Oo-la-la!' Hagen smirked.

'Baudelaire put me up for the night.'

'With or without?' said Hagen.

'With,' said Bellows, and smiled at Hagen oddly.

Hagen's eyes sparked. 'Kiki?'

Bellows shook his head. 'No. I didn't meet Kiki till three nights later. I stayed at Baudelaire's till the next night, and then Philippe came back. He talked with Baudelaire, and that's when I first heard Kiki's name. Baudelaire nearly blew his top. "Impossible!" he kept saying. "Impossible!" and kept looking at me with those greasy eyes

228

of his and shaking his head. Finally he shrugged and Philippe took over.

'We left through the back alley and cut through a yard, I remember, and over a wall; then right in the middle of a street he pulled up a manhole cover and down we went. We climbed down into the sewers.

'The place stank like slop. Every move we made seemed to echo, hollow—you know, like in a nightmare. The walls oozed with slime—I nearly threw up. And the water running just below the ledge, and smelling sour as piss.

'Philippe walked ahead with the flashlight, and I followed behind. Finally he stopped and motioned with the light. I saw a pack of rats scurrying down the ledge. There was a bundle of rags—like a bed—in the corner.

'"You must wait here," he said. "There's some bread and cheese under there, and some wine. Can you swim?" I told him I could. "Good," he said. "If you hear anyone before tomorrow night"—he swept the light to the river—"slip into there and try to hold out." That's all he could tell me, he said. "Tomorrow night we start to get you back."

'"You?" I asked. "No," he said. "Kiki." "Who's Kiki?" I said. "She will lead you," he said, "but now, you understand?" I nodded, and he turned and went back with the light.'

Bellows shivered, chilled with the memory. 'I'll never forget the cold, slimy stink of that place,' he muttered. 'And the blackness, and

229

the rats—I thought I'd go nuts. Every time I heard them, I thought it was someone coming. Once something banged against the ledge—a box—something like that floating by. I nearly dove in.

'Well, anyway—finally they came. I heard the footsteps. Then down the ledge I saw the light. Philippe came up, flashing the light in my face. I couldn't see anything except spots.

' "It is time," he said. "I will take you to the other place, you and Kiki. And from there it will be you two alone, understand? You will know the contacts one at a time. And here— the papers you will need. But understand," he said, "you must not speak a word to anyone. You speak badly in French. So Kiki will do all the talking. She understands that. And you will act as if you were in shock still. Understand? So she will lead you. She will pretend you are her father." '

Hagen startled. 'Her *what*?'

'*Père*,' said Bellows, smiling. 'Father.'

Hagen frowned.

Bellows smiled, strangely again. 'I wondered then, too,' he said. ' "Where do I meet Kiki?" I asked. And Philippe grinned. "Kiki," he said. And then I saw her. She came into the light from behind him.' He looked at Hagen. 'She was nearly seven,' he said.

Hagen stared at him. 'Seven!'

'As near as I could make out,' said Bellows. 'Her folks had been killed, like Picard, helping some guys get out, back in '40. She'd been raised by a lot of people: tossed about from one to the other. She knew more at seven than most people do at ninety.'

He leaned forward, his eyes distant with thought, and gently, 'She stood by Philippe and looked at me by the flashlight. Then all she said was, "Papa." That was her first word to me: "Papa." Her eyes were wide and brown and—sad—as if she'd never seen anything happy. Her hair was brown—shiny brown, tied in pigtails. And her face—so white. And the way her nose tilted, like a little nub—and wrinkled when she laughed. And the small, crooked teeth—' He looked at Hagen straight. 'That was Kiki.'

Hagen sat back, his mouth grim with disgust.

Bellows turned, his eyes steady on Bayer's. 'And that's where it really began, I guess.' He nodded, smiling. 'Me, I never trusted anybody. I was the only one knew all the answers. I didn't need anybody else—remember? And then, that night, out of the sewers—Kiki... But then—it was different then. "*This?*" I said. "This," said Philippe. "Jesus Christ," I said, "I might as well go straight to the Stalag-luft now." "Trust her," Philippe said. "She knows the way." "But a *kid*!"'

'She was looking at me with that strange, serious way of hers—as if she knew me—you know, *really* knew me. "He is afraid," she said.

231

Christ, I could have belted her right there. I was on edge—you know, after all that time in the sewers. But Philippe said, "Only trust her—and pretend you are her father. Your lives—both your lives—depend on it. That is all. Now, quickly—it is your only way." Then Kiki took my hand. "Come," she said. "Come, Papa..."

'And that's the way it was. Philippe led us from the sewers and Kiki led me from Paris. We stayed to out-of-the-way roads, going from village to village, from one contact to the other. They'd each give me the next directions and the next name. But it was Kiki who got me through. I acted like I'd had it—like I couldn't talk. Once we hit a road-block.

'We couldn't turn off because they'd seen us. All we could do was go straight on. I thought our goose was cooked. But she tugged me by my hand, right down the whole line of them Jerries. They stopped us and asked for our papers. I pretended it didn't mean a thing. Kiki pulled at my coat and took out the papers Philippe had given me. "He is so difficult sometimes," Kiki said, and handed the papers to the guard. "If you have a little girl," she said, looking at him, "you must never be so difficult, you know." Christ, that guard never even looked at the papers. He just looked at her and gave orders to let us through. And when he handed back the papers, he even smiled. That's the way she was.

'And then there were times we slept in the fields together—the way she'd cuddle up, snug in my arms. The way we'd talk when nobody was around—just her and me, walking down the road, her laughing at my French. And the miles in the rain, the cold—and not a whimper.'

'What happened to her?' asked Wyatt.

Bellows stared at the table. 'We got to Calais,' he said. 'A fisherman was the last link. By boat to England. I told him I wanted to take Kiki with me, but he wouldn't have it. "Too dangerous," he said. There was too much of a risk as it was with the patrols. So—I left her with the contact—and came back alone.

'We had to wait for the right night—the fog, the sea swelling, the moon down, and then it came. We got into the boat, the fisherman and me—and there was Kiki standing on the shore alone, watching. The boat pulled away and I waved, and she just raised her hand, and the fog blew between us. But just as it closed in for good, I heard her—I'll never, as long as I live, forget that cry. Just once. That's all. The way she screamed, "Papa!"'

The silence of the hut was heavy with feeling.

Trembling, Bellows raised his Scotch and drank.

Hagen leaned back, watching him with cold, sharp eyes.

'So that's it,' said Bellows softly and, setting down his glass, 'But I'll go back—someday.'

233

Wyatt looked up, quick.

'How long you going to stay here?' asked Bayer.

'It all depends,' said Bellows. 'They're shipping me to the States soon.'

'When?' asked Bayer.

Bellows only shrugged, smiling. 'When they catch me,' he said.

Hagen and Bayer laughed.

Wyatt caught his look sharply—and suddenly understood.

*　　*　　*

The hut was dark. The dull, ruddy glow from the stove flickered across the corrugated walls. Restlessly Wyatt tossed in his bunk. From the line the revving of engines cracked across the night. From across the darkness where Bellows lay, the red, still light of a cigarette brightened and dimmed again slowly. Wyatt looked at his watch. The luminous dial pointed to half past one.

Suddenly the door banged open.

'In here,' said a voice.

The lights snapped blindingly on.

'Jesus Christ!' shouted Hagen. 'Cut them goddam lights!'

Wyatt turned and saw Master Sergeant Finch in the doorway. 'The new crew,' he said.

Hagen raised up, squinting, and with a muttered, 'Sonofabitch!' reached for a cigarette and lit up.

The others stirred awake as the new crew barged in, cockily grinning, jostling down the aisle with B-4 bags and barracks bags heavily bumping.

Wyatt watched them, quiet-eyed.

'Hey, Toby, save me a bunk!' 'Christ, what a dump!' 'Here, Pop. Over here.' 'Quiet! These guys wanna sleep.' 'Where's the latrine?' 'Use your hat.'

A young-faced, bright-eyed sergeant with rusty-red hair grinned across at Wyatt and, dumping his B-4 on the bottom bunk across the way, crossed to him. 'My name's Toby,' he said brightly. He stuck out his hand. 'Toby Gordon.'

'Wyatt,' said Wyatt. 'Tom Wyatt.' He leaned over and, smiling, shook hands.

Toby began unbuttoning his blouse. 'We just come in from The Wash,' he said. 'Y'know, the gunnery school. We used to be in Section B here, near the Pool. Guess they needed us more in your squadron. You been flying long?'

'Long enough,' said Wyatt.

Toby looked up, eager. 'We're almost ready,' he said. 'Well, maybe a week more.' He cocked his head, curious. 'What's it like?' he asked.

For a moment Wyatt only looked at him, then shook his head, smiling. 'Tomorrow,' he said. 'Ask me tomorrow ... when I'm awake.'

And with a nod, he lay back, silent, waiting for them to settle in, to quiet down, to sleep ... and wondering within himself why the bright, chirpy eagerness of the boy should fill him so darkly with hurt.

The hut was still when he awoke again, and night-black. The cold had wakened him. The stove had gone out, and his blanket had slipped. He turned to pull it up and saw where Bellows lay the slow, rhythmic glow of a cigarette like a red warning beacon distant in the night.

CHAPTER TWENTY

It was a week later they made their fourth run on Berlin, and Hagen, blinded by the sunlight glancing from *The Lady*'s wing, shifted out of the angle of glare and rested by his stowed gun, his frown still focused on the jagged line of bullet holes nearly severing the right tip. Steadily the drone of the engines hummed through the blue silence. Below, the hedged, greening counties of England slid under the shadow of the homing ship.

He rubbed his eyes, stinging now with the ache of sky-searching, of having for sharp-eyed hours scanned the pure, real light of day from twenty to thirty thousand feet. He felt, too, the raw tensions of the raid grating his nerves, and

236

the straining tightness of waiting ... waiting ... expecting now something to crack, break, explode in the crew. He could feel it in his skin, the close, haunting nightmare feeling—the feeling of flying blind in a fog with Something just beyond the wingtips, unseen but there, waiting to happen ... like last Monday...

They had hit Frankfurt, their seventh run; and in the moments after target a fog had closed them in, the whole, towering formation—hundreds of bombers winging about them unseen, unreal-like, but felt, and near—like the one that had loomed suddenly in on Nelson's left, coming straight in for them from above in a rising roar of shadow; then the call—and Starrett's swift banking away, plunging blindly into the fog, lost again—with half a continent to travel back. It was the feeling of doom circling beyond sight, but near, hovering...

And this was the feeling he had even now with the clarity of all things seen sharply around him, the flashing light on the wings: the feeling of waiting ... waiting for something to happen ... to break their luck.

Their luck had been *too* good so far. They were homing on their eighth run now, their fourth to Berlin, and nothing had happened. There hadn't been a scratch on any of them, and *The Lady* was still a virgin, intact. Even the other crews were talking about her—the charmed ship, the untouched crew. But for

237

how long? How long before something *did* happen, as it almost had today...?

Right in the middle of their fourth major Luftwaffe attack, heavier than the others, just before target, Gillis and Kirby had tangled over intercom, swearing and shouting, jamming the lines as, too late, Hagen heard Cronin calling in the Focke-Wulf from two o'clock high.

Hagen looked to the bullet holes strafed across *The Lady*'s wing. If the Jerry had angled just a few degrees more, catching her in the bellyful, it would have been the end of her, of all of them... How long could that luck hold?

And the flak—Christ, every trip it seemed to be heavier, more accurate, bursting around them today every foot of the bomb run, wave after wave of shattering iron hail and bucking thunder... Yet here they were again, homing. How many times more?

He glanced down at the skimming fields, the line-of-silver river, the toylike towns, the woods.

It had been almost a week ago, the day after Augsburg, just as the long, wet grey days of waiting set in. He had been in his bunk, reading, when Wyatt had come up, a letter in hand and, grinning, had handed him a picture. 'Kay,' he said.

It was a fine, small photograph, not a cheap snapshot. And the girl—he could see her now, beautifully posed, her blond hair shining, gentle with highlight, her eyes subtle with humor, her mouth half parted in a sly, cynical smile. And across the back, in a large, friendly scrawl she had written: *This is the first time I've ever had to audition for a date. But anything for a friend. Love—Kay.*

'Well?' asked Wyatt. 'Is it a date?'

'Sure. Why not?' He pocketed the picture. 'When?'

'Next time in London,' said Wyatt.

But would there be that next time in? And if there were, would she be as in himself he had felt and wanted her to be? In his mind he had seen her stripped, her skin white, and her body firm, fresh and plowable. He could almost feel the texture of her skin smooth under his touch. And yet—there was something different about the eyes, the smile—something he wasn't sure about. And it puzzled him, as if she were not for only a night, but different, with something new. Perhaps with this one there could be between them ... between them ... Between them—how many tomorrows now between them—if ever?

He slammed his hand hard against the gun and turned away, tensed. He was getting as bad as Wyatt. Every day Wyatt had been writing to Joy, smiling over her daily letters to him. They had something going, those two, but what? How far *had* Wyatt gone in London? (If he had put it to her, it sure as hell was his first piece.) But he couldn't tell about Wyatt. There was so

239

much he couldn't tell about him.

Static crackled on intercom. 'Pilot to ball turret. Landing gears lowered. Check, Wyatt. Over.'

'Ball turret to pilot. Gears down, but can't tell for sure. Flak holes near undercarriage. I think they're flakked up. Over.'

'Roger. Climb out, Wyatt. Pilot to crew. Prepare for crash landing. Over.'

Hagen shot a swift, frowning look to Nelson. Their eyes met uneasily. Quickly Hagen unplugged from intercom and crossed to the ball turret as the armor hatch swung back.

Swiftly Wyatt reached up for the crossbar and pulled himself out. His face suddenly tightened, as if with pain.

Hagen watched, sharp, as stiffly Wyatt knelt and, locking the hatch again, started to roll the turret to aft position, his lips pressed grimly together.

Nelson and Swacey swung past them, into the radio room.

Deftly Wyatt snapped the gear lock and, with a signal to Hagen, got to his feet and hurried, limping, into the radio room.

Hagen followed, silent, wondering.

Already Swacey, Cronin, Kramer and Nelson had taken position, sitting on the floor, their knees doubled up, bracing each other like a bobsled team. Gillis sat back waiting, his back cushioned against the bomb-bay bulkhead, his knees spread out. Wyatt dropped into position and made room for Hagen.

Hagen eased down between Wyatt's knees and braced himself, his legs bent.

Golden padded his radio table with flight clothes and bent forward, his arms shielding his head.

Hagen felt the tightening of Wyatt's body. He bent his head forward into his folded arms as slowly the plane banked downward in a wide sideward dip.

Hagen held his breath, waiting. The steady droning of the engines pulsed through the quiet. His ears stopped up; the pressure built— then, with a quick pop, cleared again. The ship leveled off, easing downward.

A sudden, shivering jolt bucked through the ship, and passed.

Nelson raised up, grinning. 'We made it!'

'Get down!' shouted Gillis as a shattering quake, a screeching of tearing metal cracked through the air.

The shock snapped through Hagen, crashing him and Wyatt together. Nelson hurtled wrenching overhead, slamming against the bulkhead. The squealing of brakes shrieked through the thunderous roar of steel ripping and shearing against rock. The room spun, with a swift, jolting thrust upward; then dropped abruptly. Nelson flew back, twisting in mid-air, and struck against the waist bulkhead. A jarring shudder lurched through the ship—then the quivering stillness.

'Get out!' yelled Gillis.

Quickly Hagen sprang up and yanked open the waist door. The crew scrambled to their feet. Swacey and Kramer grabbed Nelson and tugged him out toward the side hatch. Outside, the high, rising wail of the ambulance and the crash-crew truck pierced the air. Golden and Cronin dashed through the waist and jumped free, with Wyatt and Gillis behind.

Hagen waved them to a safe distance as the ambulance screeched to a halt and the medics swung out, readying for stretcher cases. The fire-fighting team stood by, expectant, their hoses ready, but it had been a clean crack-up.

The Lady had swerved in on her right wing, her props bent under, her right landing gear shattered. Behind her lay a deep, jagged trench, over a hundred feet of plowed-up earth and runway.

A jeep careened to *The Lady*, and Miller, Greene and Bayer leaped running out. Quickly Greene looked over the crew, his face wet with sweat. 'Everybody get out okay?'

'Yeah,' said Cronin. 'Nelson's shook up, but okay.'

Greene turned as Starrett and Kirby came up. 'You okay, sir?'

Starrett nodded, grim-eyed. 'She's banged up good.'

Greene glanced at the ship. 'You brought

her back,' he said. 'That's all that counts, sir.'

Miller scratched his head. 'Look at that turret,' he muttered. The ball turret had been thrust up into the belly. 'She won't go up tomorrow, I bet.'

'That's for damn sure,' said Greene. Slowly he walked about the wing, eyeing it critically; then, with almost a smile, his hand reached out, stroking it gently. 'But she got back.' He glanced at the bullet holes, then turned to Starrett. 'You caught it this time, sir.'

Starrett nodded. 'Yeah,' he said and, his face set hard, looked swiftly beyond Hagen to Kirby and Gillis. 'I want to see you two later,' he said coldly.

'He started it!' snapped Gillis.

'I don't give a damn who started it,' Starrett shot back. 'That guy could have finished it!'

'But—'

'Not here,' Starrett cut in. 'Report to me at Squadron Headquarters, nineteen hundred. Both of you.'

Gillis glared at Kirby. 'You see—'

'Bite my ass!' snorted Kirby and spun away.

Hagen watched them, uncertain, then turned to Wyatt as Bayer came up, his face ashen, lined with strain.

'Good thing she didn't catch fire,' he said. His glance swept over the ship. Suddenly he shivered with a quick, jittery shrug. 'Christ!' He grinned tightly. 'You should-a seen it— tossing like crazy—' His look met Wyatt's, grey and uneasy, then shifted. 'Your bag still inside?'

Wyatt nodded, unsnapping his chute harness, and slid out of it. 'Just inside the door.'

'I'll get it,' said Bayer and hurried toward *The Lady* as the truck for interrogation swerved up to the wreck.

The crew started toward it, carrying their flight bags.

Hagen frowned, watching Wyatt. 'How you doing?' he asked.

'Fine,' said Wyatt.

'Then why the limp?' asked Hagen.

Starrett wheeled. 'Limp?'

Wyatt looked up.

Starrett frowned. 'What happened?'

'Nothing,' said Wyatt. 'Just a kink in the back from the turret, sir.' He straightened up, grinning. 'Getting a ball-turret spine, I guess.'

Starrett eyed him wonderingly, then crisply, 'Take care of yourself,' he said and went on.

Bayer swung Wyatt's bag over the tailgate. 'See you back at the Shack,' he said.

'Sure thing,' said Wyatt and hoisted himself up, a fleeting grimace of pain darting across his face.

Hagen watched, silent, then swung himself up and sat at the end, across from Starrett.

'Okay,' shouted Golden to the driver.

Gears shifted, and the truck bucked off to a swift start down the runway.

244

'Anyway,' drawled Swacey, 'it was a good landing, skipper. We walked away from it.'

Hagen looked at Starrett staring back, sober-faced and still, at *The Lady*, scarred now and crumpled, vulnerable like every other ship on the field.

* * *

Hagen waited as Nelson read the letter, caught by the look in his face. They were the first two back from interrogation, and alone in the Shack. The letter had been on Nelson's bunk, with a card and a V-mail.

'Something wrong?' asked Hagen.

Nelson shook his head; then, quietly, 'I'm a father,' he said. 'A seven-pound-two-ounce boy.'

Hagen grinned. 'Congratulations!'

Nelson only frowned wonderingly.

'No whoop of joy?' asked Hagen.

Nelson's frown deepened. 'I've got a son,' he said dimly.

'Don't let it rock you,' Hagen said dryly. 'It's done every day.'

Nelson looked up. 'But I can't see him,' he said. He glanced back to the letter.

Hagen's face straightened. 'You need a drink,' he said. He looked around. 'Bellows has got a bottle somewhere. Wait.' He crossed down the hut to Bellows' footlocker, knelt down and swung back the lid. 'It's—' Suddenly

245

he started. Under the shirts was a paper-wrapped package. The paper had fallen loose from the soft golden curls of a doll.

Hagen stared, puzzled; then slowly put the shirts back over it, closed down the lid and, rising, 'Nothing here,' he said. 'We'll have to wait till the club.'

But Nelson, without turning, was already striding out.

*   *   *

It was after chow when Hagen, from his bunk down the hut, saw Wyatt come in from the rear door. He noticed that when their looks met, Wyatt stiffened and walked straight, too damned straight.

Toby had also seen Wyatt, and brightly, 'Hey, Wyatt—where the hell you been?' He crossed to him, eager.

Wyatt grinned. 'Pas-de-Calais,' he said.

'Mission One tomorrow,' Toby said, excited.

'Good luck,' said Wyatt. 'On all of them.' He sat on Bayer's bunk and, slowly raising his legs, lay back.

'You all right?' Toby asked. He stood over Wyatt, looking down. 'You look kinda beat.'

'Just tired,' said Wyatt.

'Too bad about *The Lady*,' Toby said; then, blithely, 'But they'll fix 'er up good as new, I bet.'

246

'Sure,' said Wyatt.

Toby frowned. 'Ain't you gonna read your mail?' He picked up the letter from Wyatt's bunk and handed it down to him.

Wyatt glanced at it and smiled. 'Later,' he said. 'It's personal.'

'All I got was a birthday card,' said Toby.

Wyatt looked up, surprised. 'Your birthday? When?'

Toby's eyes brightened. 'Tomorrow,' he said.

Wyatt's look held, then shifted down to the letter in his hand.

'Nelson's wife had a boy,' Toby said.

Wyatt grinned. 'How'd he take it?'

Toby shrugged. 'I don't know. I just heard about it.'

The door opened, and Hagen saw Bayer come in, his face set, troubled. He watched as Bayer passed by Wyatt and, passing, gave a nod. He busied himself a moment by his footlocker, then went out the rear door.

Wyatt roused himself slowly to his feet and with a cheery 'See you later' to Toby, went down the hut and out, after Bayer.

Curious, Hagen swung from his bunk, went out the near door and, circling the hut, made his way to the corner. He watched as Bayer and Wyatt stood at a distance talking, arguing. Then he saw Bayer reach inside his jacket and pull out some things for Wyatt. Wyatt nodded and took them, and went alone, cutting back by the side path, toward the latrine, limping. Bayer stood watching, then turned and started back to the Shack.

Quickly Hagen backed away, turned and, again circling behind the hut, made his way to the main path to the latrine, just in time to see Wyatt limp hurriedly inside.

Hagen followed.

Wyatt was standing at the urinal. He half turned, surprised, then continued.

Hagen went to the washstands, turned on a tap and, taking out his comb, started to comb his hair. 'Where you been?' he asked. 'You missed chow.'

'I wasn't hungry,' said Wyatt.

Hagen studied Wyatt's reflection in the mirror as Wyatt turned, buttoning up. His jacket pockets bulged. Carefully he started to cross to the stands. A wince of pain shot across his face.

'Jesus Christ!' muttered Hagen, whirling. 'What the fuck happened?'

Wyatt looked up. 'Nothing.'

'Don't give me that shit. I've been watching you. What's up?'

Wyatt's face tightened; then, 'Something went wrong with my heated suit,' he said. 'The wires bunched up. I got burned.'

Hagen frowned. 'Where?'

'It's okay,' Wyatt said.

'Let's see.'

Frowning, Wyatt looked at him. 'Then keep

248

it quiet,' he said.

'Yeah. Sure,' said Hagen.

Slowly Wyatt unbelted his pants, unbuttoned and painfully lowered his trousers, baring his thighs.

'Jesus H. Christ!' said Hagen.

Wyatt's right inner thigh was red, bubbled with large, translucent blisters, the ugliest about four inches long.

Hagen's eyes darkened. 'When did that happen?'

'Just before target.'

Hagen stared at him. '*Before target!* You *flew* like that?'

Wyatt almost smiled. 'Well, I couldn't get out and walk, could I?' Gently he drew his trousers back on.

Hagen's look narrowed. 'Why didn't you say something?'

'Things were bad enough as they were. Remember?'

'But, Christ—' Hagen frowned again. 'You going to the Infirmary?'

'They'd ground me.'

'So? What's a few days?'

'While you guys fly?' Wyatt shook his head. 'It's not that bad. Bayer got me some salve and bandages. I'll patch it up myself.' He started to unzip his flight jacket and crossed to the corner basin by the light.

Hagen snorted, watching him. 'I get it,' he said. 'Hero stuff. All for the crew, eh?'

Wyatt turned, meeting Hagen's look evenly, then only turned again, taking the bandages and salve from his jacket pockets. He set the stuff on the shelf above the basin, took off his jacket and, hanging it on a wall hook, started again to unbuckle his pants.

Hagen stood watching, feeling—he couldn't tell why—confused and angered by Wyatt, the calm, slow way he now unwrapped the razor blade. Abruptly he turned and left.

Outside he felt his anger rising. In his mind all he could see was Wyatt in the corner, his pants lowered, studying the blisters. He would be cutting into them now, lancing them—The shock of imagined pain rasped Hagen's nerves. He wheeled suddenly and hurried back.

Wyatt was standing by the basin, his face drawn tight. He was holding a handkerchief to his thigh, catching the flow of water, daubing at it. He glanced up surprised as Hagen came striding over. 'For Christ's sake, let me help.'

CHAPTER TWENTY-ONE

Starrett got to the Squadron Headquarters just before seven o'clock, found the private conference room at the end of the corridor and, snapping on the light, crossed to the single desk at the rear. The room was small, windowless, lit by a hanging overhead light, the glow sharp against the shadows on the pale green cinderblock walls, bare but for the wall clock by the door. There was only the desk and two chairs: a stark, efficient room.

He tossed his cap to the empty chair by the desk and, unzipping his jacket, sat down facing the open door, waiting. His face was set, stern with the memory of Kirby and Gillis snapping across intercom, cutting off Cronin's call-in, as the staccato of bullets ripped into *The Lady*'s wing—a moment that could have cost them *The Lady* and their lives, if it hadn't been for Luck.

He glanced to his watch, anxious to have it over, knowing he would have to press far, yet not so far as to break their pride or set it off. For it *was* pride behind it all—the dry, stubborn yankee pride of Kirby, and the hot-tempered Texan pride of Gillis. Even from the beginning it had been a matter of pride.

Kirby had told him the cause the first morning after—at breakfast with him and Rita at the Regent's. Kirby had picked up a girl at the hotel bar, and Gillis had seen them and had moved in. He had been drinking and jokingly had told the girl Kirby had been clapped up. The girl had taken him seriously and had walked out—with Gillis going after her.

That had been the start of it. But there was also, Starrett knew, that other matter—their differences in personality: Kirby the superior, self-assured, purposeful; and Gillis, unsure of

251

himself, defensive, with a chip on his shoulder, daring the Kirbys of the world to knock it off.

They had worked so far together in the line of duty, each with respect for the other's capabilities, their differences kept separate. They had functioned in their central duty to the discipline and unity of the crew. But now they were slipping, letting their private lives intrude, jeopardizing the crew and *The Lady*.

It had erupted last night at the BOQ. With Aronson's bunch on flak leave and Kramer out, there had been just himself, reading in his bunk, and Kirby—in the middle of a letter—when Gillis came in, drunk, and, shoving the door open, staggered for his bunk.

Kirby swung about angrily. 'For Christ's sake, shut the door! You born in a barn or something!'

'Shut it yourself!' Gillis mumbled and went to his bunk.

Kirby stood up. 'I told you to shut that fuckin' door.'

Gillis glared at him. 'Is that an order, *sir*?'

'That's an order,' said Kirby firmly.

'Then go fuck yourself,' said Gillis.

Kirby tossed down his pen and started for Gillis, but Starrett swung up from his bunk and pulled Kirby back. 'Stop riding him. You're pushing too far.'

'No sonofabitch is going to tell me to fuck myself,' Kirby muttered and, shaking free of Starrett's hold, started again for Gillis.

Suddenly he stopped.

Starrett turned to see Gillis rising unsteadily with his .45 in hand, pointed squarely at Kirby, the safety catch released. 'Take just one step—one fucking step—*sir*—'

Starrett steeled himself, then slowly moved in between Gillis and Kirby.

'You stay outta this, Starrett,' Kirby said.

'Give me the gun,' Starrett said softly to Gillis. He kept his slow, even stride. 'Give me the gun.'

'Get outta the way!' Gillis muttered. 'I want that sonofabitch—'

Starrett held out his hand. 'Give me the gun, Gillis, and get to sleep.' He stood there firmly, his hand still held out.

Gillis met Starrett's look blurredly, then quietly handed over the gun, turned and, flopping into his bunk with a groan, passed out.

Starrett flicked down the safety catch, then went and closed the door.

On his way back he saw Kirby standing, staring at him. 'What if he'd shot?'

Starrett shivered, then shrugged. 'You'd've been skipper,' he said. 'But stop riding him. It's tough enough as it is.' He looked down at the sleeping Gillis. 'He'll be all right tomorrow.'

But it hadn't been all right. Today might have been the end of them all.

Both had been at fault—as officers, negligently at fault—Kirby as much as Gillis, even more so as co-pilot.

He tried not to recall his closeness to Kirby, nor, today, Kirby's actions on the crash—the way, on the first sick jolt, quick and alert beside him, he had reacted: a living and complete extension of himself, matching motion to motion, timing with the same cold, clear mind the glide and the crash impact; holding through the back-jarring, wrist-tearing shocks to keep her tight as possible in the plow-through ... a co-pilot like none other ...

And yet—there had still been that one sudden outburst upstairs—

He heard their steps down the corridor and straightened his back, his hands folded on the desk before him. He glanced up as they came in.

They both were in leather flying jackets, familiar and informal, but stood to a rigid attention on entering, eyes straight ahead, guarded.

Kirby stepped forward, snapped a clipped salute. 'Lieutenant Daniel Kirby, reporting as ordered, sir,' followed by Gillis, the step, the quick salute, the crisp, 'Lieutenant Lyle Gillis, reporting as ordered, sir.'

Starrett acknowledged their salutes, paused, eyeing them carefully; then, very quietly, very simply, 'Lieutenant Kirby, what was the girl's name—the one at the Regent's bar?'

Kirby frowned, surprised. The frown deepened. 'I don't know, sir. I don't remember.'

Starrett turned to Gillis. 'Lieutenant Gillis, what was the girl's name?'

Gillis stared long at the wall before him. Then, 'May I look in my book, sir?'

Starrett shook his head, exasperated. 'Jesus Christ!' he muttered, rising. 'You two!' He glared straight to Gillis. 'Last night you nearly killed Kirby here, and today—' looking to Kirby—'you both nearly killed off ten men, and over a broad neither of you even remembers! Why?'

'It was a matter of principle, sir,' Kirby said with dignity.

'Principle!' snapped Starrett; then, catching himself, 'All right, Lieutenant Kirby, *what* principle? What principle here is worth the lives of the crew?'

Kirby's face tautened; then, tightly, 'None, sir.'

'And you, Lieutenant Gillis?'

Gillis reddened hotly. 'None, sir.'

Starrett waited. Silence. Then he nodded. 'I think you get the point,' he said. He faced them directly, his eyes hard, piercing their looks. 'Last night was one thing,' he said. 'You were drunk, Gillis. But today—' He shook his head again; then, 'We're a crew: and you two, as officers of that crew—you, Kirby, especially— have a duty to the men. A duty that comes before anything and everything else now. Even before your pride. In fact, you haven't any *right* to pride, either of you, if it comes before your duty to them. Do you understand that? Because if you don't,' Starrett went on, '*if* the crew *is* to break this way, I'd prefer you both be transferred now—tonight—the sooner the better for all of us.'

Only the dim hum of the clock was heard as Starrett waited.

It was Kirby who broke the silence, his voice low. 'Jesus, Starrett—'

Starrett turned to Gillis. 'Any questions?'

Gillis shook his head. 'No, sir.'

'Then that's it,' said Starrett. 'Dismissed.'

The two saluted again, turned on their heels and left.

Starrett crossed back to the desk again, feeling oddly relieved, yet spent, and sat down.

'Starrett?'

He looked up. Kirby was back in the doorway.

'Yeah, Kirby?'

'You been up to the line?' It was almost conversational.

'Yeah. I just got back. Why?'

Kirby said, 'How's *The Lady*?'

'Fine,' said Starrett. 'The undercarriage got the worst of it. The wing's okay. The structure's good. Greene says she'll be up in a day or two—good as new.'

Kirby nodded. 'Great,' and smiling, turned away.

'Kirby?'

256

Kirby looked back. 'Yeah?'

Starrett grinned. 'Thanks for the landing today.'

Kirby, smiling still, nodded again. 'Any time, Dad. Any time.' And left.

A co-pilot like none other. A crew like none other. Even Hagen seemed to be working out. And Wyatt. He wondered about Wyatt's limp. He'd check with Cronin first thing in the morning, just in case it was more than the kink Wyatt had said it was. Wyatt had a way of covering things, of negating his force, of remaining remote, beyond scrutiny, never letting anyone come close to him; yet, Starrett knew, there was about Wyatt a sense of deep attachment to everyone and everything about *The Lady*, as if they were all somehow meaningful to him in a special way, with a meaning only he knew.

But who knew *his* meaning?

One day, and soon, he would get to know Wyatt—really know him. He felt there was something central to him, something important, that gave him whatever courage it took to be locked in a ball seven to ten hours a mission, exposed below ship with the least chance of survival if they were hit. Yet it was the position he had chosen—and even there, the loner. But one day, Luck holding...

Luck. There it was again: Luck, Chance, Fate. Well, so far it was on their side. So maybe *The Lady was* the Lady Luck. He grinned at the thought, buoyant almost, that even now he still had *The Lady*, a bit pranged up, as the British would say, but in a day or so she'd be up there again, shining bright and steady.

Luck and *The Lady*—and the crew still intact. Now all he had to do was to keep them that way. It was his duty. Yes, by Christ, *his* duty—to keep them together—safe—intact— whatever happened—

A quick shudder passed through him as he felt again the eerie, chilling distortion of thought. *His duty*—it was to fly the ship, to keep the crew in functioning order. Simply that, and nothing—neither in duty nor power—beyond that.

And heavily Starrett sighed, feeling again the dead, full weight of his helplessness—and futility.

Slowly he rose and, picking up his cap, tiredly crossed the room, flicked off the light switch and left, his lone footsteps echoing hollow down the corridor.

CHAPTER TWENTY-TWO

The late noon sun was warm, and the wind gentle in the deep, new grass. Hagen stretched out, his hands behind his head, his eyes half closed, watching Wyatt beside him, leaning back, resting against the mossy, lichened stone wall, his face quiet with thought.

Today, while *The Lady* was under repairs, the crew had been grounded for rest. Tomorrow it would be off into the wild blue yonder for all of them again. But now, Hagen mused, they had today—time to live, assured of one day more. It had made him feel released, alive in a free and easy way—all the more so when he thought of the other crews now getting their tails shot off over Brunswick. It didn't bother him, but it did Wyatt... Wyatt...

Ever since last night, patching up Wyatt's leg—It had been little more than a patch-up job...

Wyatt had lanced the blisters with a nick of the razor blade, drained the water, then had eased on the antiseptic salve to prevent infection. Over this they had taped a double swatch of bandages and bound them tight, to reduce friction. This done, Wyatt had simply pulled up his pants, gathered the salve, tape and bandages together, shoved them into his jacket pockets and, with a grin of thanks, had gone out as if he'd been in for only a piss.

All evening after that, he had watched Wyatt across the hut. He lay in his bunk writing the nightly letter to Joy, reading, joking with Toby—and then, that late and long conversation with Bellows, just the two of them, low and quiet, their faces close and serious, Bellows leaning on the bunk, Wyatt resting on his elbow.

259

With Bayer now on the line, there was usually Toby or Bellows with Wyatt, and of late—especially these past few nights—it had been mostly Bellows. A strange, puzzling combination—Wyatt and Bellows.

And for the first time since that first real meeting up at the armorers' shed, Hagen wanted to know—he felt he *needed* to know— what made Wyatt tick.

Today, seeing Wyatt limping off alone across the meadow east of the Shack, he had decided to follow and find out, and had found him here, sitting—as he was sitting now— resting against the wall.

It was like Wyatt to find a spot like this, with the base behind them, out of sight, and only green fields and woods before them. He had found this place the first week in, and had been coming here alone ever since—whenever he could get away, he said, to 'get quiet' and think things out ... like now ...

Only now, scanning the sky eastward, Wyatt was troubled, uneasy.

Hagen cocked an eye at him. 'Still got that feeling?' he asked. 'About Toby?'

Wyatt nodded. 'It's just the way he yelled back this morning: *'Hurry up, Pop. We'll be late.'* As if—I don't know. It's just a feeling.'

'You should've been asleep,' said Hagen. 'Then you wouldn't've heard anything.'

Wyatt pulled up a blade of grass and began to nibble it, looking off toward the trees.

'How's the leg?' asked Hagen.

'Fine,' said Wyatt.

Hagen looked at him. 'I don't get it,' he said. 'The way you cover things up like that. Why?'

Wyatt glanced off, wonderingly; then, 'It's *The Lady*,' he said. 'To me she's—luminous—with courage and hope—'

Hagen shook his head. 'Bullshit.'

Wyatt only shrugged. 'Watch the crew,' he said, 'when things get tight. Really tight. It isn't each man for himself. It's each for the other.'

Hagen lay back, closing his eyes, and grinned. 'Shit. It's their asses—'

'Spirit,' said Wyatt quietly. 'The only thing that *is* real. The spirit we are, when it grows, affirms life.'

'Is that why you're here?' Hagen asked sarcastically. 'Bomb-dropping—to affirm life?'

Wyatt's face clouded. 'We can't choose our times,' he said. 'We can only do the best we can, when we have it. But beyond this time—to see beyond and act now—to decide—' He nodded. 'Yes. In this time, for me—to fly now—it *is* still to affirm life—the life that *can* be, beyond our time. Some tomorrow—'

'Fuck it,' muttered Hagen. 'The only thing that's real is today. What we can touch, fuck, eat—that's all there is.'

Wyatt looked to him, frowning. 'But you're taking the risks with the rest of us, buying tomorrow.'

Hagen shrugged. 'The only reason I'm here

is to get out of a trap. Out of one trap into another.' He turned to Wyatt coldly. 'That's what life really is, man. A trap. You're here, then you're dead. Snap. The trap closes.'

'And that's it?'

'That's it. One great big Nothing.'

'And when you're dead, you're dead.'

Hagen raised an eyebrow. 'And when *you're* dead?'

Wyatt tossed away the chewed grass.

Hagen grunted, disgusted. 'Wyatt, what you see just isn't there.'

'Maybe what *you* see isn't there, either,' said Wyatt. 'Or maybe it's there only *because* you see it. Maybe your trap's just the way you see life. Without meaning.'

Hagen glanced up, surprised. 'Who says there's meaning? We're here, and we're stuck here. Just like we're stuck in the middle of this fuckin' war. Where's the meaning there?'

'Maybe,' said Wyatt, 'in the vision—that Man has dignity and meaning—just in being here.'

He saw Hagen shake his head again. Then, 'All right,' he said, 'how about love? Just two people. How can there be love if there's no meaning to the people?'

Hagen eyed him quickly, and with a crooked grin, 'Wait'll you try it,' he said. 'Then you'll know. Just wait.'

The low droning of approaching planes broke in at the edge of silence and neared, growing thunderously loud as the first flight of the homing bombers flew in low and over, squadron by squadron, in V-shaped formations.

Wyatt's face again darkened as he watched their own group lowering, veering for landing, the prop wash whipping the trees and the grass about them with sudden wind. Even from where they sat, they could see, here and there, the jagged wing, a sliced tailfin, feathered props.

Hagen looked at Wyatt, then back to the bombers again as they roared in low and steady on their approach.

*   *   *

When they got back to the Shack area, they stopped at the path, watching, silent.

Finch, the master sergeant, stood outside the Shack, his clipboard in hand, his face expressionless. Four men were filing out—the 'Vulture Brigade'—each with a mattress case bulging over his shoulder. A fifth followed, his arms heaped with uniforms. They plodded, quiet, down the cinder path, turned past the latrine and cut toward Quartermaster's. Finch raised his clipboard and, checking it with his pencil, went inside.

Curiously Hagen watched as the men trudged down the walk, then glanced to Wyatt. 'You sure called that one,' he said. 'They had it.'

Wyatt's eyes were strangely dark. 'There'll be others to come,' he said.

Hagen looked at him, then frowned, wordless.

Wyatt started to the Shack, limping.

Hagen followed.

A chill grey quiet darkened the shadowy hut. The bunks along the side were stripped bare, the shelves stark. The stove had gone out.

Cronin and Swacey sat at the table, a hand of poker unplayed between them. Wiggam moved uneasily up and down the aisle, his quick eyes ferreting over the bunks. Finch sat on Bayer's footlocker, talking with Bayer, a large, brown-wrapped package beside him.

Wiggam turned and came back to his corner bunk. A small pile of blank envelopes and writing pads, paper-backed books, a pair of gunner wings and two fountain pens lay on his footlocker. He glanced to Wyatt in the doorway, then to Hagen—and turned again, uncertain, wiping his hands down his fatigues.

Bayer looked up and, seeing Wyatt, 'They went down over target,' he said. His voice was quiet and dry.

'Any get out?' asked Wyatt.

'Six chutes seen,' said Finch.

Hagen glanced to the empty bunks. 'You kinda rushed things, didn't you?'

'A new crew's coming,' said Finch. He looked to Bayer, then got up. 'See you later.'

Bayer nodded to the package. 'What about that?'

'Divvy it up,' said Finch. 'If you can't—' he shrugged—'bury it.' He looked about. 'And don't forget to tell Bellows to get his ass over to Transportation.' He turned and went out.

Curiously Wiggam went to the package, his eyes cautious.

'Whose is it?' said Hagen.

'Toby's,' said Bayer.

Wiggam looked to Bayer. 'Open it.'

Bayer glared at him. 'You open it.'

'Not me,' said Wiggam. He glanced furtively to Wyatt. 'Not me.'

'Give it here,' said Hagen. He reached for it.

Cronin and Swacey swept the cards from the table. Hagen set down the package and, picking up the knife, read the address: *From Mrs Tobias Gordon, Sr, Twin Falls, Iowa*; and the red warning tag, HANDLE WITH CARE. The heavy cardboard box was sealed with taping paper. Hagen cut through the lid. The box was stuffed with padding of twisted newspaper. A circular tin box nested inside.

'Food!' said Wiggam.

Hagen lifted the tin box out and, tugging off the lid—

Nobody said a word.

Slowly Hagen set the box down, frowning at the neat white-and-pink-frosted cake. Roses and rose leaves curled about the pink ribbony words: *Happy Birthday—With All Love.*

There was a small, bulgy envelope tucked in at the side. Hagen picked it out and opened it. Tiny blue candles spilled into his hand. One by one he let them fall into the box.

'Twenty,' said Bayer. 'And one for good luck.'

Hagen looked at him, then, with a shrug, started to cut the cake. 'Anybody want a piece?' He handed it out.

'Too near chow,' said Cronin. Frowning, he started to shuffle the cards again.

Swacey looked away. 'Later, maybe.'

Wyatt shook his head.

'You, Bayer?'

'No.'

Hagen turned.

Wiggam's hand went out for it. 'Looks good,' he said.

Hagen's eyes narrowed; then suddenly he slapped the piece, frosting down, hard into Wiggam's hand.

Cronin looked up, startled.

Angrily Hagen tossed down the knife and, pulling up a chair, snapped, 'Deal.'

*   *   *

It was seven thirty by his watch as Hagen, getting ready to join the rest of the crew at the club, noticed Wyatt lying in his bunk, hands under his head, staring up at the ceiling. Today, for the first time since the letters had

266

started, there had been nothing from Joy. Hagen smiled and shook his head; then, zipping up his jacket, went down the hut.

'How about the club?' he asked.

Wyatt turned. 'No. Not now.'

'She's slipping,' Hagen said. 'No letter.'

'There's a reason,' said Wyatt. 'Maybe tomorrow.'

'Maybe,' said Hagen. 'Anyway, keep the lines open. We're due in London in a week.'

Suddenly—the door banging open—'Where the fuck's Bellows?' roared Finch. He strode down the aisle, his eyes mean, angry. 'Any of you seen Bellows?'

Hagen turned. 'Why? What's up?'

'They're shipping him back to the States, and we can't find the sonofabitch! He should have reported this morning, but nobody's seen him. Have you?'

Hagen frowned, thinking, then shook his head. 'No.'

'Wyatt?'

Wyatt shook his head. 'No.'

'Great!' snorted Finch. 'Just great! And look at his stuff! He flung his hand at Bellows' uniforms, all neatly hanging in a row. 'He ain't even packed yet. Now they're riding *my* ass!'

'Probably shacking up somewhere,' said Hagen.

'He wasn't allowed off base,' said Finch. 'But with that sonofabitch—you're probably right!' and stormed out, slamming the door hard behind him.

Hagen frowned. The last he had seen of Bellows had been last night, here, talking with Wyatt. He looked at Wyatt curiously. And vaguely he remembered something—a mist of something about all this—something on that first night... He recalled the four of them about the table, the light glistening on the bottle, the laughter ... the laughter... Something Bellows had said about shipping to the States. '*When?*' from Bayer. '*When they catch me.*' That was it! That had been Bellows' joke. Only it wasn't a joke, maybe. And Wyatt—come to see it now, Wyatt had been the only one who hadn't laughed.

Wyatt raised himself up and slid from the bunk, then, limping, went to the stove.

Hagen watched. Then, quietly, 'Where's Bellows?'

Wyatt only shrugged; then, reaching for the poker, lifted back the lid and started to stir the coals.

'Wyatt?'

Wyatt shook his head.

Frowning, curious, Hagen crossed the hut to Bellows' footlocker and, kneeling, swinging back the lid, started to search, pushing aside the neat top layer of shirts.

'It's gone,' he said and, turning, looked to Wyatt again. 'The doll's gone.'

Wyatt only met his look, then glanced away again. And suddenly Hagen knew. Finally he understood. 'Kiki,' he said.

* * *

At about ten thirty, as the door opened and a draft of cold air came in, Hagen turned in his bunk to see a brawny, bull-necked sergeant grinning into the Sad Shack. Over his shoulders were two barracks bags. Two bulky flight bags, gripped in his thick hands, bumped against the doorframe. 'Hi,' he said jovially. 'We're the new crew.'

PART SIX

INTERLUDE IN EDEN
April 8–10, 1944

CHAPTER TWENTY-THREE

By two in the afternoon on the eighth of April—Holy Saturday—the train from Thetford hurtled its way south toward London as Wyatt, seated by the dozing Hagen, stared out, unseeing, into the sunny blur of counties and villages spinning by. Only once was he conscious of focus—caught by a caravan of gypsies camping in a wooded, sun-speckled glen by the trackside. Then again, as the blur of color and shape motion-fused before him, his mind drifted inward to memory, and uneasiness, and fear.

True, there was that lightness of freedom—for three days not to face death, or even to think of death, but to enjoy life, to live and to share that living with Joy. She would show him—as she had started to that day a month ago—her England, not only London but beyond. She had written she wanted him to see The Linnet, her cottage at The Combes, just west of Sevenoaks. And Knole and a host of other places... He smiled, remembering her excited eyes, her smile, the way she had waved back from the train (that odd, shadowy look on her face—a moment only, and it was gone, lost again in her smile) ... and the train pulling out, and he alone ... and (darkly in his mind) the crushed violets at his feet... He shook his head.

A month ago, and since that time, through all the letters between, they had become, he felt, Eden, drawn by Providence, and theirs a love beyond time, space and circumstance—a love to rely on, to trust one's life on ... as he had trusted Bellows to her keeping.

He had wondered at first if he should have involved her, but she had been the only sure answer, The Linnet being just a mile from The Combes, midway between London and the Channel. And she, without qualm or inquiry, had agreed and had stood by his decision. Together, through veiled and coded letters, they had worked out the first stages for Bellows' escape.

The Linnet would be his first contact. There he would stay until she had cleared with her uncle, a fisherman out from Ramsgate. From there Bellows could relocate his last contact from France, or if he could not, the uncle would take him across, to start his return journey to Calais. Then, once there, he could by retracing his contacts search for Kiki.

And without a question Joy had followed his lead.

And yet—something, since then, had happened. Something unclear and disturbing. Since the day he had missed a letter, there had been not only a change in her usual tone but a different address. He had been instructed to send his letters to her in care of Kay at her

London address even though it was evident the two were not living together. She had evaded his questions, assuring him only that Bellows was safely en route and that the next time she saw him she would explain: that it was nothing to be said in a letter.

A chill of fear ran cold through him, of anxiety, of apprehension at their meeting, in less than half an hour now. And he was afraid that this would be the end of things for them. It was almost too clear that she had made up her mind that theirs could not be the love they had first thought it could be. Perhaps because of another love—a previous and deeper love—in her life that would—that should, of course—come first, if that was her choice.

Oh, her letters had still been intimate and warm, but more and more she had suggested caution—as if she had been afraid she had invited feelings too deep, too intense to contend with now. As if, perhaps, he had been too ardent, too sudden in his confessions. And he had wondered, now and again, in utter conflict, if he had made a fool of himself, exposing himself as naïve, foolish, too much the innocent idealist, too demanding in his open trust.

Should he have been more reserved, more New England? But with her he had thought he needed no mask, that he could be—as never before in his life he had been able to be—thoroughly himself, his truest self, singing in sunlit altitudes of freedom, in the freedom of a love lost in an answering love.

Nervously he turned away from the window and looked at the woman sitting across from him—a rosy-faced woman with the jolliest smile. 'Yer first trip into London, sergeant?'

'The second,' said Wyatt.

''Ow lovely,' the woman said, and grinned knowingly.

*   *   *

Thunderously the train roared into Liverpool Street Station.

Hagen stood up and pulled their haversacks down from the green net racks above them.

Wyatt sat back, watching the woman busying with her brood. Her suitcase, black and battered and tied with heavy rope, bulged. Two shopping bags, filled to the top with bundles wrapped in newspaper, swayed by her thick knees. Her three scrawny tykes scrambled and tumbled about, ogling out the window. The youngest wedged wide-eyed between his two older brothers, his nose pressed hard against the grimy pane.

The woman righted her hat and jabbed in a stickpin. ' 'Enry's never seen the city in ever so long,' she said. 'Bin out in the country, 'e 'as. H'evacu-ited.'

Beside her a prim, pale-faced man sat rigidly holding his neatly furled umbrella, his bowler hat snug on his long, thin head. He stared straight ahead, silent.

Hagen swung Wyatt his haversack and gas-mask kit and settled back again. 'Think they'll be waiting?'

Wyatt nodded. 'Everything's taken care of.'

'You talk with Kay?'

'No. Joy answered.'

'What about the rooms?'

'We're at the Winston,' said Wyatt. 'Kay took care of it.'

The man in the bowler cleared his throat. He stared straight ahead. His neck and face were red.

Slowly the train ground to a squealing halt. The coach bucked and shivered. The couplings rattled and clanged. A loud hissing of steam geysered out from the sides.

The woman called, ' 'Enry. You go out first.'

The youngest backed away, frightened, and hugged her knees. She sighed; then, ''Ere, h'Albert—h'Albert!' She tugged the boy nearest her and shoved one of the shopping bags at him. 'You tike this un, and, h'Egbert—p'y mind, naow—you tike this un.' She rose heftily and grinned again, swung open the coach door and, herding her brood out, her hand clutching 'Enry's, ''Ave a lovely time, sergeants,' she said and turned, yanking 'Enry. 'And you kids, ack like gentlemen, like I told ye naow. And daon't forget. Call 'im yer dada—like I told ye.'

'Come on,' said Hagen. He leaped down and stood waiting, looking about.

Wyatt stepped out, glancing around the crowd.

Finally the lanky, prim-faced man stepped coldly down. He eyed Wyatt and Hagen frigidly and, with a sniff, strode away.

Wyatt grinned.

'Let's move,' said Hagen.

They started down the platform, searching. Suddenly—

'Tom!'

Wyatt stopped. The crowd jostled against him. He looked around.

'Tom!'

'Over there,' said Hagen. He nodded toward the gate.

Wyatt turned and saw Joy, pale and lovely, waving to him—in the same tweed suit and blue sweater, her hair free—as if she had been, since last he had seen her, waiting here, unchanged and unchanging, for him. She glanced brightly to Kay beside her, and back again.

Hurriedly Wyatt edged through the crowd. 'Joy!'

She went to him, her eyes searching his face, slowly, then quickening, then in a run of wild, jubilant abandon. 'Tom! Tom!'

Swiftly he caught her and held her, and brought his lips to hers, tongue tasting tongue, and feeling the warmth, the sure reality of her body near to his, long and close. Then slowly they drew apart, self-conscious for the tears they felt. She smiled shyly and held his hand, memorizing his face and the love in it. 'Tom.'

He grinned and drew her near him gently, tenderly—possessively. There was love in her eyes only for him. No phantom of any lost love between them. It was—as he had always known it to be—Eden, drawn by Providence. Then, very quietly, he kissed her again, simply, with thanks.

Slowly her arms tightened around his.

'Well?' said Hagen, watching them. He was surprised by Wyatt's intensity.

Wyatt glanced up, then, drawing her before him, 'Joyce Cheyne, Mitch Hagen. Hagen, Joy.'

Joy smiled at Hagen, eager and warm. 'I'm very glad to know you, sergeant.'

'Thanks,' said Hagen. They shook hands. 'Same here.' He looked her over appraisingly, surprisingly impressed.

Joy turned and called, 'Kay?'

Hagen glanced up. His look suddenly sharpened. He watched Kay moving through the crowd, tall and slender in her trim WAAF uniform. Her hair gleamed in a bun, a shimmering gold. Her face was delicate and clear; her lips a warm, glistening red. Her eyes were quick to survey him, and held his look, curious.

'Kay Cheyne,' said Joy. 'Sergeant Mitch

Hagen.'

Smiling, Kay held out her hand. 'Sergeant Hagen.'

'That's right,' said Hagen. His voice was taut. 'Mitch Hagen.'

Wyatt was caught, surprised by the tightness, the uneasy defensiveness, in Hagen's voice.

'Everything set?' asked Hagen.

'Everything,' said Kay, and smiled again, watching him closely.

They started from the station.

'Where do we start?' said Hagen.

'The hotel,' said Wyatt. 'We'll check our stuff.'

'And then?' said Hagen. He glanced to Kay.

'Anywhere,' said Kay. 'Nothing's planned till six.'

Joy turned. 'Then why not get acquainted, you two?'

'What about you?' asked Kay.

'Tom and I'll go someplace—to talk a bit.'

Kay frowned. 'But—'

'It's quite all right,' Joy said quickly. 'Really.'

'You're sure?'

'Quite,' said Joy.

Kay only looked to her dubiously; then, to Wyatt, 'Your hotel is just around the corner from my apartment. We'll probably be there for a drink.' She looked to Hagen wryly. 'That is, sergeant, if you do drink.'

'I've been known to drink,' Hagen said, smiling. 'It's one of my virtues.'

Kay laughed. 'A rarity these days, sergeant. A virtuous man.'

Hagen grinned. 'Wait'll you get to the vices.'

'Oh, I have,' said Kay lightly. 'But only with the common sort.'

Hagen started, caught, uncertain.

Outside, sunlight streaked down, sharp and luminous against the swirling grey turbulence of clouds. The buildings loomed massive and dark against the afternoon sky. Shadows lengthened, dusky and blue, down the streets. People thronged by, tweeds and uniforms merging and shifting in the hurrying flow. Traffic honked and blared over the drumming staccato of footfalls. Whistles shrilled. Newsboys hawked the latest headlines about the latest raids on Germany. Hagen stepped to the curb. 'Hey, taxi!'

A rickety black cab swerved up from the side.

'No use all of us going,' Hagen said. He turned, smiling to Joy. 'You two go ahead. I'll check the bags. Okay?'

'Sure,' said Wyatt. He unslung his haversack and gas-mask kit and swung them to Hagen. 'Thanks.'

Kay got into the cab. 'Don't forget now. My apartment, at six.'

'Six it is,' said Joy.

Hagen stepped in and, slamming the door
281

hard, 'The Winston,' he said.

The sallow-faced cabby nodded. 'Righto, guv,' and, grinding his cab into gear, shot rattling off.

Smiling, Wyatt turned to Joy. 'You ready, Joy?'

'Always,' she said and, holding his arm, 'Where shall it be?'

'You name it. Where we were happiest last.'

Joy looked at him, then quietly, 'St. James's Park, then. You loved it there last time. The gardens.'

Wyatt nodded, and, stepping to the curb, signaled a taxi.

* * *

She was silent for most of the ride, looking out the window, preoccupied, it seemed; and Wyatt, holding her hand gently, studied her in silence, noticing she seemed paler, more fragile, than he had remembered her.

Then quietly out of the silence, 'He's safe, you know,' she said.

'Oh? You've had word?'

'Yesterday. My uncle said the crossing was quite uneventful.'

Wyatt pressed her hand. 'Thanks,' he said.

'Tom—can I ask about him now?'

'What?'

She met his look evenly. 'Was he a deserter?'

Wyatt frowned. 'No. Not really. If they had

282

caught him here, he might have been up for AWOL.'

'And if they catch him there?'

Wyatt shrugged. 'It all depends. He was wearing your brother's clothes?'

'I suppose so. I'd left them for him.'

'Then,' said Wyatt, 'if he's caught, it could be the firing squad. He could be considered a spy.'

Joy frowned, disturbed at the thought. 'Was it all that important, then?'

'To him it was.'

'And to you?'

Wyatt only looked at her. 'To help him was the right thing to do, if that's what you're wondering about. The way our lives crossed—it seemed the only purpose.'

'And to you,' she said, 'there's always a purpose, isn't there, Tom? Even in us.'

Wyatt smiled and his hand tightened around hers. 'Especially in us,' he said. 'Especially in us.'

*　　*　　*

The park was cool and green. Wyatt lay in the grass, staring up at the trees. The din of the city's traffic seemed muted and distant. The laughter of children chasing over the green rippled across the air fragrant with April. Strollers wandered the paths and, to the left, the broad, tree-lined boulevard of The Mall.

The Admiralty Arch stood guarding the eastern approach, with Trafalgar Square beyond. To the west, the Victoria Monument rose, sovereign and austere, before the classic majesty of Buckingham Palace.

He turned, watching the swans across the shadowy water beyond. Nearer, the tulips stirred in the wind, banks of them blazing in scarlet and deep orchid, yellow and smoky purple and delicate pink. He glanced at Joy beside him, her knees drawn up, her eyes meeting his, and smiled.

'That was the first real smile today,' said Joy.

'How so?' said Wyatt.

'Relaxed,' said Joy. 'Contented.' She cocked her head at him.

Uneasily Wyatt frowned.

Joy studied him; then, quietly, 'Want to talk about it?'

Wyatt shrugged. 'Toby went down on his first run. Maybe that's it.'

Joy listened, silent.

'I had a premonition he would,' Wyatt said; then, frowning, 'I guess it's always like that. You know that everyone can't make it, but you keep wishing they could. And then—you think: if a crew has to go, you don't want it to be yours. You hope it'll be the other one. You even expect it—' He broke off, shrugging again.

Joy looked at him, her eyes shadowed with thought. She turned away, glancing at the strollers going by. 'And they—the other crew, Tom—they hope the same way, I suppose. That it'd be you, not them?'

Wyatt frowned. 'I guess so.'

'It rather evens out, then,' said Joy gently, 'doesn't it?'

Slowly Wyatt sat up. 'I guess I just wanted to get away,' he said, 'from war—death—'

Joy's eyes darkened. Her face tightened, as if with doubt, uncertainty. She stared at the grass before her; then she looked off, glancing distantly across the Mall, decided. 'But you can't, Tom. Not with me.'

'Why not?'

She looked at him evenly, deeply, a searching moment. 'Because I'm going to die.'

He stared at her, stunned, shaken. 'You? Die?'

Her eyes saddened, watching his. 'It's not so bad really, once you get used to the idea.' She almost smiled. 'I've been used to it for some time now.'

Wyatt felt his body chill. His mind tried to block out the jolt of shock, the jagged, cutting hurt.

Joy shook her head. 'Kay told me not to tell you. She said it would be better that way, but—I could never lie to you, Tom. Or pretend. It wouldn't be fair.'

'But how—?'

She almost smiled again. 'I'm one of the chosen ones,' she said simply. 'I've leukemia.

And now—what's left isn't quite enough for a long-range plan.'

Her breathing was quiet and slow.

'Last week the doctor said there were signs—new signs—of progressive deterioration.' She looked up again, but not at him. 'He gave me this week-end, Tom. He said—he said there should be lovely weather this week-end.'

She waited, her hands tight in her lap.

Wyatt's voice was low. 'You've been hospitalized, then—the change of address?'

She nodded.

'And you never told me?'

'You had your missions. How could I?' And looking at him, 'I had to tell you, face to face, so you could—just go off—if you wanted to. Forget—' Her face was taut and white. Suddenly her voice broke. She turned away quickly, her hand to her lips, her shoulders quivering with sobs. 'I—I'd thought—when first we met—there'd be time—much, much more time. But—Tom, do go away. Now. *Please?*'

Wonderingly Wyatt stared at her, then slowly the wonder altered. His eyes grew strangely deep. 'But I can't,' he said softly. Gently he reached for her and drew her to him.

'No, Tom. Please, not out of pity.'

Tenderly he turned her face to his. Her cheeks were wet. Tears sparkled on her lashes. Her eyes searched his. He smiled and nodded, his voice breathless and trembling. 'I've never

286

been in love before.'

She looked at him. The wind stirred cool between them. Then slowly they kissed, as if for them there were no such thing as time.

CHAPTER TWENTY-FOUR

Hagen stood amazed in the doorway of Kay's apartment. The main room was regal, with a high-arched ceiling, tall windows, thick carpets and a marble fireplace at the far end. The chairs and settees were of satin and damask, the tables and cabinets delicate, set with silver ornaments and figurines. A large, gilt-framed picture dominated above the fireplace—a glowing portrait of a lady in an old fashioned gown, pink, with lace about the shoulders. Sunlight streamed through the high windows, flooding the room, flecking it with silver reflections and porcelain glints: a room of rich, warm ease.

'It's really our town house,' Kay said. 'Or had been before the war. Dad and Mom live out at Essex now, but I stay here—close to quarters.'

Hagen crossed to the portrait. 'An ancestor?'

'The Duchess of Knowlton, 1817. On my mother's side. But she's very like my mother, so I keep her there.' She tossed her hat to a chair.

Hagen turned. 'She's also very like you. The eyes.'

'Thank you, sergeant. But what'll you have? Scotch, gin or bourbon—all black market.'

'Bourbon,' said Hagen.

'You've settled your room, have you?' Kay asked, going to a corner cabinet. 'At the Winston?'

'Yeah. For the whole week-end.' He looked about the place. 'How many rooms have you here?'

'Four,' said Kay. 'For ourselves, I mean. We let out the other part to some Whitehall people.'

'What do you mean "for ourselves"?'

Kay glanced up, caught. 'I *am* sorry. I didn't mean that. It's just—well, Brian and I—this used to be our place. I forget sometimes.'

'He was Joy's brother?'

'Until Dunkirk.'

'How long had you been married?'

Kay brought Hagen his drink, and one for herself. 'Two weeks.'

Hagen raised his glass and drank. 'Some time,' he said, 'since Dunkirk.'

'For some.'

'Don't you—well, miss it?'

Kay looked at him evenly, then smiled wryly. 'Now and then,' she said. 'But I get over it.'

'Don't you—'

'No, sergeant.'

'Call me Hagen.'

'Why not Mitch?'

'I don't like the name.'

'All right then, Hagen—no, I don't.'

'What are you holding out for?'

'The right man again, maybe. Or the right time.'

'You got anything against sex?'

'Not if it's not confused.'

'With what?'

'Oh, with a lot of things. Manhood, for one.' She looked at him curiously. 'I've met so many—Americans mostly—who think sex is manhood. They think if they can—well . . . you know.'

Hagen looked at her oddly. 'Have you ever known a man—a *real* man?'

'I married one,' Kay said crisply. 'A *very* real man.'

Hagen studied his drink. 'I'm sorry.'

Kay smiled. 'You're forgiven. You're young and you're forgiven.'

Hagen felt uneasy, defensive. 'I'm older than you.'

'By a year, I'd say. No more.'

'That makes—'

The door opened and Joy came in alone and, seeing Hagen, stood uncertain, glancing to Kay.

Kay turned to her, and an instant darkness clouded her face, disturbed, waiting.

Joy looked uneasy, then, 'I'm sorry, Kay,

289

but—but there's been a change of plan.'

'You've told him,' Kay said quietly. 'Oh, Joy, I told you not to.'

Joy nodded. 'I told him,' she said simply. 'I told him everything, Kay. And it's all right.' Her face glowed. 'We're going to The Linnet—just the two of us, for the whole week-end.' She came to her, beaming. 'It'll be our time, Kay.'

Kay frowned. 'But—if something goes wrong?'

Joy smiled, knowing. 'There'll be Dr Forest at The Combes. And if necessary, London again. Tom'll see to that.'

'It's risky, Joy. A chance.'

Joy nodded, smiling. 'Yes, Kay. It's a chance.'

Gently Kay put down her glass and, holding her, kissed her cheek. 'Oh, God, be happy, Joy.' Then, 'Where's Tom?'

'He had things to do. I don't know what, but he'll pick me up in an hour or so—here.'

Kay nodded decidedly. 'Then I'll help you pack.'

Hagen frowned, puzzled. 'You mean, it's off? The week-end?'

Kay looked at him. 'Just a change of plan,' she said. 'A slight change of plan—for them.'

Hagen's frown deepened. 'Wyatt's going off? For the week-end?' He looked at Joy, intensely curious.

Embarrassed, she avoided his look and hurried into the bedroom to pack.

The porcelain clock on the mantle chimed as the doorbell rang, and Joy, with a look to Kay, hurried across the room and let Wyatt in.

He smiled and, with a bow, handed her a full bunch of violets. 'With all my love.'

Tenderly Joy took the violets and, looking at him a moment, gently kissed him on the cheek.

Hagen's face was caught with confusion, seeing Wyatt, with gas-mask kit and haversack slung over his shoulder, entering the room. 'I checked out at the Winston,' Wyatt said. 'But I paid for the room, so you're okay.'

He turned to Kay, his voice quiet. 'Thanks, Kay—for looking after her. Maybe there'll be another time—for all of us.'

Kay met his look evenly, then slowly smiled. 'The blessings of the family, Tom. Welcome.' And embracing him, kissed him on the cheek, then whispered, 'God love you, Tom. Be happy.'

Wyatt nodded and, glancing to his watch, 'We've time for the train, Joy. The taxi's still downstairs.' He looked to Hagen. 'Have a good week-end, boy.'

Hagen only stared, curious, and raised his drink. 'You, too,' he said wonderingly.

Kay pinned the violets to Joy's coat, then embraced her.

Quickly Joy turned away and, taking Wyatt's arm, 'Ready, Tom?'

Wyatt nodded and, picking up her bag by the door, left, closing the door behind them.

Hagen turned to Kay and startled to see tears. 'Now, what the hell—?'

Kay looked after the closed door. 'I'm just a sentimentalist, I guess.' She shrugged; then, softly, as if to herself, 'Their courage—it really shines...'

*   *   *

It was eleven thirty by the porcelain chimes when Hagen unlocked Kay's door and brought her gently into the darkened room. The blackout curtains had not yet been drawn, and moonlight flowed through the shadows of the room—a luminous darkness. He pressed her evenly against the door and laid his lips on hers, and slowly his body eased against hers sensually, the length of hers.

She returned the kiss, but pushed him slowly from her.

'Why not?' he asked. 'You said it's been a long time since Dunkirk.'

'Because I'm afraid,' said Kay.

'Afraid?'

'In almost the same way you're afraid.'

Hagen drew back as she slipped by. 'Me? Afraid?'

Kay nodded. 'I'm afraid to love again because I'm afraid of being hurt again. And you're afraid—simply to love, because you don't know what love would mean to you.' And suddenly she laughed, facing him, silvery in the moonlight. 'It would mean freedom for you, if only you knew it. All the freedom and wonder you could handle. And you *could* love, Hagen, if only people—somewhere—meant something to you.'

'But you *do* mean something to me.'

'Do I?' Kay smiled. 'Only for the night, I'm afraid. No, I meant *really* mean something. Oh, I don't know. It's like—lives touch—out of nowhere—you never know when or how— but you're never the same after. A meaning— something you'd never known or seen before— touches you, and you're never quite the same again. Like Joy and Tom. Like—'

'Us?' asked Hagen.

She only looked at him a long moment; then, with still the same smile, she shook her head. 'The way we've met—here and now, as we are—we're just two misfits on a blind date. So what do we do about it?'

Hagen stared, confused.

Kay touched his hand. 'We've had a wonderful evening, Hagen. We could be friends and have fun—like tonight. But that's as far as it would go.' Her eyes met his evenly, lightly. 'I'm probably the first honest woman you've met. I see you as you are. You don't have to prove anything to me. And maybe—in time—if we ever have time—maybe you'd even learn to trust me. But—' she shook her head—'I won't let myself love again—not as you mean it. Not in our time. It takes courage to love in our time—like Joy and Tom. But I haven't got that courage.' She shrugged, her eyes still on his. 'So there it is, Hagen. We'd have to keep it light. Or, if you wish, Piccadilly's full of women. Go to them. Maybe that's better than love, after all.'

Hagen frowned, studying her look. 'What is love to you, then?'

Kay's face shadowed with thought, then quietly, 'When I can feel needed again—to belong fully to one—to share—to lose myself, my fear, in that belonging.' She looked to him. 'And in your way, Hagen, there'd be no meaning to me. You'd give me none. You're on a one-way ticket to nowhere. And you want me to share that ride?' She shook her head again.

'You'd be afraid to love me.'

Kay nodded. 'As you are, yes.'

'Why?' He met her look intently.

'Because, as I said, you're afraid of love. It'd be a conquest, someone to break—because unless you broke me, you'd always feel I could break you. To be safe, you feel you *have* to break the other person. Then you feel strong and all of a piece. So you go through life—breaking people—or trying to break them—except—'

'Except?'

She looked to him wryly. 'I was about to say, except people like Tom.'

'Wyatt!?'

'Or maybe even Starrett.'

'What the hell do you know about Wyatt or Starrett?'

Kay turned wonderingly, then, 'Joy reads his letters to me—parts of them. And I see him—and Starrett, too, the way he writes about him—as the unbreakables. People bigger than themselves—involved with life—linked together—as your crew is—except for you.' She turned again, to face him. 'You stand apart from them. Independent, you call it.'

'Is that what he said? Did he write that?'

Kay shook her head. 'No. Actually he said very little about you, but I don't need letters about you, Hagen. I've had the whole evening with you, and right off I knew your type. You are a type, you know.'

'And you've known them all, I suppose.'

'I said we could be friends.'

Hagen shook his head. 'Friends like you I don't need.'

Kay shrugged. 'If ever you do, you have my phone number.'

'Thanks,' he said. 'But I'd have to be in one hell of a mess before I'd use it!'

And with that, he wheeled and strode slamming out.

CHAPTER TWENTY-FIVE

They went by train to Sevenoaks; then by rickety cab to the hilly hamlet of The Combes, and from its cobbled square, a winding country mile to the cottage at the edge of a road.

'There it is,' said Joy. 'The Linnet.'

Wyatt helped her from the cab, took down the luggage and, paying the driver a tip of a pound, cheered him on his way back to Sevenoaks. The cabbie veered sharply about and shivered off in a dusty rumble, leaving them alone outside the gate.

There was a low stone wall about The Linnet, overhung with ivy, and from the country around, wild odors, soft and sweet in the dusky quiet. A white picket gate opened into a small enclosed garden, kept lovely and fresh in its deep hyacinth smells of early flowers and earthiness.

'Mrs May does the gardening for me,' Joy said. 'She lives next door, but—well, she's a lonely one, and needs to do for people, to keep her busy. I'm afraid I'm her pet project.'

'She knows?'

'Yes. She keeps a close eye out for me, the dear.'

Wyatt smiled. 'Do you think she'll object—to my being here?'

Joy shook her head. 'Quite the contrary. I

daresay she'll love it when she finds out. It'll give her two to do for then. And she's a romantic.'

They crossed the small garden to the door—weatherbeaten, in thick walls, with a heavy thatch roof shading low over the latticed windows.

'If she knew we'd intended coming back, she'd have had a fire going,' said Joy. 'As it is, she keeps the cupboards filled, so there's no wanting there.'

Inside, Joy closed the blackout curtains and lit the central lamp. The room was raftered, simple, with a fireplace at one end, and wing-backed seats. Wyatt turned and noticed that actually there were two rooms—the one he had entered and, to the left, up a step, another room, with another fireplace, a desk, settees and a library wall. 'You read a lot,' he said.

'As much as I can,' Joy said. 'Right now I'm on Emily Dickinson. Do you know her?'

'Some. But not much.'

'She reminds me of you. Quite a lot, in fact.' She turned. 'Do you like the place?'

Wyatt unslung his gas-mask kit and haversack to a nearby chair. 'More than I can say. Joy?'

'Yes.'

'Come here, please.'

She crossed to him slowly, then gently he kissed her. 'Thanks,' he said, 'for bringing me home.'

*　　*　　*

It was after dinner, a small meal, and the dishes done, they went into the garden. The night was cool, sweet-scented, the air star-clear, and they stood close together. Then quietly, 'I was raised a Quaker,' he said.

'I know.'

'But I'm not a very good one. Too much of me in me. And yet I do believe, Joy. In the Light as I feel it. It may not be as the Friends feel it, but I do. And—if I'm wrong—' he shrugged—'then Christ will be my Advocate.'

'Do—you feel this is right, now, Tom?'

Gently he encircled her shoulders, drawing her nearer to him. 'In certain circles of Friends, the young marry each other. They merely declare their love at Meeting, and it's heard and approved. But here—' He turned, dropping his arm, and, reaching into his shirt pocket, he pulled out a tiny box. 'I had a hard time finding the jeweler's. But I did,' he said. 'That's why I was late at Kay's.'

He handed her the box.

Quivering (whether from the cool of the wind or the gentleness of the thought, he never knew), she opened the box. Inside were two plain gold rings.

Looking into her face, he took out one of the rings and held it poised. 'Here, in the presence of—our love, I, Thomas Benton Wyatt, do profess my love for thee, Joyce—' He looked to her.

'Joyce Anne,' she whispered.

'Joyce Anne Cheyne. So I, Thomas Benton Wyatt, do take thee, Joyce Anne Cheyne to be my wife, promising through divine assistance to be unto thee a faithful and affectionate husband until Death shall separate us.' He slipped the ring onto her finger.

'And I, Joyce Anne Cheyne, do take thee, Thomas Benton Wyatt, to be my husband—'

'Promising through divine assistance—'

'Promising through divine assistance—'

'To be unto thee a faithful and affectionate wife—'

'To be unto thee a faithful and affectionate wife—'

'Until—until—'

'Until Death shall separate us,' she concluded and slipped the ring onto his finger.

There was silence in the garden. Then, 'Oh, Tom—'

'I do love thee, my Joy.'

'And I thee, my love.'

PART SEVEN

'THAT SUCH HAVE LIVED'
May 9–28, 1944

CHAPTER TWENTY-SIX

Leisurely Starrett drove the commandeered jeep down the perimeter track toward *The Lady*'s revetment, his jacket unzipped, open to the early May warmth. Ordinarily only he took up *The Lady*; and when he did, the raid would be, nine times out of ten, a Deep Penetration run. In fact, more and more lately, his crew had not gone on the lighter raids over France. And that, too, had become part of their reputation—as the DP crew; and as much a part of *The Lady* herself as the superstition that she was, somehow, a charmed ship, that she always came back.

But today's run had been a late, short-range one—Juvincourt, France—and more as a token of luck than as a chance assignment (their own ship, *The Queen O'Reno*, having gone down over Germany when Aronson had been on leave), Aronson and O'Hara had taken up *The Lady* on their final, thirtieth mission—the end of all these months of agony, suspense and fear. When they landed, it would be the sudden sunburst moment of release—the open passport to all the tomorrows to come. And Starrett had wanted to be there, to share it with them, to be the first to congratulate them.

The jeep moved easily, veering through the

sunny calm of the late afternoon, passing bomber after grounded bomber; for today's raid had been only a minor one. If it had been a major one, as in the month past—

Starrett frowned.

April had been a rugged month for *The Lady*. Since Easter Week—a month ago—all their runs but one had been Deep Penetrations: Poznan, Poland, eleven hours; Augsburg, nine; Lippstadt, seven; Friedrichshafen, ten. And the men were beginning to show it. The tensions of the raids were grinding tempers to a fine, sharp edge, honed all the finer by the latest communiqué, that all tours of duty consisted of, no longer twenty-five, but of thirty missions over enemy-occupied territory—which still meant the whole of Europe, Hitler's *Festung Europa*, from Russia to the Channel.

So far *The Lady* had put in eighteen missions. Now it meant twelve more to go— five beyond their expected tour. It seemed, too, that the men, not only of *The Lady* but of the other crews as well, had braced themselves for twenty-five raids, as if they could take twenty-five without snapping. But now it meant five more chances to press their luck, to stretch it with shortening odds—five more gambles against Fate, any one of which could be the breaking point—the emotional point of no return to courage or normalcy. Already he had seen it happen—to too many.

He idled the jeep to let a crippled bomber

taxi across to her revetment; then, at a signal from the ground chief, and with a wave, he geared in again and continued his way.

True, the air war was now in its declining phases. The air part of the war seemed nearly over; time now for the ground offensives—the invasion—soon to begin. The fierce, turbulent air battles of Schweinfurt, Regensburg, the early Berlins were decreasing. And so far as their objective had been concerned, they had cracked the Luftwaffe and severed the pride of the Germans who had shouted, 'Tomorrow, the world!'

But while the raids, especially the Deep Penetration raids, were still intense and costly, with the Germans hurtling all they desperately could against any and all onslaughts, the balance of Chance had swung to the Allies' favor; and while there was still no such thing as a 'milk run,' the American losses had been down and the victory in the air was becoming, raid by driving raid, more assured—for the price.

And the price, as Starrett saw it, was in terms of his own men.

Cronin, Swacey and Kramer were holding together beautifully, and Golden—the easy, resilient kind. But Nelson was getting edgy. Natural enough, of course. He had never been a father before, and was sweating out seeing his son. Still, he hadn't gone to London last month to unwind.

And Wyatt... Still the puzzler, the loner. All the more so since the Easter pass. Something had happened then to make him even more remote, more one with himself.

But as for Hagen—

Starrett's frown deepened, his hand tightening on the wheel.

Something had happened to Hagen, too, since the last London pass. Something was smoldering inside him. His cocksureness wasn't so spontaneous anymore. He was more withdrawn, sulky and, when stirred, more aggressive, belligerent—as if it was now he, not Wyatt, who had a fight fuming inside him. One day, one way or another, he would explode.

Starrett shook his head and veered wide on a perimeter turning. He would have to sweat Hagen out, just as he was still sweating out Kirby and Gillis. Between them there was still that armed, guarded truce, the undercurrent conflict; but the threat of the bounce had held them in check. There hadn't been any further outbursts. Yet they, too, were taut.

If only their pride in *The Lady*, the crew, could hold them in line for twelve missions more. Yet Hagen—that was another matter. Hagen still had no pride in anything but himself. Or—suddenly Starrett wondered—or *did* Hagen have that now? Was that what had happened in London? Had Hagen lost that pride in himself? If so, how?

Starrett sighed and settled back, wondering

darkly if anyone ever really knew anyone in this world. Here he was, skipper of a crew—yet what did he really know of them? The old question again. And all he could do was guess. And yet their lives—all of them—were inextricably bound together in *The Lady*.

As for himself, he had to admit now he felt tighter than usual, more alert, quicker to sense things (sometimes things that weren't even there). But when he got wound up, there was always Aronson to talk with, or a letter to Rita.

Still—and he had faced it weeks before—the men were tightening. They needed a rest. Yet that had been precisely where he had had to block them—the most difficult personal decision he had so far made. He had deliberately refused the Old Man's suggestion that *The Lady* take flak leave, and had decided himself to take the crew the full limit of their tour without any let-up, to keep them intact.

Starrett slowed down the jeep to let a gas truck pull out from a revetment and circle back toward the line. Then, pressing the gas, he started up again.

About the flak leave there had been many factors involved, not the least of which, he knew, had been his pride. He had seen too often how after flak leave a crew would crumble—fatally. They got out of gear, or they lost that tightness, the momentum—maybe even the nerve—that had keyed them to combat demands. To some it gave too much time to think, to brood. To others it renewed a sense of self too sharp for the good of an interdependent unit like a crew. And to others it merely prolonged the tensing agony of sweating out a full tour duration; so that the days, instead of being of rest and recuperation, were only ones of more tensing strain.

He had also seen it in Aronson's crew, or what had been left of it. In fact, it had been Aronson himself who had urged Starrett not to take the leave, not while he still had his full crew intact. Four of them—the only four left of the original Aronson ten—had gone on leave; and after the leave, only he and O'Hara were in shape for their final missions. The other two, while at the rest home, had simply cracked. One had shot himself, a suicide.

Also, Starrett had had to consider the Old Man's offer to himself and to Kramer as navigator. *The Lady* was now the oldest intact crew on the field, and they, two among the most experienced officers. The Old Man had offered each—after flak leave—a captaincy, to take over lead-ship positions. Starrett himself had refused on the instant, and Kramer had followed his lead.

It was his duty, Starrett had said, to bring *The Lady* through as a crew. He had insisted on that. True, he could be ordered to other duty, but he knew the Old Man had never considered that an honorable tactic. The Old Man had understood Starrett. He had, however, thought that after flak leave—

'There'll be no flak leave, sir,' Starrett had said firmly. 'We'll ride through, as far as we can, as a crew, sir.'

And that had been the decision. He himself had decided that for *The Lady* as their skipper, and his decision was both determined and definite. They would ride through as a crew; and nothing, if he could help it, would jeopardize that unity. That was his duty—and his pride. Their luck was holding, and Fate seemed on their side. He would trust to that Fate—and to that one central conviction of duty: to keep the crew together and to bring them through—as far as he could.

The only question now was, Could they go the limit? Could he—and *The Lady*—hold them together all the way?

The Lady!

Quickly Starrett glanced to his watch. It was nearly three thirty. He stepped on the gas.

* * *

He sat on the hood of the jeep, waiting, Greene beside him, when—the first of the bombers roaring in from beyond the eastern hills—Greene stood suddenly tensed, watching, just over the height of the far trees, a silver bomber uncertainly, erratically veering and dipping recklessly toward the base.

Starrett leaped to his feet.

309

Two flares shot skyward, spiraling smoke.

'It's *The Lady*, sir—she's headed toward the emergency strip!'

Swiftly Starrett spun, leaped into the jeep, with Greene vaulting in beside him. He started up, shifted into grinding gear and, jerking the vehicle about, sped careening across the field to the emergency strip.

His foot jammed to the floor. He heard the screeching of tires as he rounded the perimeter track and shot, angling, down a link runway toward the strip. Already he could hear the wailing sirens of the crash-crew trucks and the ambulances, and from the rise, saw them, far ahead, plunging for the strip from the line side, almost riding under the lowering *Lady*.

She was yawing in low, left wing high; then slowly swung up on the right, with full flaps lowered, shivering and veering for balance as she swept in for touchdown. Suddenly there was a high screeching of brakes, a jolting bounce, up—then down again, jarring—and the shrilling, braking to a shaky stop.

'She made it, sir!' Greene yelled.

Starrett's hands clenched the wheel as he sped down the linkway, veered, and in the emergency strip ahead saw *The Lady* as the ambulances and crash crews swung around her.

Swiftly he slammed on the brakes and, stalling the engine, jumped from the jeep.

Already he saw some of the crewmen

outside, clustered under the tail, one of the men throwing up violently. He swung into the side hatch and hurried through the waist. At the radio room he saw Reed, the new engineer, sitting at the radio table, his face streaked with dirt and tears, his coveralls smeared with blood. He glanced ahead, through the bomb bays, and saw two medics rolling up a body in a blanket.

'Who?' said Starrett.

'Aronson,' said Reed. 'He got it in the neck, sir. Flak. It came right through the flight-deck panel. O'Hara—O'Hara tried to hold the windpipe—' Reed's face cracked with agony. 'Jesus, sir—O'Hara—he stuck his hand right into the throat to hold it together—but he couldn't. The blood squirted all over him. We—we had to drag him away... We got Aronson out of the seat—and O'Hara— we—he and I—we brought her in. Only—oh, Christ, sir—O'Hara—'

Starrett looked up as the two medics made their way back through the bomb bays, maneuvering over the narrow catwalk with the blanket bundle that was Aronson bumping and knocking between the bomb racks. They passed Starrett, sober-faced.

Starrett eased back to let them pass and stared, tight-throated, steeled, down at the cumbersome load, lumpy and bulging, shapeless, with a mass of blood starting to ooze through.

'You'd better see to O'Hara, sir,' said the second medic. 'We'll be back with the needle soon's we can.'

Starrett turned. 'Reed, go with them now.' It was an order.

Reed nodded and, rising heavily, wiping his face on his sleeve, followed.

Starrett swung through the radio door onto the catwalk and made his way to the flight deck. Blood glistened everywhere, sticky now, darkening, congealing.

He looked to O'Hara—and his face froze. *O my Jesus!*

O'Hara was staring straight ahead, seeing nothing. His coveralls were soaked with blood, and his face and hands. His hands gripped the controls, motionless.

'O'Hara?' He reached to touch him, then drew back. He sat in the pilot's seat—suddenly aware he was sitting in a pool of blood. He pulled his hand away instinctively from the bloodied back. 'O'Hara?'

O'Hara nodded, hearing. 'We'll make it, Pappy,' he said. 'We'll make it.'

Starrett felt his eyes burn with tears, his throat constrict, but he showed nothing. 'You've already made it, boy. You've already made it.'

'—and when we land,' he said, 'just think, Pappy—when we land, it'll be all over. For both of us. All over...'

'But it *is* all over, O'Hara. You *have* landed.'

312

'I'll take it from here, Pappy. You rest—I'll take her in.' He smiled his old wry smile. 'Starrett'll kill us if we don't bring 'er back. Remember—'

'O'Hara—'

'Lower flaps.'

The second medic came back, a long needle poised in a vial. 'Lieutenant O'Hara—'

'I said, lower flaps!' O'Hara yelled. 'For Christ's sake, lower flaps!'

'Give me your arm, sir.'

O'Hara snapped him off. 'Get your goddam hands away. Give me flaps!'

The medic appealed to Starrett. 'Please, sir, his arm—'

Starrett looked to O'Hara; then with a nod to the medic, 'Flaps lowered,' he said evenly. 'Steady throttle, O'Hara.'

O'Hara's arm reached out for the throttles. Starrett grabbed it tightly and tore back the sleeve. O'Hara struggled. 'God-dammit, you sonofabitch! We'll crash!'

The medic swiftly inserted the needle.

'Jesus Christ!' yelled O'Hara.

The medic pulled away. 'Easy. Easy, sir.'

'Flaps down,' said Starrett. 'Landing speed, one-twenty.'

O'Hara nodded. 'Don't worry, Pappy. Don't worry. We got all the luck in the world.'

Starrett waited, his hands sticky on the controls; then slowly O'Hara started to slump forward.

313

The medic called behind him. 'Grearson, give me a hand!'

The first medic returned, and together they hoisted O'Hara out of his seat, from the flight deck, into the bomb bays and out of *The Lady*.

Taut, Starrett sat in the pilot's seat. Blood besmattered everything he saw. He stared at the lower instrument panel—the jagged edges where the flak had burst through. From a memory—of years and years ago—he heard Greene's voice ... *They didn't armor the flight deck, sir.*

I know. She's heavy enough.

But, shit, sir. That leaves you wide open.

She's heavy enough...

So that had been his decision, too. If it hadn't been for that, if he had listened to Greene, Aronson would have made it. But he hadn't made it. Because of one simple decision...

Wearily Starrett held his head in his hands. How much was he responsible for the deaths of this war? Deaths like this, for all the deaths, because of his decisions? How much would he bear himself—because of what he did, even innocently? And the flak leave, too—what would be the results of that decision? Had it been the right one, all things considered? Would he ever know—ever? Or would always—always would he see—the blood-spattered cockpit—and the lumpy, shapeless, bloodied blanket—to make him wonder?

He felt his throat hurting, tightening again. He shook his head, and rubbed his eyes. Suddenly he saw it—in the dark, sticky, congealing pool at his feet—the glitter of the blood-covered harmonica: Clementine.

CHAPTER TWENTY-SEVEN

Their luck was still holding, in spite of Aronson's death in *The Lady* three weeks ago and O'Hara's crack-up. But the raids now had been steadily DPs: Brux, Czechoslovakia; Osnabruck; twice more to Berlin; and today Strasbourg, an eight-hour run the whole way across France—with Nelson, his ears frost-bitten, in agony half the way back.

On landing they had immediately shipped him to the Infirmary. Now, toward nine thirty, since the others of the crew had already been in the ward, Hagen had made his visit alone, not for any personal affection, not even because he was curious, but simply for somewhere to go, something to do. Actually, they had little to say to each other, so after the usual 'See you later, man,' Hagen had left. Nelson had seemed fit, and the reports had been good: in two or three days he would be back to flying again. Still—

The stars were sharp white, the night clear and warm, as Hagen stood on the Infirmary steps, putting on his cap. Grimly he looked up and, noting the brittle clarity, knew tomorrow would bring another raid and, with their luck, another DP. Tensely he shoved his hands into his pockets and, sensing his way in the blackout, started down the stairs and along the path to the main road.

He shuddered, chilled with a strange, dark disturbance, all the stranger when he realized it had nothing to do with Nelson. He had had it earlier when, passing on to Nelson's ward, he had glimpsed O'Hara through the glass-and-mesh panel of the psychiatric room—just sitting in a chair by half-light, staring at his hands like a man not quite dead. They had had to fight to get his blood-soaked coveralls from him. But he was at least a man at rest now, and well out of it. A man without feelings—

Feelings!

Swiftly Hagen quickened his pace. Again he felt the anger, the blind turmoil driving inside him, whirling him into a restless, desperate need to—run. Tensely he felt the cold chill of perspiration on his face. And for the first time in his life he knew he was afraid.

Christ! It wasn't the war. That he had taken in his stride. That was his kind of fighting. Not this—these feelings crashing through him he couldn't understand, tearing at him, driving him to strike out desperately, violently—at what? Why?

Tightly he clenched his fists. Never before had he felt this way, fighting shadows

316

threatening, overwhelming him—almost like those of long ago, of the trap closing in.

Shadows ... Feelings ... Ideas he didn't know what to do with, that didn't make sense ... Memories...

He shook his head. But the memories came back ... of a high-ceilinged room shadowy with moonlight, of a gentle, lovely girl silvery, with a quiet voice in the darkness.

It always came back to Kay.

Christ—he had left her that night and had picked up the first chippie he could find at Piccadilly. They had fucked the whole night, desperately, furiously; and in the morning he had paid her off, and she had left with a grinning 'Ta-ta, Duckie.' And all he could think of was that it was over—and that it had had no meaning. He was alone again. Alone as he had always been; only, this time there was an emptiness inside him, an aching and a longing for something more...

You're on a one-way ticket to nowhere... And you want me to share that ride?

Why the hell not? All the others had. Always they had given themselves to him without question. What had he given to them? He frowned, suddenly puzzled. Himself, wasn't it? Sex...

I've met so many ... who think sex is manhood.

Well, wasn't it? What more was there? And yet—the way she had looked when Wyatt and

317

Joy had left. It was sex with them, too, wasn't it? Just that. Nothing different, nothing that he could see. Still—the look, the tears...

Their courage ... it really shines...

What had been the difference there?

Swiftly the anger pressed in on him again. He could feel the sinews in his arms tighten. And again the feeling that life was going on, a deep, rich, wonderful life he had never known—something he wanted, something he needed to find! It was going on, but without him; and he couldn't reach out to it. He couldn't find it. He was missing out on something, something vital and shining maybe—and time was running out. *He had to find it before it was too late!* But where? How?

Quickly he shook his head again and took in a slow, deep, quieting breath. No. No, the trouble was with her, not him. She was the unliving one. She had said so herself. She was afraid to love. She was afraid...

... the way you are because you don't know what love would mean to you. It would be freedom...

What *was* love to him? His mouth grew tight. What was love to him? And he had no answer. And how would it free him? For what?

What is love to you? he had asked.

When I can feel needed again—to belong fully to one ... to lose myself, my fear, in that belonging.

But he didn't *want* to lose himself—in
318

anyone or anything. He was all he had, all he was sure of. Hagen, and him alone. As it had always been. Even on the crew.

You stand apart from them—independent, you call it. But lives touch—out of nowhere—you never know when or how, but you're never the same after...

as their lives had touched, his and hers; and ever since, his life had been one seething tearing apart inside. Nothing seemed centered anymore, the way it used to be, the way he had seen things. He had been thrown off balance—by a dame he had seen just once.

A meaning—something you'd never known or seen before—touches you, and you're never quite the same again. Like Joy and Tom.

Hagen's face tautened. Wyatt again, and yet even that hadn't lasted. Even that had busted up, and in just a few weeks, at that. He remembered—about three weeks ago now, about the time Aronson had died—Wyatt had received just a book in the mails from Joy—an old, worn book, poems by Emily Dickinson. He had seen it lying on Wyatt's bunk, with the blue book-marker in it, but—He frowned, remembering, remembering the way, without a word, Wyatt had taken off, suddenly, as soon as he had opened it. No letter. Nothing. Just the book. And never another letter after that, from either him or her. That had been the end of it for them.

He hadn't seen Wyatt for the rest of that day,

nor all that night. Then late, about eleven, just as he was coming in from one of his night walks, he had looked off across the fields. There had been a bright moon that night, a bomber's moon, and he watched as Wyatt came slowly across the moonlit meadows—from his spot beyond the wall. He moved slowly among the shadows, in a halting, broken way—as if he couldn't see too clearly. They passed each other without a word; in silence and the dark they went into the Shack.

Three days later, noting Wyatt had received no letters, he had gone up to Wyatt. 'How come no letters? You and Joy bust up?'

Wyatt had been reading the poems. He only looked at him, a still, deep look. 'We have an understanding,' he said. And that had been all he had said.

So Kay had been wrong about them, and wrong about love, and about meaning.

If only people meant something to you...

Like Bellows and Kiki! He shook his head. No. She had been wrong, whatever she thought. And he had been right to stand apart. And yet—oh, Christ—

That feeling that life was going on, somewhere, just beyond him—all around, just beyond him—and he couldn't touch it! Everywhere he turned, there was a sense of life he couldn't see. He could almost feel it. But it was beyond him. He was missing out. Jesus! What if he were missing out on life itself—and it was going by, day by day? And time passing. Time. He needed time. But there was none, not this way, not on Starrett's crew.

Starrett!

Every day now the missions were deeper, longer, worse, it seemed. Their odds were cutting. They had flown twenty-three raids so far and he was tired. If only they had taken their break. Gotten their rest. Taken that flak leave.

But no! Jesus H. Starrett himself had told them that was out. No flak leave. They'd ride it through as a crew.

Crew! That's all he ever thought about. Him and his crew. Keeping them together, no matter the cost. He'd bring them through, all right, piece by piece if he had to. It wouldn't do for Christ Starrett to fail now.

And that crew—they followed him. They went along without a word, whatever he said. To them he was the Lord God Almighty, skipper now of the oldest crew on the base— the DP crew—*Starrett's Crew*, as if it meant something.

And all the time, life was going on and time was running out on them—all because of Starrett. They couldn't see, as *he* did, that they didn't mean a damn thing to Starrett, that all Starrett really cared about, really *used* them for, was his own pride and power—his record. The pride and the glory of the Lord God Starrett, the crew.

321

Well, fuck the crew!

*   *   *

Angrily Hagen swung open the door of the Shack. The other crew had gone up on a night-practice flight, so only *The Lady* was there, with Bayer as usual, and Wiggam in his sack. They turned as he came in, and nodded. Swacey and Cronin were at their cards. Wyatt was reading, and Golden. Bayer was writing a letter.

'Mission tomorrow,' Cronin said. 'Early call.'

'So? What am I supposed to do? Shit green?'

Cronin frowned up; then, 'Something bugging you, Hagen?'

'Sure,' snapped Hagen. 'All you ass-holes.'

Swacey lowered his cards and turned. 'Better quiet down, man. We'uns understand English.'

'The fuck you do!' muttered Hagen and jerked off his jacket.

'The flak getting to you?' Swacey asked coldly. 'I mean, the way you been acting lately—'

'No. Not the flak. Just you guys—you and Starrett.'

Cronin shook his head. 'Still on that flak-leave stuff?' He looked at Hagen as Hagen started to undress. 'Starrett was right, there, Hagen. It's no guarantee we'll get through, no matter how you look at it. But look at what happened to the *Miss Fire* and Aronson's bunch. We have a better chance as a crew. We operate better that way. We all know each other—how we act, and react. It's just that much safer—to stay together and ride it out. If we'd gone on flak leave, we might have busted up.'

'Starrett gave up a captaincy for it,' Swacey said. 'So did Kramer.'

'Bullshit!' said Hagen.

Cronin rose, then quietly, 'Do you want out?' he asked.

Hagen turned, surprised.

'Hagen, don't.' It was Wyatt coming forward. 'Don't break up the crew. Not this way. The spirit's good—'

'Spirit!' Hagen laughed suddenly, a short whip-snap of a laugh. 'Look who's talking about spirit!' And fronting Wyatt directly, 'You little sonofabitch—you get your piece of ass just like the rest of us, and then you talk about *spirit*. You're lucky to know what hole to put it in.'

Swacey got to his feet, between Hagen and Wyatt.

Wyatt eased Swacey back.

'Like I said,' said Cronin quietly, 'do you want out?'

Silence.

Hagen looked at them uneasily, the tension mounting within.

'They're calling your bluff,' said Wiggam,

323

smiling from his bunk.

Hagen whirled. His eyes met Wiggam's and in that instant all the fury, the desperate, driving rage to strike out burst through. With a cry of utter disgust at what he saw in Wiggam, Hagen lunged for him and, grabbing him by his thick neck, pulled him from the bunk and started slamming and back-handing him across the head.

Shouting and crying, startled, Wiggam fought fiercely to ward off the blows as viciously Hagen swung him bodily about and hurtled him at the rushing Cronin and Swacey. Then, in a frenzy, Hagen grabbed up the upper deck of the bunk and snapped it free and, kicking open the door, shoved and hurled the bunk—mattress, pillow, blankets, all—out into the night; then, swinging back, picked up Wiggam's footlocker and, lifting it with all his strength, tossed it into the darkness.

'Get the fuck out and stay out!' yelled Hagen. He grabbed the cringing Wiggam and, with a swift, hard kick, shot him headlong into the night and slammed the door.

He was sweating, panting, exhausted when he turned again and looked over the crew, feeling spent but strangely released and quieted inside. 'Now—is there anyone else?' he panted. 'Because if there is—' He waited.

The crew turned away. Anything more now, at this point, would be useless. They started getting ready for the night, in silence.

It was almost midnight by his watch when Hagen, smoking, thinking, had calmed down enough to go back over the night's explosion. He felt better now, quiet, and in a way at rest. Then slowly, as he thought about it, it dawned on him why he had so viciously, so mercilessly turned on Wiggam. No: not really on Wiggam himself, but on all that Wiggam had seemed in that instant to stand for, with his ferret-cold eyes, his fat sense of self, his sloven indifference to all around him. And suddenly—with a start—Hagen realized that in Wiggam, in that instant, he had really seen himself.

*　　　*　　　*

The chill pre-dawn darkness was greying, the first flickering glints catching on *The Silver Lady*, as Hagen, his waist gun checked and secured, swung out the side hatch and into the way of a strange gunner, bulky and slow-moving, coming out from the semi-darkness, from under the right wing, his flight bag over his shoulder.

'Is this Starrett's ship?'

'Yeah,' said Hagen. 'Why?'

The gunner shifted his bag. 'I'm your new waist gunner,' he said. 'From the Pool.' He looked *The Lady* over, silent; then, 'Where are the guns?'

Hagen pointed to the armament tent. 'Left lower rack.'

The gunner nodded, hefted his bag and tossed it in through the side hatch; then turned toward the tent. 'By the way,' he said, 'the name's Cable.' He held out his hand mechanically.

'Hagen,' said Hagen, and shook hands.

The gunner looked at *The Lady* again. 'Sure hope she can fly,' he muttered. 'How many runs?'

'Twenty-three so far,' said Hagen. 'And you?'

'Four,' said Cable, and went to the tent, sulkily.

*   *   *

It was grey light now, and the morning tensed with waiting. The props had been pulled through, and all was in readiness but for Starrett.

Anxiously Kirby paced the revetment, looking off disturbed toward Operations, glancing to his watch, then off to the line. Starrett had never been this late, this near to takeoff.

Gillis and Kramer were under the nose, checking the nose turret. Cronin, Swacey and Golden were sitting and lying about, talking in low tones beyond Hagen's hearing. Wyatt was just now swinging his turret aft, readying it for takeoff. The new gunner, Cable, sat sullenly by himself, picking absently at the grass. Hagen

326

stood by the tail wing watching, apart and alone.

Today, Sunday the twenty-eighth, the target was another DP, Magdeburg, a nine-hour run at best, straight to the middle of the Northern Reich. The tension since target disclosure at briefing had only intensified in the waiting.

Suddenly, careening down the perimeter track, a jeep veered squealing in before *The Lady*, and Starrett, leaping out, waved the driver on.

Kirby grinned. 'Jesus, man, you almost missed this one.'

But Starrett, with only a nod to Kirby, swept by him, his face set with anger, and ducking under the wing, 'Hagen!'

The crew turned and watched wonderingly as Hagen straightened. 'Yes, sir.'

Starrett's voice was sharp. 'What the hell happened last night?'

Hagen's eyes swept the watching crew. 'What did they tell you happened?'

'Nothing,' snapped Starrett. 'But I've just had one hell of a time with Sergeant Finch. He said you nearly killed a Sergeant Wiggam.'

'He had it coming—'

'That's not the point!' Starrett cut in. 'The point is, he wanted you up for court-martial— for criminal assault.'

'That sonofabitch Wiggam! When's the court-martial?'

'There's not going to be any,' Starrett said.

'I've just seen them both.' He paused, then, 'I apologized for you. I told them how rough the missions have been and how—'

'You apologized for me?'

Starrett's eyes narrowed. 'Why not?'

Hagen shook his head, the anger coming through his voice. 'The Lord God Starrett. He speaks and the world is made whole.' He tensed, aware of the eyes of the crew on him. 'I don't need your apologies,' he said brittly. 'I don't need anything from you, or from anyone else. I stand on my own two feet.'

Starrett's look quickened; then tightly, 'They would have busted you—grounded you—'

'And that would have really busted up the crew,' said Hagen. 'That's what you thought about.'

Starrett eyed him searchingly. 'That's right, Hagen. That is what I thought about—the crew.' Then with weighed words, 'And Hagen thinks only of Hagen—still.'

Hagen nodded. 'You're goddam right I do, because when I'm dead—and the way you're pushing, we're bound to be—I'm dead forever. But so long as I'm alive, I'm Hagen. I do what I want. And nothing else counts.'

'Not even the crew,' said Starrett. 'Not even now—after all this time.'

'It's your crew,' said Hagen coldly. 'Not mine.'

'It's every man's—'

'Bullshit,' said Hagen.

Starrett took this in silence; then, with a deep breath of decision, 'Get your things, Hagen.'

'There are the flares!' yelled Kirby. 'Ready for takeoff!'

Starrett met Hagen's look. 'After this run,' he said softly, 'you're off *The Lady*.'

'I'm due for flak leave, sir.' It was a demand.

Starrett looked back at him. 'Maybe we all are.'

*   *   *

Gently *The Lady* teetered into position, number three in the lead element, paused, balancing for flight; then, the signal given, the thunderous gunning of the engines, the forceful, even thrust forward; the swift hurtling down the runway, the ground blurring; and the slow rising, the low, clean skimming of air beyond the runway, beyond the edge of trees, beyond the squares of meadows, and into the new sky.

Hagen breathed more freely as he always had on cleared takeoff and turned, smiling, to signal. But Nelson wasn't there. The stooped, lanky Nelson, sweating out the takeoff from his position, had always nodded and signaled back. But today as Hagen turned, the smile went from his face.

Cable was strapping on his flak vest, then picked up the spare. 'Yours?' he asked.

329

Hagen shook his head. 'His.' He thumbed toward Wyatt. 'He never uses it. Too bulky.'

Cable nodded and spread it on the floor beneath him; then, leaning on his gun, looked out the waist gate without expression or response.

Hagen turned back and looked out, seeing nothing sharply, but realizing slowly that there would never be a Nelson to signal to now, to share the relief of takeoff with; that this was his last trip with *The Lady*; and that from now on he, too, would be, like Cable, an extra gunner, a stranger to whatever crew he flew on, with nothing shared.

And suddenly, from the long-ago past, he remembered Ralegh, the old gunner he had met at the Pool those days before *The Lady*...

It's like fighting the whole fuckin' war alone...

'Hagen!' It was a kick of sound. The sharpness of the intercom crackled in sparks, startling him. 'Yes, sir!'

'The tail wheel!' snapped Kirby.

Hagen wheeled and checked. 'Tail wheel up and locked, sir.'

'Roger.' The intercom cut.

Hagen glanced to Wyatt, not resting as usual, curled about the walk, but sitting up, looking at him, straight and intently.

Hagen turned away, his back to Wyatt, and started out as *The Lady* banked slowly, rising into her element position.

*   *   *

The intercom sparked again. 'Ten thousand feet. Go on oxygen. Over.'

Hagen turned to Wyatt and, meeting his even look without expression, signaled to the turret.

Wyatt nodded, got to his knees and, engaging the hand crank, started to roll his turret into position. The wind whipped off his knit cap and blew his hair about. Wyatt ignored it as the hatch rolled into view.

Briskly the wind blew Wyatt's knit cap toward Hagen. He reached down and, picking it up, crossed over to Wyatt's flight bag and stuffed it in. The wind from the turret well flapped against his body. They exchanged looks; then Wyatt nodded thanks as, holding the brake, he opened the hatch, reached in against the whipping wind and secured the turret in position.

He then reached for his helmet and oxygen mask, snapped them on; then—as always—braced himself a moment at the crossbar, tested the seat, then descended, stooped forward and, reaching above him, pulled the curved iron door shut behind him with a loud clank.

Like a trap closing, thought Hagen. He frowned, disturbed, uneasy, and, seeing the latches lock into place, crossed back and plugged into intercom and oxygen again. For the first time he felt the tightness, the closeness, the trap of Wyatt's position. For that's what it was, wasn't it? What it had always been right along, all these missions: nothing more than an iron trap. One that Wyatt entered knowingly, deliberately, every flight. Why? Why, with those odds? Because, as he had said, it was his duty, his part of the crew.

But all the same, a trap.

He glanced across to Cable. Cable, his oxygen mask on, was leaning on his gun, looking over the gathering formations.

Slowly, whining, the turret started to revolve. Hagen watched the hatch slide below the ship line and out of sight.

'Ball turret to skipper. In position, sir. Over.'

'Roger.'

Hagen's face tightened, remembering that first flight—his own voice to Nelson...

Supposing he gets stuck or the turret jams—then what?... So it's two of us then... Right?

And Nelson's strange, even look. *Wrong... It'd be three of us then...*

Hagen looked again to Cable. Cable turned, shrugged and glanced away again.

Hagen frowned. An iciness beyond wind or thinning air suddenly chilled his blood.

*　　　*　　　*

Time and the mission droned on—beyond the North Sea, over the Zuider Zee and beyond the

Netherlands, straight into Germany. So far the mission was routine—the test-firing of guns over the North Sea, the checking in of positions, the icy lashing of the wind through the open waist gates; the burning clarity of scanning pure sky; the blue and the glinting of the sunlight from *The Lady* stinging the eyes; the tension of the still waiting for the sharp and sudden attacks; the flak bursting—the sudden, silent shocks of black cloud, the buffeting of the shock waves, the side-sliding of *The Lady* easing in evasive action; and the sight of the bombers—more and more of them silver now—wing on wing of them, in high box formation forging defiant through sunlit time.

*   *   *

'Fighters,' Swacey called in. 'Seven o'clock high.'

Hagen turned to Cable and caught a sudden startled look.

'Ours?' asked Hagen.

'They're hitting the high group,' said Swacey. 'Messerschmitts, 109s.'

A gun blasted, shocking thunderously behind Hagen. He whirled. Cable's hands were tight, rigid to his gun, his bursts long, the links spraying into the hold.

'Cut it!' yelled Swacey. 'They're out of our range!'

'Cable!' shouted Hagen.

The gunner stopped, his eyes fixed on the high group. 'Jesus, look!'

'One ship in high group—split,' said Swacey; then slowly, 'Six chutes, Kramer.'

'Ball to Hagen. Watch it. Low at four, coming in high. Six, in formation.'

Hagen sighted them. 'Got it, man.' He started to track the rising ME-109s. They were beyond range, but bearing in for the group.

'Looks like we're it,' said Swacey. 'Ready, Hagen?'

'Ready,' Hagen said. 'Wyatt?'

'Ready.'

'They're flying like they're new 'uns,' Swacey said. 'By the book.'

'Yeah,' said Cronin. '*Mein Cunt.*'

Swiftly the ball-turret guns started, the twin fifties hammering as the fighters rose spiraling in toward the lead group.

The Lady's guns thundered. Hagen's whole body swayed in a low, rhythmic arc as he tracked one of the fighters rising in and high.

Suddenly—a burst of orange flame and flung debris—

'Got him!' shouted Hagen.

'Watch it!' called Swacey. 'They're splitting up. Nelson—on your side.'

'Cable!' snapped Hagen. 'That's you—your side. Watch it.'

'He's barrel-assing through!' yelled Swacey.

Behind him, Hagen heard Cable's gun, the staccato roar rising, too long, too—He spun, saw—Shocked, he yanked Cable away. 'Cut your fire!'

The ME hurled past, between *The Lady* and *The Little Lass*.

'You nearly got the Fort!' cried Hagen.

Cable only looked at him, bewildered, his gun swinging loose on its mount.

* * *

'Bombardier to crew. On IP. Target ahead.'

'Christ, look at that flak,' muttered Kramer.

Hagen peered out. Between them and target, the air was smoky with black-bursting patterns of flak, solid and sudden before them, saturating the altitude. He turned and motioned Cable down behind the armor plates.

'Bombardier to ball turret. Clear below.'

The turret whined down and around. 'Ball turret to Gillis. All clear below. Flak straight ahead. Accurate. Over.'

'Bomb-bay doors opening.'

The first shocks of flak waves suddenly caught *The Lady*. She veered up, yawing, then righted again. The old, familiar iron hail of the fragments shattered against her. The concussive shocks were violent, wrenching her from her level flight-through.

'Golden to Gillis. Bomb-bay doors down and locked. Over.'

'Christ!' cried Kramer.

A sudden shocking explosion flung *The Lady* high up on her left wing. Cable hurtled, slamming against Hagen, pressing him against the side.

'Number-one engine hit,' Cronin called in.

'Feather one,' said Starrett.

The Lady bucked, righting to level flight, the flak bursting jagged around her.

Hagen pushed Cable off and frowned, taut.

The Lady evened off rockily, jolting through the concussive waves and droning steadily forward, closing in on target through the exploding walls of flak.

'Bombs away!' Gillis reported.

The bombs dropped, train by steady train.

Suddenly another shocking burst tossed *The Lady* high on her left wing, almost in a complete half-roll. The force rocketed through the ship.

'Jesus Christ!' muttered Gillis.

'Number two hit,' said Cronin.

'Feather two,' cut Starrett.

The Lady reeled abruptly, shivered and dove, veering, rocking through the shock waves, the iron rain of fragments, the strain of the plummet quivering through her.

The force of the plunge sent Hagen spinning, slamming high against his gun mount. He tried to move, but the pressure of the drop pinned him useless as Cable again spun against him, jamming him hard against the armor plate.

The Lady strained against the plunge.

Slowly the dive started to even out, forcing against the pressure.

'Five hundred feet!' Kirby called in. 'We've dropped five hundred.'

Abruptly the pressure cut.

Cable rolled to the side, startled.

Hagen dropped, sliding to the floor, shook his head once; then swiftly, in the instant, was on his feet again.

'Ship leveling,' Starrett called in. 'But losing altitude. Strip ship. Repeat: strip ship. Get her as light as you can. Jettison everything—repeat: everything—possible.'

Hagen looked up and saw Cable yank free of his intercom and oxygen, then bolt for the side hatch.

Swiftly Hagen grabbed his arm and spun him about. 'Where the fuck do you think you're going?'

Cable, in panic, fought and clawed to get free. Sharply Hagen belted him hard across the head and, slamming him back into position, replugged him into intercom and oxygen. 'Now you stay the hell where you're supposed to!'

'Starrett to Hagen. Any trouble?'

Hagen glared down at the gasping Cable. 'No, sir. No trouble.'

'Starrett to crew. Check in.'

'Tail. Still here.'

'Hagen—both still here, sir.'

'Ball turret. Your oil line's hit, sir. Spraying

337

upper sighting-pane. Otherwise, okay.'

'Radio. Fine.'

'Top turret. Still going.'

'Bombardier. Okay, sir.'

'Navigator to pilot. Out of formation, Dad. How're we fixed for return?'

'Engines three and four still turning. Fuel— we'll see. Plot us back shortest—repeat: shortest—way.'

'If he can't,' Gillis called in, 'we can always jettison him.'

'Top turret to pilot. Should we jettison ball turret?'

'Wind drag. Not worth it,' Starrett said; then, 'Starrett to crew. All gunners, throw out half of all ammo. Hagen, half of ball turret ammo, throw it out. Jettison all flight bags— everything that'll go.'

'Radios included?' asked Golden.

'Radios included, except for essentials. Remove all armor plate. Swacey, help forward. Wyatt, get out of turret.'

'Ball turret to skipper. If Swacey comes fore, the tail will be blind. If I get out, we'll be blind below. That'll leave *The Lady* wide open in case of attack, sir. Suggest I stay in as observer. Over.'

Pause.

'How bad is your sighting-pane?'

'Usable. Also, there are the side panes.'

'We'll have to cut turret power.'

'I'm already on manual, sir.'

338

Pause. Then, 'Roger.'

Already Hagen was tossing the flight bags out through the waist gate. He glanced to Cable. 'Come on, god-dammit, and give me a hand.'

Cable rose uncertainly, confused; then suddenly, snapping to awareness, started into action. Out the waist gates went the flight bags, the ammo boxes, half the ammo, the flak vest—

'Here!' shouted Golden.

Hagen glanced up.

Golden held out a radio set.

In a moment the line was formed. Set after set went down the chain, from Golden to Cable to Hagen, and out into Germany.

Swiftly—his own work done, the tail stripped clean—Swacey crawled his way forward and, with tool kit in hand, plugged into the spare oxygen outlet by Hagen and into intercom; then, with a nod, tossed Hagen a screwdriver and started deftly, desperately, to unscrew the armor plating.

The intercom crackled. It was Kramer. 'I can't get this armor out the nose hatch.'

'Hand it up through,' said Cronin.

'Keep bomb-bay doors closed,' Kirby said. 'Wind drag.'

'Golden,' Cronin cut in, 'get ready. It's heavier than a sonofabitch.'

Hagen glanced up through the radio room. Golden was at the edge of the catwalk, reaching in for a massive bulk of armor plate. Hagen signaled to Cable.

Instantly Cable unplugged from the main oxygen line and, plugging into the portable, dashed into the radio room. Together he and Golden maneuvered the heavy plate to Hagen and, with Swacey's help, heaved it through the waist gate. It spun, spiraling down, like a part of the ship falling away.

Swiftly Hagen got down on his haunches again, shoulder to side with Swacey, and went on unscrewing the armor plates while slowly behind them the ball turret moved, revolving, searching.

*   *   *

The Lady was stripped clean. Everything that hadn't been bolted down (and even some of the things that had been) had been strewn out over Germany, including cameras and bombsight, scattered in a pattern of haphazard wreckage from Magdeburg to—

Hagen frowned, leaning spent and exhausted against the side of the waist gate by Swacey. He hadn't the vaguest idea where they were now, nor any idea of time. To hell with it. All he knew—in flashes of broken ideas—was that they didn't have a chance: They were somewhere west of Magdeburg, square in the middle of the Northern Reich; they had a whole fucking continent to cross—alone; and not only alone, but in a crippled ship with two engines already dead, a broken oil line and a questionable amount of fuel; yet here they were, naked as skin, fighting for altitude, time and distance. Why? One more burst of flak in the right place or, if they were spotted, one more Luftwaffe attack, and they would be done for, for certain. How long could their luck hold? Wearily he turned to Swacey.

Swacey only nodded and held up his hand, his fingers crossed.

But, Christ, why didn't they bail out now? The worst it could mean would be capture, a stalag. But at least they'd be alive. And the war couldn't last forever. Someday they would have to be released. And to be alive was the thing—the only thing that mattered. And yet when Cable had tried to do what he himself had wanted to do, he had blocked him. Why?

I got out, said Bellows. *I jumped. And left them.*

Good thing, too.

Was it?... If I'd stayed, if I'd helped—maybe they'd all have made it.

Too much of a chance.

The chance they took, said Bellows. The chance I ran out on...

And suddenly Kay... *If only people— someone—meant something to you...*

Hagen's frown deepened. He glanced to Swacey beside him, then to the turret, still slowly, slowly searching.

341

Suddenly he jumped to his feet, tensed with anger.

*　　*　　*

'Pilot to crew. Fuel still holding. Altitude low, but holding. Avoiding radar range.'

'Kramer to crew. Over the Netherlands. Repeat: over the Netherlands.'

'Ball turret to Hagen. Hagen, check three o'clock.'

Hagen's eyes swept the sky. Suddenly, 'Jesus Christ!'

Swacey leaped to his feet, scanning out toward three.

Far in the blue were thin white vapor trails: fighters.

'Reckon they can see us?' Cronin asked.

'We're hugging pretty low to ground,' Kramer said. 'I doubt it.'

Pause. Then, 'They're headed east,' Hagen said.

'Keep your eyes on them,' Kirby called in. 'We're looking for Little Friends to escort us in—if they can find us.'

'How's it going?' asked Gillis.

'Nothing so far,' said Kirby. 'But keep checking.'

Tensely Hagen stared until his eyes burned with watching.

'They're fading,' Swacey said. 'They didn't see us.'

'What kind were they?' asked Kramer.

'I don't know,' said Swacey, and smiled. 'And from this distance, I don't give a shit.'

*　　*　　*

The Lady started to buck.

'Transfer fuel,' Starrett cut in.

'Roger,' said Kirby. 'But I don't know—'

'Try it!' said Starrett.

The Lady veered sharply, then caught again and righted.

'She's holding,' Kirby said. 'She's holding.'

'Off oxygen,' Starrett ordered. 'Off oxygen.'

Eagerly Hagen tore off his mask and threw it down. The smudge lines were deep, streaked with sweat.

Swacey and Cable pulled off theirs. 'Jesus, that feels good,' Swacey said.

'Ball turret to Cable. Planes, nine o'clock level.'

Cable looked out his waist gate.

Hagen crossed to look over his shoulder.

'Ball to Kirby. What kind of Little Friends expected? Thunderbolts? Over.'

'Kirby to Wyatt. Yeah. I think so.'

'Hagen to Kirby. Thunderbolts. Nine o'clock.'

'Escorts!' yelled Cronin.

'Do they see us?' asked Swacey.

'They sure as hell do!' said Gillis. 'They're tipping their wings.'

343

Suddenly, 'Ball turret to crew. Flak, twelve o'clock level. Heavy. Over.'

'Kramer to crew. Coastal guns.'

'Coastal guns!' Swacey swung to look out toward twelve, excited. 'You mean we've made it?'

'Just about, man,' Cronin called in. 'Just about.'

'Pilot to crew. Nearing coast, but low on fuel. We'll have to fly through it. Over.'

'They've got our range,' Gillis reported. 'Over.'

Steadily *The Lady* droned on, straight toward the darkening barrages.

The first shocks shivered her level flight.

Hagen startled to see fragments bursting through her, piercing her tail with jagged holes of sunlight.

The concussive shocks rocked her, but she bore on. Wave on jarring wave buffeted her, the tearing fragments ripping through the waist walls.

The gunners crouched to the center.

Suddenly a shattering burst of flak broke directly under her, near and shocking. There was an explosive, bucking shock that spun *The Lady* high on her side, and the acrid smoke of black, swirling powder filled the ship. Slowly she strained to right again. Then—the shock waves subsided, and the hailing of iron fragments. Slowly, windily, the black smoke cleared.

'We've made it!' Kramer yelled. 'We've made it!'

'Jesus, Starrett, she did it!' Gillis shouted. 'There's the North Sea!'

Hagen rose and glanced out the waist gate. Behind him the wind blew the flak clouds into a grey haze against the blue. He turned to Swacey and pointed to the Thunderbolts buzzing the waves, shepherding them in, and signaled, thumb up.

'Gillis to Wyatt. Get out of the turret, Wyatt. We made it!'

Silence.

Hagen wheeled.

'Wyatt?' called Gillis.

The turret was motionless, down, the hatch locked.

Swiftly, catching Swacey's look, Hagen pulled free from intercom and leaped to the turret. He knelt to unsnap the turret locks. The wind from the turret well blew wet against his face. He brushed away the wet with the back of his hand, and stared at it. It was splattered with blood.

He looked up and saw Swacey staring at his blood-streaked face.

'*Wyatt!*' It was a shriek from the depths of Hagen.

His hands tore at the locks and pulled back the hatch.

A wind-blown fountain of blood erupted over Hagen, drenching him, spattering him

345

steadily till his face and front dripped with blood as wet as baptism. The wind blasted up through the shattered pane, and what had been Wyatt was only a mess of blood-clotted clothes and wires, glass and metal—no front, no form. The flak burst had been too near, too direct, and Wyatt—

His eyes were blinded by the blood flowing over him, bathing him. Desperately he reached in to pull him out—and gasped in horror, jerking suddenly away, as the arm came loose, and swiftly slammed down the hatch, and knelt there tensed as rock.

How long he knelt there, Hagen never knew. He looked up and met Golden's eyes. Golden wheeled away. He turned to Swacey, but Swacey had his back turned, his face buried in his hand. Cable only stared at him, white and sick.

Hagen's eyes burned, wet without tears, with only drying blood. Stiffly bracing himself, he again drew back the hatch, reached in and checked the manual clutch; then slowly he closed the hatch again. Carefully he locked the latches into place. And kneeling there, his face set, tight against feeling, he engaged the outside crank and gently rolled the turret into landing position.

The wind from the turret well, flapping against him, was already congealing the blood.

Then rising slowly, like a man in a mist of motion, he crossed to the intercom and, slowly plugging in, 'Hagen—Hagen to Starrett.' His voice was dead, unreal. 'We'll have to land—with Wyatt in the turret.'

'O God!' Starrett's voice was caught, soft.

'Jesus, Mary and Joseph,' murmured Kramer.

'I—I tried to—to take him out,' Hagen went on. 'But he—he started to come apart.'

Only a muffled cry came over intercom, a groan.

Hagen released the intercom switch. It felt sticky in his hand. The wind from the waist gate felt fresh against his face. *If only ... someone ... meant something to you ...* He stood there gripping the waist-gate frame hard, and harder, the tears streaming in the wind, streaking across the blood.

*   *   *

Drawn and spent, Hagen stood in the public telephone booth in the canteen and waited for the base operator to clear his call to London, his little black book before him. It was late afternoon, and the smell of soap was clean about him. He had bundled his bloodied clothes into Quartermaster's—'Burn them!'—and after he had bathed, he had walked, and had walked, and had walked. He couldn't go back to the Shack—not yet—not yet. He hadn't eaten since breakfast, but he felt no hunger—only the tensed, dry ache inside, and the confusion. He felt stricken. Blind. Alone, as never in his life before. And out of the blur of ideas, he realized Joy should be told. He had Kay's number... *I'd have to be in one hell of a mess before I'd use it...* Words to burn a man's pride, but only ashes were left of that now.

The phone clicked. 'Kay Cheyne, here.' The bright, silver-gay voice.

'Kay—' The word scratched in his throat.

A puzzled 'Yes? Who is this, please?'

'Hagen.' He waited for the click-off, but there was only silence. 'Kay?'

'Yes.' The voice was silver-cold now.

He paused. 'I've a message. For Joy.'

'For Joy?' She seemed startled.

He nodded, as if she could see him. 'Wyatt—' He felt his throat choke tight. He forced his words, shaken. 'Tell her—Wyatt had it. He's dead, Kay.'

There was a gasp, the tap of the phone gripped differently.

'He didn't suffer,' Hagen went on. 'He—caught it—all at once. All at once. Tell her that.'

'I can't,' Kay said. Her voice was broken. He could hear the tears in her tone, the strain to speak. 'Joy died three weeks ago.'

The words shocked him; they were senseless. 'What do you mean, died?'

'She had leukemia,' Kay said. 'She died three weeks ago.'

Hagen shook his head. His mind reeled back

three weeks ago. The book of poems that had come from her, and Wyatt coming back by late moonlight, from over the meadow...

How come no letters? You and Joy bust up?
We have an understanding...

'Hagen?' Her voice was anxious.

'Yes. I'm still here.'

'Tom had said nothing?'

'Nothing... Had he known—about the leukemia, I mean?'

'That was why they had gone to The Linnet. They knew.'

'Wyatt was full of secrets,' Hagen said. 'He always was. And now—they don't count anymore. Wyatt. Joy. It's all nothing, Kay. Just like I said.'

'Oh, no, Hagen. No.' Her voice deepened, strong and steadying. 'I was there when she died, and she went simply—at rest—in his love. And that counts, Hagen. It counts for a lot. Maybe it's the only real thing that does count in life, Hagen. Love.'

'But they died before they'd even lived! Both of them!'

'Did they, Hagen? Are they really dead? I mean, even now, talking about them, thinking about them, don't you *feel* them—their lives, their courage, their victory?'

'Over what!' snapped Hagen.

'Time,' Kay said gently. 'Time and the world. They're beyond them now. Maybe they've always been beyond them. Maybe that

349

was their secret. That love *is* beyond time and the world...Do you see what I mean, Hagen?'

Hagen rubbed his head, tensed, uncertain. 'Kay—'

'Yes?'

'Can I see you again—to talk with you? I need to, Kay. I *need* to. Can I see you again?'

There was a hesitant pause.

'Your way,' Hagen said softly. 'On your terms.'

'I—don't know that I've the courage, Hagen. It would take courage to see you now.'

'I know...'

The silence was deep, weighted. Then—

'On your next leave,' said Kay. 'I'll be here.'

The phone jolted shut.

Hagen hung back the phone and leaned, tired, against it.

*　　*　　*

He climbed the crumbling stone wall and for a long moment stood looking out across the twilit fields to the far range of trees. He had come here now because here, in this quiet, lone spot, he had come nearer to Wyatt than he had ever been, nearer to knowing him, to knowing the secret that had made him such a part of life... Life again, and meaning. They were— they *had* been—such a part of Wyatt.

He saw a hare, sprung with life, leaping through the grass; and, oddly, he thought of

Bayer. He had seen the look in Bayer's face when they had landed—first, beaming that *The Lady* had made it; then, seeing the turret, the death look shocking his face. Suddenly he had whirled and crumpled, retching into the grass... The grass swayed after the bounding hare.

Life still went on its useless way. Useless? He wondered.

What you see just isn't there.

Maybe what you see isn't there, either.

And that was strange, the way that memory came back, because here in this spot now, grey in the quiet of a day dying, the memory was sharper than that day had actually been: as if in the moment of time when it happened there was no focus, no meaning; that it was only *after* the moment, *after* things had passed, that the meanings came—if ever. Always after. Or, at least, that had been the way for him. Maybe people like Wyatt knew the moment and the meaning all at the same time. Maybe that was their secret.

But with him—The dark, restless tension stirred up again. Always the feeling, more and sharper lately, that somewhere, somehow, life—real life—was going on without him— just beyond him, and he couldn't touch it, and it couldn't touch him—

No: that was wrong. It *had* touched him— today. It had torn him apart, and he could feel it. He could *feel* it, but it had no meaning, only hurt. And the futility of it all, the anger of knowing how useless it had been—how senseless the death of Wyatt! Wyatt of all people, when a hare could go leaping through the grass. Where was the meaning there?

Maybe in the vision ... that Man has dignity and meaning ... to affirm life—the life that can be, beyond our time...

What you see just isn't there.

Maybe what you see isn't there, either.

Swiftly Hagen turned away. He ran his hand hard over the rough, lichened rocks. He needed to feel something solid, real, like rock and briar. Something he could touch, that in its way made sense. How could a man die for a vision? A vision that was only a dream, against the fact of death—the fact that Wyatt was dead.

Are they really dead? asked Kay. *I mean, talking about them, thinking about them, don't you feel them?*

as he was feeling it now, Wyatt, as if he were still alive. He shook his head again. But the *real* Wyatt *was* dead! He was a mass of blood and bones and stringy veins, all tangled with wires—

He whirled, his face tight, his hand against his mouth. *Was* that the real Wyatt? Was that all that Wyatt had been—the blood, the veins, the bones? Or was there something more—beyond all that? The spirit...

Had Wyatt been right? Because if he had

been, then all *his* life he, Hagen, had been wrong. If reality was more than the physical, death more than an end, then all his life—*all his life*—he had been wrong.

A still, wondering, bewildered look crossed Hagen's face. Slowly, aimlessly, he started to ramble across the fields, his mind forcing through darkness, forcing to follow an idea like a faint, far star... The spirit...

Watch the crew, Wyatt had said, *when things get tight. Really tight. It isn't each man for himself. It's each for the other* ... as it had been today; and even he himself, side by side with Swacey and Golden, had been one with them, one spirit.

That had been what *The Lady* had meant to Wyatt. Not just ten men fighting to save their asses. They were, to him, the spirit of all men who flew and fought for a vision ... *luminous with courage and hope...*

He understood that now because, for the first time in his life, today he had lost himself in others, in the crew.

And yet—

No! Wyatt was too idealistic. Too unreal. Life wasn't what he had seen it to be. It was really as he, Hagen, had always known it to be—a trap.

That's what life really is, man. A trap. You're here, then you're dead. Snap! The trap closes...

Maybe your trap's just the way you see life—

Hagen startled. The trap—the way he had

seen life. The gutter view of the stars—out of reach. And yet—

Quickeningly the ideas flowed. That *had* been the trap, the way he had seen things, forever closing him in, isolating him, cutting him off. No. Life hadn't been cutting him out. *He* had been cutting life out. He had made it too narrow, seeing it as he had. It was more than just Now and Things—just as Wyatt, the *real* Wyatt, was more than the mess in the turret. And Man was more; and he was a man, more than he had ever been before—so much more, with depths and dimensions he had never before known, that now he felt he could give, and give, and still be Hagen. But a new Hagen, free, released into life flowing all around him and through him, vital and alive— maybe not so great and so golden a life as Wyatt had seen it, so luminous with dreams and visions. But life that meant others, the whole wonderful miracle of others, of lives touching lives with meaning, and even death—

Suddenly he slowed. Even Wyatt's death hadn't been meaningless, not now, not after this... *Lives touch... A meaning—something you'd never known or seen before—touches you, and you're never quite the same again...*

as Wyatt's had touched his life; and in the touching, in the sunbursts of insight, the trap had been shattered. And he was free, free forever ... with new dimensions of life to fathom ... with Kay ... and possibly even love, a love that had meaning for him. And there was the crew—

He stopped abruptly, remembering this morning, Starrett's low voice: *After this run, you're off The Lady.* Swiftly Hagen turned and started quickly back across the fields, hurrying, hoping he could still get to Starrett in time.

CHAPTER TWENTY-EIGHT

Starrett stared at the small, white, lidless cardboard box on his desk—Wyatt's personal effects—and turned away. As senior flying officer, he now had his own room at the BOQ—an end, narrow room with only one window, a desk, a chair, a bunk and the quiet of being alone. Now in the lone stillness he stood tensed by the window and stared out across the darkening field, seeing nothing, feeling only the jagged loss, the irony of blind questions and the sick awareness of time and a man gone forever, too late for him ever to know now—and against all this, the hollow futility of his own worn helplessness.

Why had it been Wyatt—the quiet, gentle Wyatt? Out of all the ten, what touch of Chance or Luck or Fate had marked it the end for him in such a way? And why now at this late point, and not before? Why—

But he knew his mind was drifting. Ever

since they had brought him the box with its odd, meager contents, he had been resisting the questions. He had been deliberately avoiding them, obvious and immediate as they were, and the more painful because now he *had* to answer them. And he had no answers.

Who was Wyatt? What kind of person had he really been? Was there anyone who knew him—who could explain the box?

Slowly Starrett closed the window and drew the blackout curtain. He turned and crossed the room in darkness, darkness within and darkness without. It was up to him to write the letter home, to justify, if he could, Wyatt's death—or simply to sympathize. But how could he only sympathize with them when they, from what he had gathered, had been estranged from Wyatt? They were Quakers, and Wyatt had died on a combat mission, violently amid violence—and on the Sabbath.

He turned on the lamp over his desk and sat down again, drawing the box to him. One by slow one, he took out the contents and again examined them: A legal packet from an Enderby Firm, Solicitors, Sevenoaks, Kent—a deed turning over to Thomas Benton Wyatt the property at The Combes called The Linnet, from a Joyce Anne Cheyne. (A deed of property willed. So she had died. When?) He had remembered, as censor for crew mail, Wyatt's letters to her—love letters, innocent, true; and now—to learn that she had died.

(And all along Wyatt had known.)

Next, a packet of her letters. He had read one or two for some clue, but they were like Wyatt's own, intimate ... innocent. Yet in the letters of both, time and again, the reliance on Providence, the insistence their lives had been guided by God. (It was strange to read such letters, of a God so personal in their lives, as if they had really believed. Always, with him, it had been Chance or Luck or Fate. But God—in people's lives, in these days? *Providence*?) He wondered and set the packet aside.

A personal letter from Wyatt followed, dated the day after the postmark from the Enderby Firm letter. It was addressed simply, quite common among airmen, *To Be Opened On My Death*. So he had opened it. It was a basic will, notarized by Lieutenant Waverly, transferring The Linnet to a Mrs Brian Cheyne, Ilford, Essex. (Who was this one? He couldn't recall from the Wyatt letters any Mrs Cheyne. Nor, frankly, could he recall any passes issued beyond London. Yet here, somehow, apparently Wyatt's life had touched both The Combes and Ilford.)

Next, there was a worn English copy of *Poems* by Emily Dickinson, with the curious inscription in the flyleaf: *For Tom. With all my love, my legacy... Forever your wife, Joy.* It was the word 'wife' that had jarred him at first. He had signed no papers for marriage; and according to regulations, no American soldier could marry an alien without clearance from his superior officer. Yet here, simply and clearly, was the word—apparently in its fullest meaning—'wife.'

Then the bookmark, a slip of blue silk. He had turned to the page. One poem had been circled.

That such have died enables us
The tranquiller to die;
That such have lived, certificate
For immortality.

An odd poem—circled by whom?

He closed the book, puzzled, and put it aside.

Next was a well-marked pocket Bible, worn, dog-eared. Natural for one of Wyatt's background.

And then, strangest of all, at the bottom of the box, found on his dog-tag chain, a plain gold wedding band, of male width.

The puzzle plagued Starrett. He would, of course, turn the whole matter of the Enderby letter and Wyatt's will over to the Judge Advocate General's Office. Let them act on it. But—if only there had been someone who had known Wyatt—to explain all this—

If only there had been someone who had known Wyatt. Once again the ache within him. That should have been *his* duty. He had (how often?) *meant* to get to know Wyatt, but always there had been other things to do.

Wearily Starrett stroked his eyes, tired, wondering again, with the hurt tight inside him, if anyone ever knew, *really* knew anyone in this world—so quickly it goes.

He sighed, worn, and stared at the contents before him; then slowly he put them back into the box again, one by one.

They had told him nothing, really; and knowing almost nothing of Wyatt's parents, how could he communicate with them? How could he explain Wyatt's death to them when he couldn't even explain Wyatt to himself? Wyatt—the gentle. Had he been a victim of his own idealism fed by propaganda and a drummed sense of patriotism? (He himself had known the hysteria of the spielers in the early years, back in the Old Army days.) Or had Wyatt chosen his way, out of principles and conviction? (From what he had seen, this had seemed the truth, ever since the first Berlin run. But he would never know what had happened then. Not now. Not ever.)

So here he was, back to the same questions again: Who and what was Wyatt? A fool? Or simply a boy who had died, like so many, too early and unfulfilled—another war statistic? Or—

Abruptly Starrett wheeled away from the desk and rose, rocking back the chair.

Or maybe he himself was really responsible

for it. Maybe if they had gone on their scheduled flak leave, they wouldn't have been on this run. Then Wyatt would have been still alive.

But he had wanted to keep them together, to keep them intact, to bring them through—and he had thought that only as a crew could they do it. It hadn't all been pride. He had just wanted them—wanted them all—to come through it. He had thought it his duty—

But he had failed. Failed because what he had wanted—only the gods could have done. And he was so mortal, so very, very mortal. And they—

They were a broken crew now. He had never seen them so low, so shattered, as he had this afternoon. They were worn, too worn perhaps. Maybe he *had* pushed them too hard. Maybe he *had* been wrong about flak leave, wanting to keep them together.

And now—could they ever go up in *The Lady* again? Or would they always see her now with the blood of Wyatt dripping from her sides? (He himself could still see the blood-splattered panels of the flight deck where Aronson had died. But he had to think of the crew, first and foremost.)

Still—maybe the rest would do them good. Maybe it was time to break up *The Lady*. They had only six runs more to go. And maybe a new shuffle of luck was in the cards for them—on other crews, other ships, each to take his own chance, and not risk the lot of them. Not anymore. Not when the luck of *The Lady* might have run out. As Hagen had said that morning, they were due for flak leave.

As for himself, if he took over lead position, the crews would always be changing. He would have no reason to give himself to them, to feel—as he felt now.

Don't give them any more than you have to, Aronson had said. *Every time they get hurt—or die—something goes of you... And for what?...*

Yes: that would be the wisest move for all now.

Brusquely Starrett crossed back to his desk and, shuffling among his papers, found the forms he needed, requesting flak leave for all *The Silver Lady.* With their record, he could force the Old Man. Within two days they could be on leave. He'd see to that. He sat again and, taking his pen, started to write, pausing only long enough to weigh out the answers for the blanks. His writing was rapid and sure.

Suddenly the abrupt knock on the door.

He turned, annoyed. 'Who is it?'

'Hagen, sir.'

Starrett's voice cut sharp. 'Come in.'

The door opened, and Hagen entered, his hair windblown, his jacket unzipped, his face gaunt, flushed. He closed the door behind him.

'Well?' asked Starrett.

'I've come to apologize for this morning, sir—'

Starrett glanced up.

'—and to request permission to stay on *The Lady*.'

There was a thoughtful pause; then, quietly 'Why?'

'Because it's a crew, sir. A damned good one. Wyatt's kind.'

Starrett frowned. 'Did you really know Wyatt?' he asked wonderingly.

'Better than anyone else did, I think. Except Joy.'

'Joy?' Starrett's frown deepened. 'Joyce Cheyne?'

Hagen startled. 'Yes, sir. Why?'

Quickly Starrett reached for the box again. 'Hagen, come here.' He pushed his papers away and, spilling the contents of the box onto his desk, picked up the Enderby letter and, handing it to Hagen, 'Can you explain this?'

Hagen went through the pages slowly. 'Only The Linnet, sir,' he said. 'That's where Wyatt and Joy went Easter week-end. It was her place.'

Starrett frowned, disturbed. 'I didn't think Wyatt was that kind,' he said.

'He wasn't,' Hagen said. 'Joy had leukemia. They had only that week-end. If they had had time—But they hadn't.'

'And this?' Starrett handed the Wyatt will to Hagen. 'Who is this Mrs Brian Cheyne, Ilford, Essex?'

'Kay,' said Hagen. 'Her sister-in-law.'

'And the ring?' He held up the plain gold band.

Hagen looked at it, puzzled; then a slow, dark smile. 'I'm not sure,' he said. 'But I can imagine.' He looked to Starrett. 'One way or another, they were married, sir.'

Starrett frowned again. 'Then that would explain this,' he said, and handed Hagen the book of Dickinson poems, open to the flyleaf.

Hagen read the inscription. 'Yes, sir. That would explain it.'

'And the poem inside? The marked one?'

Hagen flipped to the blue silk marker. This had been the book—the last thing sent to Wyatt by Joy. It must have been a sign for him—the sign to know. Slowly he read over the poem, then, finishing, closed the book.

'They lived—and died—in love, sir. Beyond time and the world.'

Starrett looked up, questioningly.

'Everything was spirit to Wyatt, sir. Even the crew. It was the only thing that was real to him, he said. The spirit that we are.'

Starrett eyed him squarely. 'And you believe him?'

Hagen met the look evenly, then slowly nodded. 'Yes, sir. I believe him. I believe that the mess in the turret wasn't Wyatt. Not the real Wyatt. The real Wyatt is still as much a part of *The Lady* as you or I, sir, because the crew to him wasn't just the men; it was their spirit—luminous with courage and hope, he said. And I believe him.'

Starrett turned away, shaking his head, tensed. 'But the men need the rest. Flak leave—'

'At *this* time?'

Starrett whirled. 'Can you think of a better time, Sergeant Hagen?'

'Yes, sir. After six more missions.'

'Six!' muttered Starrett. 'Didn't you see them today? They're broken, shattered. They're dead inside, falling apart.'

'All the more reason you keep them together,' said Hagen. 'You've been right so far. The only thing that kept us together today was each man thinking of the crew first—whether he wanted to or not—depending on it—as we depended on Wyatt. And he knew it.'

Starrett sighed, tired; then, after a long moment, 'So I was right, you think.'

'Yes, sir.'

Starrett leaned forward, his chin in his hand. To bring them through intact was for—he mused on the word—Providence. But to bring them through with the spirit intact, to keep that idea alive and part of them (as Wyatt still was)—that he could do. That he *had* to do from now on: not to manage Fate, but to show them how to meet it, how to make even of this shattered moment, this darkness and despair, a growing time, a time of victory that could be won only from within. To keep the spirit—how was it?—luminous with courage and hope...

364

But first he had a letter to write, one simply of thanks and gratitude—and of deep regret for their loss.

His eyes caught on the flak-leave forms before him. Quietly he picked them up and tore them through. His look caught Hagen's and he smiled. 'Six more, Hagen,' he said. 'Reckon we'll make it?'

Hagen grinned. 'I'll bet my life on it, sir.'

We hope you have enjoyed this Large Print book. Other Chivers Press or Thorndike Press Large Print books are available at your library or directly from the publishers. For more information about current and forthcoming titles, please call or write, without obligation, to:

Chivers Press Limited
Windsor Bridge Road
Bath BA2 3AX
England
Tel. (01225) 335336

OR

Thorndike Press
P.O. Box 159
Thorndike, Maine 04986
USA
Tel. (800) 223–6121 (U.S. & Canada)
In Maine call collect (207) 948–2962

All our Large Print titles are designed for easy reading, and all our books are made to last.